I0635924

CLUBBED THREE
Darkness and Light

Robert A. Karl

Self-published by the Author

First Edition: March 2023

ISBN: 979-8-9879126-4-5

Cover Design: Nirkri (fiverr.com/nirkri)

Dedicated to victims of
anti-LGBTQ+ violence.

PROLOGUE

The CLUBBED series consists of three novels. The author strongly believes in the importance of keeping alive the stories of LGBTQ culture from the pre-AIDS era to the present day. This is not just the story of one or two individuals. Instead, the narrator takes us on a journey, a guided tour, through the many varied aspects of LGBTQ lives by telling the stories of characters who are drawn together via their connections to the main setting, Club Sanctuary.

The first two books were narrated by Joey, a gay white male who owns the club. His omniscient viewpoint allowed the readers to see into the lives of other characters, whether they were included in his main focus, or were just mentioned briefly. This was done purposely, as the intent was to simulate the feeling of being inside a gay club. Some characters are known by everyone, while others are on the sidelines, or just appear briefly, as they go on with their lives.

Everybody at the club has a story, and every story deserves to be told.

Themes include coming out, self-acceptance, self-loathing, internal and external homophobia, racism, classism, ageism, assimilation, and many other examples of human frailties and conditions. But it's also about connections - sometimes weak, sometimes strong, that people make with one another. And of course, the most important connection is love.

Joey, from the suburbs, first met Henry, a Black man from Philadelphia, in 1976. They have already traveled a long road together, and their relationship was being put to the test when we last heard from them. Although they were married, they had agreed to only play with others when they were together, as a way to keep their relationship fresh while also trying to stay safe from HIV infection. At the end of Book Two, Joey violated their agreement by having unprotected sex with a young man he had just met, and without Henry being present. Henry was furious, and he walked out on Joey.

In a departure from the first two books, Henry's voice will be brought to the forefront, providing a different perspective to their story. Other voices will also be heard, with various characters sharing their stories as they experience the variety and diversity of Queer life into the 2000s.

Book Three begins with the story of how Joey and Henry first met, but this time, that part of the story is told from Henry's perspective.

Here, the story continues in

CLUBBED THREE: Darkness and Light

CHAPTER ONE

HENRY

"No Fats. No Femmes. No Blacks."

I wasn't paying attention, so the words hung in the hot, humid air, as if the brushstrokes of the artist working near us had captured the words in a still-life.

"No Fats. No Femmes. No Blacks."

The awful words were repeated, once again unheard by me, hanging in the air like the smoke from our Kools, refusing to drift away from our spot on the Rittenhouse Square park bench.

I was scanning the park for potential hook-ups, hoping to find some fine young thing to enjoy that afternoon. Or, if no fine young thing was ripe for the picking, at least a guy with some extra cash he could afford to lose.

"No Fats. No Femmes. No Blacks."

Trying to retrieve the words before they escaped my grasp, sensing their importance, my failure to comprehend the message was an emblem of my preoccupation with my physical environment. My attention should have been focused on my companion, but I was failing him at that particular moment.

1

That's when Shawn slapped me upside the head with the rolled-up newspaper he'd been scanning, checking out the classifieds in the latest July 1976 issue of Au Courant.

"Henry, listen! Did you hear what they said in this ad? No fats. No femmes. No Blacks. What's a fat, black gurl like me supposed to think about that?"

I started to laugh, but a quick look at the hurt in Shawn's eyes caused me to quickly adjust my attitude. Placing my right arm around his broad shoulders, sighing deeply, I took the paper from his hands. Opening back to the classifieds section, I quickly scanned the text.

Seeing what people had written in their search for sex partners wasn't new for me, but I understood that some words cut deeply. I was trying to find an ad that would make Shawn feel better, one that would recognize the value inherent in his qualities, sighing at the hopelessness of this quest. Tossing the paper to the side of the park bench, I took a more direct approach.

"What would you write in an ad, Shawnie?" I asked, referring to him by the nickname I had used since we were kids in elementary school. It was too hot to maintain that physical contact, and we both laughed as I peeled my sweaty arm away from him.

"First, I don't like those negative ads. No this. No that. What the hell kind of way is that to meet somebody, anyway?"

"Good point," I replied. "But give me more details. Maybe we can put an ad in there for you."

Even as I said the words, I knew we wouldn't go through with it. Neither one of us had the money for something like an ad looking for sex in the back pages of the local gay paper. But still, we could pretend.

"Ok, let's see. I guess I'd start off describing myself, then describe what I'm after."

2

"All right then. You can start with 'Handsome Black stud looking for'...what is it you're looking for? Black cock? White cock? C'mon, help me out here, Shawnie."

He was already laughing as the air of tension eased away into nothingness. We both knew what he wanted. Friends know those kinds of things. And I always made it a point to get to know as much as possible about my friends. Sometimes, I thought I was being nice, but other times I realized that this was a way to hide my insecurities, doubts, and negative emotions.

Men just love to be fawned over, to be the center of attention, to hear compliments strewn in their direction, whether there's an ounce of truth in the words or not.

I remembered those words of advice from my spiritual guide, the Tarot card reader on 9th Street, explaining how to move a conversational topic from myself to avoid scrutiny. It was a technique I was happy to use on many occasions.

Although my public mask was one of self-confidence, I had spent time examining my insecurities, tracing them back to the words and actions of my Pops when I was just a kid.

"You gotta beat the devil outta that boy!" he'd drunkenly slur, wielding his belt as a weapon against the evil that he believed resided within me. "Beat the devil out and let Jesus inside!"

Those were times that I tried so hard to forget and that I never shared with anyone new that I met. Shawnie, however, was all too aware of my family difficulties, a common history that occurred all too frequently in our community. Fathers were very strict with boys who were perceived as being different. And at a very young age, my father already recognized what he would describe as "the evil" in me. At the time, I didn't know exactly what Pops

3

meant. Now, I realize that he saw my queerness as a sign of evil.

"Look at that guy over there. He must be new. I wouldn't mind getting a piece of that fine white ass," I said.

"Henry, I thought we were talking about what I want!" Shawn replied, slapping my knee with his large, sweaty left hand.

"Ow, gurl, you gonna hurt this delicate flower if you're not careful," I teased, rubbing my knee, pretending to be injured.

"You? A delicate flower? My ass!" came Shawn's reply.

As our laughter subsided, I picked up the paper again, opening back to the ads. I already knew that Philly was a segregated city, and we were sometimes rudely reminded of that fact. There was no lack of ads specifying that the guy wasn't interested in making any connections with a Black man. Honestly, that was the part that bothered me the most, though the references to 'fats and femmes' also rubbed me the wrong way.

Shawn wasn't wrong about me being far from a delicate flower. My physical appearance reflected my past as a star pitcher on my high school baseball team. I stretched my long, muscular legs in front of me, looking and feeling confident. Combined with my outgoing personality, as perceived by friends and acquaintances, I had a feeling that I could make a mark in the world.

Trying to ignore the guy sitting on one of the short walls in Rittenhouse Square, spreading his legs wide as he swung his legs, I scanned the ads again. Leaning in close to see what I was reading, the scent of Shawnie's Paco Rabanne cologne comforted me, like the scent of a mother's cooking on Thanksgiving day or the scent of the freshly-fallen rain in one of the urban oases in our city, such as our current location in the Square.

"I think this is the best one I can find," I said, pointing at a very short ad that simply said, "White gay male seeking Black gay male."

Shawn scoffed at that, clearly unimpressed with the lack of specificity.

"Probably short, old and ugly!"

Laughing, I realized that there are plenty of types of prejudices in the world. But Shawn had enough to deal with, so I wasn't about to lecture him about that.

Out of the corner of my eye, I saw the new young white guy stand up, stretching, and I thought he was checking me out. But without saying a word or giving any signal that he might be interested, he turned and walked away from me. Craning my neck, I tried to keep his fine-looking ass in my sights for as long as possible, but he eventually disappeared.

I didn't know it then, but that boy's name was Joey.

Shawn and I spent more time that afternoon just hanging in the park, smoking Kools and talking shit. Just a regular afternoon. I was off from school for summer vacation, heading towards my goal of a college degree. My shift at the pizza shop didn't start until later that evening. And I was horny. Yes, definitely horny. Especially after seeing that white dude who interested me.

Most of the guys in the park that day were regulars. Some were homeless, needing a place to be during the hours when the shelters were closed. Others were office workers, wanting to spend their lunchtime outside, some with packed lunches while others ate from nearby food trucks or delis.

Rittenhouse Square was also a well-known place for gay men to meet other gay men. That's why I was there. And if I couldn't meet that one guy, well, it would be easy enough for me to hook up with someone else.

But before I chose my next conquest, Shawn and I saw our friends Malcolm and Quincy entering the park, heading in our direction. Music loudly boomed from the box on Malcolm's shoulder as they approached, sauntering and sashaying to the beat of the music. They always had the best mixtapes, so we thought we'd be hearing the best of today's new music.

But instead of some recent radio hit, the song was one that I only heard played in the clubs. "Soul Makossa" by Manu Dibango was released in 1972, and that beat is not only contagious, but unforgettable. Any DJ who kept that song in their rotation knew it was sure to pack the dance floor. Years later, some people called "Soul Makossa" the very first disco song. All we knew back then was that it was the jam.

I was sure the guys would be putting on a show. After all, it wasn't like we had never met in the park before. And that song, with its heavy African beat, was almost enough to get me to dance this early in the day.

Malcolm, wearing a vest with no shirt and tight cut-off jeans, made little yelping noises, teasing us as he drew closer. Quincy wore an orange crop top with very short, tight cargo shorts. His lip gloss glowed in the early-afternoon sun and his hair gel shone sleekly. He wasn't one to shy away from attention.

Shawnie, also in short shorts, jumped up from the bench, eager to join in the fun. Maintaining my position as an observer, I had to smile admiringly at their moves. If people had paid any attention, they would have seen real talent on display here. Not just in their ability to move fluidly, but in the actual choreography. Not rehearsed, but taking cues from one another, they moved in a way that wasn't synchronized, but harmonious, each one able to anticipate and respond to the movements of the others.

Quincy, the smallest in stature, was nevertheless athletic, lithe, and filled with boundless energy. Watching Malcolm, with his expressive face matching his graceful movements, I admired how he embodied what I thought of as masculine femininity. Or feminine masculinity. A combination of the best of those genders could be seen not only in his dance movements, but in how he lived his life.

Not to be outdone, Shawn moved with an ease that belied his size. Moving, shaking, popping, catwalking, duckwalking, creating a scene in the park that drew the attention of more than a few passers-by. Of course, they were voguing, long, long before Madonna made it popular in the white clubs. Even before Malcolm McLaren released his hit "Deep in Vogue."

Sensing an opportunity, Quincy took his cap and placed it on the lawn next to the boombox, just in case anyone might be in a generous mood and leave a tip. Without missing a beat, the trio continued the show as the song transitioned to Disco Inferno by The Trammps. For just a moment, I considered getting up and dancing with them, but then I remembered that I would be setting myself up for getting read by these sharp-tongued queens. There was no way I could match their moves, not even close.

Regular visitors to Rittenhouse Square can be a jaded group, easily ignoring the sights and sounds of three young Black men voguing on the pathway. However, during the show, a few folks, surely visitors, dropped a few bucks into Quincy's collection cap.

"Whew! That was hella fun!" Shawnie wheezed out the words, settling back onto the bench beside me. "Did you see how every movement had meaning, how we were vibing? Damn, I love you guys!" Shawn gushed at our two friends.

As the three dancers chatted about the fun they had, I chose to be careful with my words. I felt somewhat removed from the group, though all of us were close friends. But I felt like I was different. Not in a bad way. Just different.

I could see their movements; I saw the way they moved together, but I didn't think I could feel what they felt. My mind was more analytical, more calculating, more business-like. I mean, I could hold my own on the dance floor, but I lacked the confidence to move with others in a dance that could be characterized as something with meaning and purpose.

I chose to keep my thoughts to myself. This wasn't the moment for a total nerd-out.

Instead, I turned my attention to a guy who had watched them dancing for a minute, dropped a fiver into the cap, while keeping his eyes fixed on me, making sure I noticed that he was checking out my body, moving his gaze from my eyes to my clearly large package and then back to my eyes. It was no secret what he was thinking, what he wanted.

I was sizing him up, too. He looked like the type that would submit...and not only submit but probably pay for the honor. And judging from his business attire, he could probably afford to be quite generous. Just what I was looking for this afternoon.

This was the guy's second time around the park pathway, and when he had walked a respectable distance away, I started my move. This was a dance that I understood completely. Just like my friends took their cues from one another during their routine, I took the non-verbal cues from the one I was following.

At the park entrance, he turned and slyly looked back to verify that I was in pursuit. When he saw that he had the fish on the hook, he started reeling me in, walking about half a block, pausing to look into a shop window, catching my reflection as I was getting closer, but on the opposite side of Walnut Street. Nodding slightly as he turned to face me, his lips forming a small smile, then looking away and continuing his walk down the street, slowing his pace, silently inviting me to come closer.

When he paused at the Holiday Inn Express, lighting a cigarette as he leaned against the wall, I knew that the next step in the dance was mine. I walked past him, pretending to ignore him, but stopped before I walked too far away. Then I turned back in his direction, noticing that he had turned his back to me. Tossing the remnants of his cig into the street, he walked into the hotel lobby.

That was the step I was waiting for. That was my invitation. I wasn't going to turn it down.

Approaching the hotel entrance, I planted myself in the exact same spot that he had previously occupied. Striking up a match and lighting a Kool, I peered inside and saw him waiting at the elevator, but I could see that he hadn't pressed the call button.

My heart beat just a little faster as I saw him hesitate, turn back towards me, and then start to walk outside for our meet and greet.

As much as I enjoyed our dance, I wasn't going to be the one to approach him first. He had to come to me, like the little bitch that I wanted him to be. That was his role in the play. He was mine; I wasn't his.

"Hey, whatsup," were his first words to me, as he lit a fresh Marlboro and exhaled in my direction.

"Disrespect me like that again, and I walk away," was my curt reply. "The only words I really wanna hear out of your bitch mouth is 'Yes Sir,' you hear me?"

Hiding my pleasure with a frown, I did enjoy it when he answered without hesitation, "Yes Sir."

Bingo! I had him now.

I'm not sure if he felt awkward as we stood there, smoking in silence, but I felt confident, in control, masterful. Dropping my Kool to the ground, crushing it out with the toe of my shoe, I finally spoke again.

"Pick that up and follow me, dog," I said, as I turned and headed into the hotel lobby.

Silently, he did as he was told. Not a word was spoken as we rode the elevator to his room, after he obeyed my gesture to toss the cigarette butt into the receptacle between the doors of the elevators.

I was disappointed that the room was small, not a suite of rooms. But this hotel was of the budget variety, so it lacked the amenities of the better-quality places in Center City Philly. I made myself at home, stretching my lanky frame on the bed. My host simply stood silently near the door, awaiting my instructions. I was glad he wasn't a newbie at this, saving me the bother of teaching him how to behave properly.

"Listen, dog, I want you to strip naked and kneel at the foot of the bed. But first, I want you to put my gifts on top of the dresser right here," I said, pointing to the side table. "I hope you got at least 2 Cs for me," I continued, indicating that I expected to be paid at least $200.

"I wanna let you know I ain't here to rob you, so no worries about that. You can put everything else in the bottom drawer over there, but I gotta say I admire your watch and I think it'd make a very nice gift for me. Oh, and that necklace too."

I watched carefully as he removed two $100 bills from his wallet. It was clear he had plenty more, so I felt confident he could afford to give me what I wanted. His eyes were on the outline of my rigid cock in my very short, blue satin gym trunks, as he removed his watch and necklace, placing both on the table beside me.

"You're a good boy, aren't you?"

"Yes Sir."

"Now go back to your spot and start strippin'. Make it sexy if you can, though it don't really matter to me," I said, feigning disinterest, humiliating him as much as possible.

It was disappointing to see him in his saggy, boring white boxers when he dropped his pants. I hoped he might surprise me with some sexy underwear, but no such luck.

"Take 'em off, dog. Let me see what you got hidden in there. But first, you forgot to take off your wedding ring. Put that piece of junk in your drawer. I don't want you thinkin' about your wifey while you're bein' my bitch," I scolded.

"Yes Sir," he whimpered, realizing his mistake in wearing the ring.

For me, the ring had been a good sign. I knew that a married man was more likely to want to be submissive, with all that pent-up desire to be with a man, when night after night was spent with a female who could never provide what these men really wanted.

And my preference was for men to be as submissive to me as they possibly could.

Looking at him totally naked, his pale skin sprinkled with freckles, his pointy nipples surrounded by wisps of hair on his pecs, had my cock straining within the confines of my jockstrap, yearning for release. I could already feel the wetness inside.

His hard cock pointed straight up, though it was just visible through the thick bush of hair that almost completely hid his balls.

"I want you to service me, dog. Start with my boots."

He started to reach for the tops of my Timbs, as if to take them off.

"Not like that, dog. Use your tongue. Just like my doggy."

"Yes Sir!"

He knelt and licked the bottoms of my Timbs, and the moan that escaped from him let me know he was getting

11

what he wanted. Pulling my legs up towards me on the bed, he was forced to crawl forward, giving me a better view of the show. He was salivating as he licked and kissed my boots, from the soles to the tops, deeply inhaling the scent of the leather. A string of pre-cum dangled from the tip of his little white dick.

Removing my tank top, I pulled him on top of me, pushing his face into my erect nipple, gasping as he swirled his tongue around it, flicking it with his teeth. This one knew what he was doing, opening his legs in case I was ready to invade his privacy.

"Fuck me, Sir" he whispered into my ear.

That pissed me off.

"Who's givin' the orders around here, dog? You?"

Recognizing his mistake, he waited in silence.

"Am I the man in charge here? Am I the only one who can make the decisions?" I demanded to know.

"Yes Sir," he whimpered, then went back to giving my hard nips a good workout.

Letting my anger subside, I leaned back to enjoy the service I was receiving. "Take my boots off. Then my shorts," I told him, then watching him obey me.

"Leave my socks on, but get 'em wet."

Reaching inside my jock, I stroked the length of my nine inches as the man-dog licked, sniffed and sucked my feet through my white socks. My breathing was getting hot, building up towards the climax I knew I'd quickly reach.

I smacked his hot ass a couple times, heard him groaning, and watched as he took hold of himself, quickly stroking and then gasping as he shot a jet of man-cream on my socks.

"You know what to do."

I watched as he licked up his mess.

"Get ready to catch this. NOW!"

12

He quickly turned as I pulled my erection out of my jock, pointed the uncut head in the direction of his mouth and unloaded the cream that had built to an unbearable pressure inside me. "Eat it, pig!" I grunted as the last jet landed on his lips, which were quickly licked clean.

Flopping back on the bed, I took a moment to regain my composure. Then, sitting up abruptly, I handed him my new necklace. "Show me what this looks like on me."

As he fastened the jewelry around my neck, I asked him, "This is real, right? It won't turn green on me if I wear it in the shower, right?"

"Yes Sir, it's real," he assured me.

I wrapped the watch that used to belong to him around my wrist, pulled on my clothes and headed for the door. "Nice knowin' you, dog," was my way of saying goodbye, as I opened the door, just after tucking the money inside my boots.

I didn't know if he was disappointed or pleased. I didn't even care. He was just an opportunity for an afternoon nut to me. Yes, we had just had sex, but we hadn't made love. He had no way of knowing that while I was shooting my cum on his face, I was thinking about that younger white guy I'd seen in the park earlier. If the guy in the hotel would think about it later, he'd realize that I never even asked for his name. To me, he was just "dog."

***

In just a few minutes, I was back in the park with the guys. Back to relaxing, hanging out, gossiping, chatting, enjoying the company of friends. Life seemed pretty damn good that day. As a bonus, I had an early sex romp to release that particular type of tension, plus two bills hidden away in my boots to treat myself to something nice later.

13

I spent some time that day wondering what my life would be like. Barely 20 years old but already in college, estranged from my birth family. I had enough self-awareness to realize that I was gay at an early age, and I made no effort to hide that fact from my strict, old-fashioned religious family. Though I was sleeping on the sofa, I was already living with a gay roommate on Spruce Street, the gayest street in Philly.

I was living in the moment, but that didn't mean that I had no thoughts or dreams about the future. I just really didn't have anything specific in mind.

My thoughts kept drifting back to that blonde kid. The one I had seen earlier. I can't even explain why. Yeah, he was attractive, but that wasn't really it. He was also someone new, maybe even a tourist, but that wasn't it either. Lying on the bench with my head in Shawnie's lap, feeling him gently stroke my hair as he chatted incessantly about fashions, music, celebrities, boyfriends, dance, and then more about music, music, music, my mind centered on that young boy. I hoped I'd run into him again sometime soon.

Before I knew it, the afternoon had flown by and it was time for me to report to the pizza shop for my shift. Before I left the park, I took my new watch and handed it to Shawnie.

"I don't need that watch, Henry. You know I don't need it. I don't live on any set schedule, where I need to know the time."

"I know, gurl," I smiled. "But take it anyway. Sell it on the El or something. Then buy yourself something. You know I like my bestie lookin' fly."

Shawnie blushed under his dark skin. We weren't a couple, but he was my bestie for real. We had a long history together and I always enjoyed his company. I called him my broster. He was definitely a bro, the best of the best. But he was also like a sister to me. His softer side was a comfort, a blessing, and helped to keep me grounded.

I knew he'd take the watch, and he did, carefully placing it into his shoulder bag. After hugging and air-kissing Shawnie, Quincy and Malcolm, I headed towards 12th Street, ready for a night of slinging pizzas.

No one had to tell me I was a horndog. Before I even got to Broad Street, I decided to make a quick detour to stop by Mahmoud's apartment, a second-floor walk-up at 13th and Pine. I needed a quick blowjob and Mahmoud was good enough to get me off in just a few minutes. I didn't even undress, just unzipped, pulled it out, watching him lick, slurp and suck before busting a quick nut down his throat. Zip up, quick air kiss and back out on the way to work.

I was working from 6 to midnight. Ten minutes before my shift, I was in the back room, pulling on my uniform black pants, and quickly buttoning the uniform shirt. My Paulie's Pizza cap completed my "fashionable" look.

Around 10 PM, one of my regular customers came in and ordered to go. Just as I placed the pizza into the oven, he nodded in the direction of the back alley, raising his eyebrows, asking a silent question. We didn't need words. I knew what he wanted. Cock.

I smiled and nodded. Thirty seconds later, we were in the alley, my cock buried down his throat, gagging him. Just the way he liked it. Two or three minutes later, he swallowed my third load of the day. As I was about to put myself away, he begged me to give him some yellow dessert. Laughing to myself, but scowling on the outside, I gave that pisspig what he wanted, shaking the last few drops on his upright face, wiping my cock clean in his hair.

I left him in the alley, quickly returning to my place behind the counter, before he followed me inside a few moments later.

As he left with his pizza, I knew that he was one happy customer who would return again and again, hungry for pizza, but also hungry for me and the all-meat special I could provide for his satisfaction.

Customers like that, always ready to service me plus adding a generous tip, provided the green I needed for my living expenses.

By 12:15 AM, I was already dressed in my regular clothes, heading home for a quick shower. Passing by TRAXX, a very popular club in Center City, I almost tripped when I spotted him. The object of my desires. That boy, the one from the park, in line to enter TRAXX.

Looks like we won't be meeting tonight, I thought, already knowing that I wasn't exactly welcome at that club. Almost exclusively the domain of the white gays, TRAXX had an unwritten policy to keep out what they'd consider "the riff-raff." That's what they thought of me. When I was in the mood to joke about it, I would ask my friends which one of us was "riff" and which one was "raff." But in reality, it wasn't a joke to me. It was hurtful.

Instead of partying in Center City, I headed to North Philly after I'd cleaned up at home. Sharkey's was my favorite place. Plenty of hot, Black men here. To be honest, including me. I was an object of desire here. Some of the men adored me. And I loved every minute of it. There, I felt like I was a star being born, a young god to be worshipped and desired, a king among queens.

***

The next night, I saw him in the park again. As I made my second pass along the concrete pathway, I felt a crush of disappointment. He was already talking to a guy who was sitting very close to him on the bench. I mean very close. Even though I didn't even know this dude, I felt the jealousy beginning to rise in my heart, thoughts of me dueling for the love of my fair maiden, winning his hand in a happily-ever-after marriage.

Coming to my senses, I could almost slap myself for having such ridiculous thoughts. Dueling? A fair maiden? A happily-ever-after? Living in a fool's paradise, indeed!

***

The third night I saw him in the park, I was prepared. No wandering around, no waiting for the right moment. This was the right moment. I'd either meet him or go on and totally forget about him. I approached him with all the confidence I could muster, sat down beside him, and introduced myself with a simple, "I'm Henry. What's your name?"

I was delighted by the sound of his voice, sweet, gentle, but masculine. "Joey," was all he said.

I liked the simplicity of our first meeting.

I don't think Joey remembers very much about our first night together. I mean the part after we went back to my place after I took him to Sharkey's.

It was a night of passion. Long, hot, sweaty sex sessions. Streams of cum everywhere. Groaning, moaning, whispering, breathing, grunting, pounding, thrusting, and both of us cumming and cumming and cumming.

With my usual tricks, I liked to degrade them, verbally abuse them, talking nasty and humiliating them. But with this one, I was mostly wordless. I didn't need to humiliate him to get to my goal, my orgasms, my points of no return.

I remember every second of it. And what I remember most clearly was the moment just before I fell asleep. My last thought was that we didn't just have sex. I dared to think that maybe, just maybe, we had been making love.

I knew that Joey was already asleep, so I felt safe whispering these words into his ear. "I love you, Joey."

I liked the feeling of saying that. One day, I hoped to be able to let him hear me say those words.

I love you, Joey.

CHAPTER TWO

JOEY

"I know it, Jando. I fucked up big time."

Alejandro, one of the Board members at Club Sanctuary, had of course heard all about what I had done to Henry, and he called to check up on me. I wasn't really in the mood to talk, not even having time to process what had happened yet. However, I could appreciate that he was concerned about me, especially since everyone in the community was already stressed out about AIDS, and any additional stress only added to the weight we all carried.

Ever since Henry walked out on me, after catching me violating our agreement to only play with others when we were together, I alternated between moods of deep depression and anger directed at myself. I couldn't, I wouldn't be angry at Henry. After all, I was the guilty party, and though I might try to justify my actions, there was no real way to do that.

I'd also been spending a lot of time thinking about our life, our relationship, going all the way back to when we met on that dark park bench in Rittenhouse Square. It was so random. A guy I had never seen before just comes up, sits down next to me and starts a conversation.

We went out on our first "date" that very night, out to a Black club in North Philly, then back to Henry's apartment for a night of sex on the mattress of his pull-out sofa.

That night, I had no idea about what would follow. Henry and I built a life together, something I didn't think possible back in 1976. We also built a very successful business.

I considered our club, Sanctuary, to not only be a place for gays to congregate and have fun. I also thought of it almost like a cultural center, providing resources for our community in times of need, like now.

Thinking back to how we had worked together to turn Club Sanctuary into a successful venture, I recalled how we had collaborated on so many different projects. One example that comes to mind is when we designed the club logo together. Throwing ideas out for each of us to consider, laughing at some of the more ridiculous suggestions, such as the flaming phallic symbol, or the martini glass with tiny dancers in and around the drink, or the two ruby red lips, slightly parted, tongue just barely visible, with "Welcome to the Club" stamped at an angle across the lips.

"Why don't we just have a long tongue licking a pair of balls?" I had suggested, as we continued having fun with our ideas.

"Or we could draw a logo with you kissing my ass!" Henry replied.

That was a conversation that eventually got us both horny, ending in a most satisfying fuck session. There was no lack of sex in our lives.

In the end, we decided to keep it simple, designing a stylized "S" inside a disco ball, with the name of the club both above and below the image.

The design looked fabulous on tee shirts, note cards, menus and other club items.

Even after we had our unofficial marriage ceremony on Christmas Eve in 1980, we had plenty of adventures, including flings with others. Monogamy wasn't really important to either one of us. However, the epidemic made us reconsider that, and we had vowed that we'd only play with others while we were together. We both agreed to this arrangement in order to protect ourselves and each other.

That leads me to my current situation. It's the Spring of 1992, and I'd just been caught red-handed, or more accurately, bare-assed in bed being barebacked by a hot young guy I'd picked up in the park on the same block as our house in the Queen Village neighborhood in Philly.

Now, I had to deal with the consequences. Henry had left me, while I was sleeping fitfully, brutally leaving behind his wedding ring, the sign of our commitment to each other.

Clearly, the next step was up to me.

"Jando, please do me a huge favor. Call Henry and ask him to meet me at our spot, the same place we met for the first time. Eight o'clock tonight. Please!" And then I quickly hung up.

My nerves hit about an hour before I was to meet Henry. We had been together for four years before the wedding, which was 12 years ago, and this was the worst situation we had faced as a couple. Potentially, it was the end of us. I wasn't sure how angry he still was with me, unsure of his reaction tonight.

***

Deciding what to wear tonight was a major decision. I thought about wearing the tux I wore when we married, but then I worried how I would feel, wandering back home by myself in such a sentimental outfit if he ended up rejecting my attempt at reconciliation. Casual attire? Then he might think I was being casual about my apology. Slutty? No, that might remind him of what caused this entire problem. My slutty behavior. Digging through my closet, I wanted to find something that was both comfortable and would send the right message.

Do straight people have problems like this, I wondered. *Or is it just me?*

I took a cab to Rittenhouse Square, anxious, humbled, a little ashamed. I got out at Broad and Walnut Streets, opting to walk the last few blocks, trying to calm myself. Approaching the entrance, I felt heavy, like I could barely move my legs. I wondered where was that happy, confident, young man that I used to be.

Unsure of myself, I thought, just momentarily, about turning around and walking away. Pausing in the shadows, between the lights casting down from the street lamps strewn haphazardly along the walkway, I looked down at myself. I knew I looked elegant. Perhaps it was a bit much for a casual stroll in the Square, but this was anything but a casual affair. The arc of my future hung in the balance of Henry's decision, whether he would take me back or not. My mind had been made up from the moment he caught me in my infidelity. I wanted him. That was the all-consuming thought in my mind since that awful moment in time.

A small tear in my eye caught the light streaming from the nearby lamp, causing a rainbow that was visible only to me. A private rainbow. *It's a sign*, I thought.

Each color seemed to reflect something about our love, an aura that must mean something.

Red - That was our passion. My undying love for Henry, which I now worried might be rejected. The color of blood, rushing from my heart to every part of my body, now pounding in my head as I dreaded this meeting.

Orange - Our optimistic outlook when we joined together to accomplish something. The energy that exuded from Henry, heightened when we worked together as a team.

Yellow - The joy that Henry brought into my life, bringing light as literally as the sun brings light to the Earth. But it's also a color of caution. I have to remember that I could lose everything if I continue to act irresponsibly.

Green - For the growth we experienced during our years together. Henry had been the impetus for my growth, my maturity, my better understanding of the world and our place in it.

Blue - The color of inspiration. There's no doubt in my mind that Henry is my inspiration. Everything I do is for him. Why did I put myself in this position? Why did I betray the one man who inspired me in ways that no other man possibly could?

Indigo - The color of wisdom. Possibly one of Henry's greatest traits. It was his wisdom that guided us. Certainly not mine. I was the fool. I needed Henry to guide me. What will I do if he turns me away? I cannot even bear that thought.

Violet - Royalty. Henry is my King. I worship him; I adore him; I obey him.

Each color reminds me of why I need to fix this problem. As the tear falls from my eye, the colors of the rainbow melting into nothingness, I worry that our relationship might meet a similar fate, melting away, out of my grasp, unable to maintain the steady force that I needed in my life. I was more afraid right now than ever before in my life.

I stayed in the half-shadows, drawing in a slight gasp when I saw that Henry was already there on our bench, waiting for me to arrive. Staring impassively ahead, he gave no hint of his emotions. I couldn't tell if he was still angry, nervous, or what.

"Babe!" I heard him say, knowing he had spotted me.

He stood, casting a shadow larger than life as he waited for me to come closer.

My single tear, now replaced with a flood, blinding me as my emotions became too strong, overwhelming all my senses. My legs felt weak, trembling, as I looked into his eyes, those beautiful eyes that I had fallen in love with so many years before. That's when I truly felt the sorrow that I had caused him. It seemed to me that the spark in his eyes had disappeared. I had done that. I had stolen that from him and I wanted nothing more than to give that spark, that joy, back to him.

"I like your outfit. It's very...serious."

Oh no, I thought. *It seemed that I had made the wrong fashion choice, after all.*

"Thank you, my King," was all I could manage to say.

There were many times during our years together when silence between us felt very right, totally comfortable. This was not one of those times. Awkwardly, I sat down as he sat next to me.

"Do you really like it?" I asked hopefully.

Scanning me from head to toe, slouching in my grey, flowing, oversized silk shirt matched with black lightweight wool slacks, both by Armani, and my highly-polished black dress shoes with the ultra-pointy toes by Kenneth Cole, all accessorized with sterling silver earrings, necklaces and bracelets, he tugged at my Gucci belt.

"You know, I oughta take that belt off you and turn you over my knee right here."

That helped to break the tension, and for a moment, I thought maybe we'd just go back to normal, without even talking about the past. But I did realize that wouldn't really solve anything. We had to talk about what I had done.

I laughed quietly, knowing that if that was what Henry wanted to do, I would submit. Right here. In public.

"Is that what you want?"

"No, we have to talk."

His voice sounded ominous to me. The fright I had experienced earlier came rushing back, filling my head to the point I felt the world swirling around me.

Taking hold of Henry for support, leaning into him for the support I had counted on for years, he instinctively held me in a protective embrace. It took all my effort to pretend I had courage, to pretend that I was ready for any decision he would make, but in the end, I couldn't do it. I sobbed as silently as I could, my emotional guilt taking over, although this was not my intention.

Henry held me more firmly, silently, until my tears subsided. He knew me well enough that waiting for me to stop was the only option for us to discuss our situation rationally.

I often wondered how and when Henry had learned to handle difficult situations, difficult people. People like me. Because as much as I tried to be an equal partner in our relationship, to provide the same support to Henry as he did to me, I knew the truth. It was Henry who was the pillar, the rock, the strength in our lives.

When I would ask Henry about his youth, before he met me, seeking clues to his remarkable qualities, he would respond with "Palms and Psalms."

At first, I had no clue what those words meant. I thought he was referring to the palms of his hands, or maybe palm trees. The word "Psalm?" I couldn't have even spelled it if I tried.

As our relationship grew, Henry taught me what he meant.

"Palms were used in our church to praise the lord," he'd explain. "In my family, church attendance was mandatory, and not just on Sundays. My Mom's a true believer and Pops was the enforcer, until he finally left us."

Palms to praise the lord.
Palms folded in prayer.
Palms for punishment.
Palms across the face.
Palms folded up into fists to beat the devil out of bad boys.

Continuing my education, he would say that "Psalms are all about the Old Testament. That was the focus in our church, where they believed in a god who's unforgiving, demanding, and judgmental. I don't know why our church was that way, but I did know that I couldn't be part of it."

From the King James version, The Book of Psalms:

Psalms 10:15 *Break thou the arm of the wicked and the evil man: seek out his wickedness till thou find none.*
Psalms 10:16 *The LORD is King for ever and ever: the heathen are perished out of his land.*

Over and over, Henry was told that he was wicked, evil, a heathen. Who wants to hear talk like that from a preacher? Or from a parent?

Henry was never involved with any organized religion after his childhood, but Palms and Psalms had a long-lasting effect on how he approached life. Rejecting both of those ideas, he embraced a life of materialism, independence and being as non-judgmental as he could. To me, it always seemed that he valued true friends more than anything else in the world.

But right here, right now, Henry was acting more like the stern father, giving me space to grieve about my infractions, but not quite ready to just forgive and forget. Not yet.

Once I had recovered sufficiently, I choked out the words. "Do you want to talk here or go somewhere?"

"I'd be happy to stay right here, though a storm is supposed to move in soon. That's if you can trust that weatherman."

"We're both dressed okay if you wanna walk over to Chinatown. I like that new Vietnamese spot where we had pho a few weeks ago."

"Sounds good," he agreed. We got up, heading east to Chinatown, and I reached for his hand. Ignoring my effort at physical closeness, he walked slowly, giving me a gentle touch, indicating that he wanted me to walk a half-step behind him.

That's a bad sign, I thought, but I silently obeyed.

Chinatown is so interesting, so different, a world unto itself right in the midst of Center City. That walk would be the inspiration for a new dance party at the club, The

Dragon Ball. I had the idea as Henry and I walked through that night, but it was kept in the back of my mind, an idea to be explored later. I had more important things to consider right now.

We ordered our food or more exactly, Henry ordered for us. I was being put in my place and I knew it. Actually, that was a place of comfort for me. Maybe there was a chance for us to still have a future together, after all. If Henry just let me do as I pleased, that could be a sign that he didn't care about me anymore, that he was letting go.

Once the waiter had taken our order, Henry looked me in the eye for the first time this evening.

"I have a lot to say," he told me, "but first, I want to hear from you. Why? Why'd you do it?"

Although I'd rehearsed this conversation at least a thousand times in my mind, I seemed totally unprepared to explain anything. Why did I let some random guy from the park fuck me bareback without Henry being there? How do you explain that kind of action to your man?

"Don't just sit there like a dumb fuck. Tell me. Explain yourself, boy."

Now I knew he was getting angry with me. The scowl, the stern voice, the fists clenched on the table in front of him. My head hung low as I felt the weight of my shame, forcing me to avoid looking into his beautiful, blazing eyes.

"King, can you forgive me?"

"Sometimes you're so goddamn pathetic," he spat out.

The waiter arrived with our soup, the aroma teasing me with the scent of exotic spices. Henry ladled the soup into his bowl, refusing to serve any to me. Sipping from his spoon, glaring at me, he simply stated a fact. "I'm still waiting."

"I wish I could explain, but I just got caught up in the moment. He was so sexy, so demanding, I couldn't stop myself..."

"You couldn't stop yourself," came the sneering reply. "You couldn't tell the dude 'No' or 'Let's wait till my man gets back home' or 'I only play with others when my man tells me it's okay and he's here to watch me.' You couldn't say nothin' like that, huh?"

Tears rolled down my cheeks. He made it sound so easy. And he was right, it should have been easy enough to do any of those things. Instead, I was a traitor, a thief, a dishonorable excuse for a human being.

The waiter arrived with the second course, removing the soup, along with my unused bowl and utensils.

Henry started serving himself, and once again refused to offer me anything. I dabbed at my face with my napkin, trying to look composed, as my mind was reeling from the mix of shame and embarrassment.

"I'm not saying what you did was right, because it wasn't. But I will say that I might understand what happened better than you think I do."

Henry paused to let that sink in, as he continued to enjoy his meal. My hands remained clasped in my lap, clearly not being invited to share, at least not yet.

"I mean, look at what we've been doing. At first, I couldn't imagine why you would act like that. Cheating on me," he said, the disgust so apparent it might as well have been written on the menu.

"But I've had a lot of time to think. And I think that maybe we were setting ourselves up for failure."

I had no idea what he meant by that.

Between bites, he began to explain.

"Let's remember two things. First, what it was like when we first met. Remember?"

Of course, I remember, I thought, remaining silent, subservient, obedient, being taught a lesson by the Master. My eyes were still averting his steady gaze, pretending to be interested in the empty plate in front of me.

"We didn't enforce any rules. I was your main man and you were mine, but other than that, we did what we liked, with anyone we liked. Am I right or not?

"Yes Sir," I whispered.

"Tell me that louder," came the order.

"Yes Sir," I repeated, loudly enough for every customer in the small restaurant to hear. The background chatter seemed to suddenly go silent, as people became aware of our presence and my obvious position as submissive to the Black man sitting across from me.

"Maybe your pea-brain can remember why we decided on our current arrangement, where we decided not to just fuck around with any street whore we find." His voice was raised so anyone who wanted to continue listening to us could easily do so.

"Do you remember, pussyboy? Why don't we just fuck around anymore?"

Slouching into my chair, subconsciously trying to escape the gaze of the other diners, my mind was blank except for the feeling of being completely and publicly humiliated.

I was crying again.

"Holy fuck!" was all Henry could say. "How can you forget when we're living right in the middle of all this sickness, all this death? Dude, it's all because of AIDS. How can you possibly forget about Lonnie, the way he looked when we saw him in Frisco? He was nothing but skin and bones, wasting away right in front of Stephen's eyes, in front of our eyes. And how about BJ? How long did we know him and then there we were, at his funeral?"

Henry's eyes were on fire, in a passionate rage at my stupidity and selfishness.

"And you know those were just the tip of the iceberg. So many people. So many friends. Gone, gone forever! Is that what you want to happen to me? Do you wanna watch me waste away and die? Is that what you want for yourself? For both of us? Because that's what you did. You put everything at risk! And you know you did it! That's why I'm just a little upset about your little trick the other day!"

It's possible, even probable, that many of the patrons in the Vietnamese restaurant spoke little to no English. But it seemed that everyone knew the word "AIDS." At the mention of the "gay disease," it seemed that all eyes were on us. I heard a customer in the back telling the owner, "Kick them out. They have the AIDS."

Something hit me in the back of the head. A customer had thrown something at me. No physical harm, but certainly a blow to my self-esteem and surely meant as an insult. Looking towards the back of the restaurant, there was no indication of which customer was guilty of the assault, and Henry just looked at me impassively and shrugged his shoulders.

He went back to eating, adding spices to his pho, leaving me once again with empty plates and bowls in front of me. Again, something hit me from behind. I was about to get up and confront anyone who looked suspicious, when the owner of the establishment rushed over to our table. Much later, I would find that the owner's name was Tuyen.

"Please excuse me," he said hurriedly. "My restaurant is just a small place, where my people come to enjoy a meal. We don't get too many outsiders here, and some of my customers are already nervous around Americans and..."

He paused. I thought he was about to say something like "Black people," but he never finished that thought.

"Everyone here heard you talking about the AIDS and now some of them think you might be sick. That has them worried. I don't mean to be rude, but I'd like to wrap up the rest of your meal for you to take with you."

Henry stopped and thought for a moment. This time, he decided not to make an issue of it, mostly because he was already preoccupied with the problems between us, and he was in no mood to argue with the owner here.

"Give the bags and the check to the girl," he told the man, pointing at me. "I always make my bitches pay for my meals."

Looking at me with a mixture of ridicule and pity, he hurried away to prepare the meal for take-out.

By the time I got outside, Henry had already flagged down a cab. He stepped in first, instead of holding the door for me, as usual.

"Gimme that," he said, grabbing the bag.

"Now take off your shoes and socks. I want you to walk home in your bare feet. With every step, I want you to think about what you did, how you hurt me, how you hurt us."

I stood there, stunned.

"Dog, don't make me tell you twice. Do it. Now."

I obeyed. Like I always obeyed. Or, I should say, as I almost always obeyed.

Before I took the first step, on my way home, barefooted and humiliated, I saw the owner of the restaurant, Tuyen, watching me, seeing me in a state of total humiliation.

Never before did I realize how many pebbles, twigs, papers and just plain pieces of trash were on Philly's sidewalks. Not to mention all the gum that passers-by had disrespectfully spat out just about everywhere. Luckily, the pavement had cooled from the heat of the day, so at least my soles weren't burning.

Watching the cab head towards Queen Village, our little neighborhood located a few blocks south of South Street, it occurred to me that I could easily get my own ride home. But before I'd walked three blocks, I saw Henry passing by me, checking to be sure I was still walking. So much for that plan.

It didn't take long to get home. Henry was waiting for me in the living room, having changed out of the outfit he had worn for our meeting, a patterned silk shirt with black cotton pants.

Clad only in boxers, he was clearly making himself at home. He motioned for me to sit across from him.

"Just sit and listen. This isn't a conversation right now, not a discussion. I want to tell you a few things."

My head and my heart sagged.

"You put both of us in danger. Real danger. And that isn't right, and you don't have the right to do that. Understand?"

"Yes Sir."

"But I've been thinking a lot about our lives. What we've been doing. And I think that maybe we should think about that, and maybe change direction."

I wasn't exactly sure what Henry meant by that. Did he think we should break up and go off on different life paths?

"We'll talk more about that later," Henry stated matter-of-factly. "Right now, I want you to know, in case you haven't already figured it out, that you're going to be punished. Just like a little boy has to be punished to learn a lesson. Hear me?"

"Yes Sir," came my meek reply.

"Strip," was the simple command.

I was led by my dick to a chair in the kitchen, pushed down onto the seat, my arms pulled behind the back of the chair, feeling the cuffs snapped on tightly, ensuring that resistance and escape were both impossible. My dick betrayed me by quickly growing hard, though Henry paid no attention to my excitement. That wasn't his intention; this wasn't foreplay.

Less than a minute later, I heard the buzzing sound of the razor. My longish locks were being shaved off, leaving me with a buzzcut. My beautiful blonde hair littered the kitchen floor, which brought me again to tears. Admittedly, I was ashamed of myself, and I knew that this was a way for Henry to be sure my shame wasn't just something that I would feel, but that others would be sure to see. He would expose me publicly as penance for my sins.

I felt a tug at a length of hair left hanging over my left ear, and then my right. Henry held a mirror so I could see the results, my reflection showing a man with red swollen eyes, with pink bows tied around the length of hair over each ear.

"Pigtails for a pig. Seems appropriate, don't you think?"

I was dying on the inside. Not only was I filled with shame, but Henry was rubbing it in, seeming to revel in his role as my tormentor, and though I had earlier thought that blaming myself was hard enough, it was so much worse having Henry treat me like the traitor that I was.

Though I felt so guilty, a secret, sometimes hidden part of me was finding pleasure in my punishment. My erect throbbing cock gave me away, and I wondered if Henry might get turned on and eventually turn this scene into make-up sex. An image of him lowering himself onto my erection flashed through my mind, and a sigh escaped my lips.

Make-up sex was nowhere in Henry's thoughts. Standing in front of me, arms crossed, glaring at my downcast face, he used his strong fingers to take a flick at my dick, making it swing wildly in front of me.

"You are a fuckin' dog, aren't you?"

I looked up with my best impression of puppy-dog eyes, hoping for the best.

"I got some news for you. Bad news. If you think you're gonna be using that pathetic excuse for a cock anytime soon, well, think again."

Averting my eyes from him, I was staring at my dick, pointing straight up at my face. Everybody, and I mean everybody, teased me about its size, though it just isn't all that small. I knew that to be true, having seen hundreds, if not thousands, of hard dicks in my lifetime. Of course, it paled in comparison to Henry's nine inches, with mine when fully erect still an inch, ok, two inches, below my belly button. But ever since a Halloween party years ago, when Henry shaved me completely bare, I had continued to keep that smooth, hairless look. Honestly, I thought that made me look bigger than I really was. Still, for whatever reason, other guys made fun of it, most probably just as a way to feed my need for being dominated.

"Look at me," he commanded, and I obeyed instinctively.

"We don't know right now if you're a poz pig or not. You understand that, right?"

"Ohhhh."

In my guilt, I hadn't thought about that possibility. Of course, Henry was right. I might have been infected with HIV during my bareback fuck session with the skateboarder from the park.

What was that guy's name again, I thought. *Oh yeah, Xander*.

"I'm not gonna let you do any screwing, at least not until we get new test results. And you already know there's a waiting period before we can know for sure."

"But there's more," he continued. "I'm not gonna let you cum, not even once, till we find out whatsup. Tell me how long you hafta wait. I know you already know the answer. We've been to enough safer sex workshops and read enough about this. You better get the right answer, or your time's gonna get doubled."

"I remember they called it the window period. For most people, it takes 4 to 6 weeks."

"True," Henry said, "but are we 'most people'? Are you willing to put me at risk after 6 weeks?"

I wanted to bury my face in my hands, but they were restrained behind my chair, preventing me from putting my feelings into action.

"How long does it take to be certain? How long are you setting your punishment for? It's up to you. Tell me how long you're gonna hold your cum inside till we know for sure that your test will be accurate."

"I know it can take three months in some people before the test will let us know for sure."

"You sure about that? Three months?"

"Yes Sir. I'm sure, my King."

Henry stood in front of me, gently rubbing the top of my buzzed head. My emotions were a mixture of regret and humility, yet I also felt comforted by the stroking. If I could, I'd be purring, rubbing my head against the strong man in front of me.

"That dick of yours refuses to go down, huh boy?"

The rigidity of my erection answered for itself. Henry always turned me on, but never more than when he was being strict with me.

"I read about this in one of my magazines."

I had no idea what he was talking about.

Reaching between my legs, his stroking hand was now working my cock rather than my head. Though he had just told me I'd be going without shooting my jizz for the next three months, I'd already forgotten that, as I felt the sensations of pleasure beginning to rise within me, closing my eyes in anticipation.

"This'll keep that bad boy soft."

I wasn't looking at him, lost in the sea of sexual emotions flooding my brain.

Then, very suddenly, a painful burning sensation.

"Owwwwww! What the fuck?"

36

Henry had grabbed a pepper shaker from the nearby kitchen counter, pouring grains of black pepper on the tip of my dick, a few grains falling into my open piss hole. Rather than the pleasure of the expected orgasm, my dick immediately went limp, as my excitement was replaced with the agony of denial.

Not yet recovered from the shock of this sudden change in my situation, I watched as Henry then reached inside the shoulder bag he had brought with him from the restaurant. Groaning, I realized how Henry planned to keep me in a state of chastity, feeling his hands pushing my flaccid, limp penis into a plastic case, feeling it snap closed around my manhood, and then latched tightly with a lock.

"That won't be coming off for at least three months, maybe longer," he smirked. "Except when I want you to shave down there. I'm not gonna let you grow your hairs. That might give you the idea that you're a real man, and we both know you ain't nothin' but my little bitchboy. Right?"

My silence irritated him.

"I asked you a question. Am I right, boy?"

"Yes, my King. You're right."

Henry positioned himself in front of me, his manhood hard and wet, just out of reach of my mouth. I wanted him inside me so much, I tried to lunge forward, opening my mouth, inviting him to enter me.

He did no such thing. Instead, he slowly massaged his meat, gently at first, but then more quickly, as he sought the release of his pent-up desires. It wasn't long before I felt his creamy milk splattering against my face, with the final spurt deposited on the top of my head.

My mind was now in a state of confusion as my sexual desires were burning hot, with no way to reflect those desires into manly hardness. My cock, securely caged, remained soft and small.

"We still have a lot to talk about. But that's enough for now. I'm tired. and I wanna sleep," he said, walking behind the chair to release me.

He led me by the hand into the bedroom. "You sleep down there tonight," he told me, pointing at the floor. "No pillow, no blanket, nothing. Just a naked, pathetic pig on my floor. No, not even a pig. A whore on the floor. That's you."

Those words, meant to cut deep, hit their intended target. Curling up on the hardwood floors, I tried to get comfortable, failing miserably. I knew it would be a long night for me.

As soon as Henry got into bed, I could hear his breathing change to that of a man sleeping contentedly, as if he didn't care about any of my troubles.

Though I was physically uncomfortable, part of me was happy that, at the very least, Henry was back home. We had never slept apart like this before, but being in the same room was a step in the right direction.

"I love you, Henry," I whispered. He remained motionless, giving no hint whether he heard me or not. He slept on, gently snoring, and I comforted myself, wrapping myself in his embrace, although it was only in my imagination.

CHAPTER THREE

MISTER GQ

"Good morning, Sir. My name's Harvé."

That was how I introduced myself to the owner/editor/personnel manager at the Philadelphia Gay News, aka PGN.

In my opinion, he didn't need to know the pesky details, like that my name is actually Harvey. That day, I was Harvé, with a silent H and a second syllable that rhymed with "Oy Vey," reflecting my Jewish heritage. I was trying to make an impression, but also a name for myself.

By the time I'd left the office, I had been offered a position as a general assignment reporter. Despite the title, I had gotten the impression that it was going to be up to me to find the topics for my stories. And that was just fine with me. I saw myself in the role of a columnist, specifically, a gossip columnist.

Arranging my pencil holder, coffee cup and Rolodex filled with blank cards around the typewriter at my newly-assigned desk, I could imagine my first headline:

Mister GQ
The Gossip Queen
By Harvé

Perfect, I thought. *They're gonna eat this shit up*!

The year I dropped out of college, 1985, and started working at PGN, was a big year for gossip. Major national stories included the death of Rock Hudson from AIDS, the courtship of Sarah Ferguson (aka Fergie) and Prince Andrew, and the fabulous musical artists appearing at Live Aid that year, including Madonna, Led Zeppelin, Mick Jagger with Tina Turner, and our own Patti LaBelle, all live at JFK Stadium on July 13.

I covered those stories, of course. But my specialty was gossip of the local variety and even more specifically, all about gay society in Philly. I lived it and I loved it!

For at least two years before I started working at PGN, I'd been a regular at the clubs in town, particularly Club Sanctuary. At that point, I was still trying to find where I fit in. I didn't have anything in common with the druggie crowd, since taking any kind of illegal substance generally made me feel sick rather than flying high. The glamorous queens didn't even notice me, with their glittery sequins, feathery boas and exotic make-up designs not really feeling like my style.

The leather crowd? They scared me a little.

The older men? Same. A little scary.

The hustlers? In a word, no.

Where were the literary men, the educated, the refined gentlemen, I wondered. Maybe they met in some secret gathering place, away from the clubs, away from this club, anyway.

Or, more likely, those men were intermingled among the various groups and cliques at the club. Perhaps they had just put that part of their lives aside as they enjoyed the club atmosphere. My goal was to seek them out, to join them, to be one of them.

I had to think of a way to find them. My first thought was to check out the library, so to speak. The Main Branch of the Free Library of Philadelphia was the logical starting point. Sitting at a table there, browsing the stacks, flipping through card catalogs, those were fun times for me. I was interested in titles by authors such as Faulkner and Hemingway, though I will also confess to getting absorbed in titles by E. M. Forster (*Maurice*), Truman Capote (*Other Voices, Other Rooms; In Cold Blood*) and Edmund White (*A Boy's Own Story*).

But far from finding a soulmate, or even a like-minded literary soul, it always ended the same. A quick encounter in a bathroom stall, with no follow-up. No one there seemed interested in continuing contact, not even as a friend.

Discouraged, but not deterred, I decided that maybe this would just take more time than I originally thought.

If I was being honest with myself, I'd admit that I enjoyed those trips to the Free Library, because at least I found some physical relief and release. But while satisfying a physical need, they didn't provide any sense of community. At least not for me.

Bookstores were also on my list of places to visit regularly. Mostly, I would spend time browsing places like Robin's Book Store on S. 13th Street and Giovanni's Room on S. 12th Street. But again, if I'm being totally honest, I'd also hang out at spots like Adam and Eve, Doc Johnson's and other adult bookstores. I liked porn; I still do. Plot, setting, characters, motives, themes, I simply adored those aspects when I read literature. But give me descriptions of sweaty sex sessions between two perfect male specimens with gigantic horse cocks, and that was just fine when I was reading purely for sexual gratification and fun.

I think what I'm saying is that I like a lot of things both ways. One side of me had a definite taste for the finer things in life, while my other, darker side sometimes wallowed in sleaze and filth, enjoying every vile moment of it.

Slowly, I was building a name and a reputation for myself through my columns, now a regular feature of PGN. Some of my more memorable columns chronicled the many parties held at Club Sanctuary, particularly those that drew the biggest crowds, the AIDS fundraisers.

I remember when, at the end of a column about the first Snow Ball fundraiser, I planted a blind item about a new bartender at Sanctuary, writing:

"Rumor has it that a new bartender at a certain nightclub "blew" his way into town and a job behind the bar. How high up the ladder will he climb? Or is the real question, how far did he crawl to get where he is?"

Where did I get ideas like that one? Honestly, some of them were just totally made up in my fervid, evil mind. But that one came straight from the horse's mouth, as a drunken bartender bragged to me about exactly how he'd gotten hired at Sanctuary. A back room blow job. Though he refused to say whose cock he had in his mouth, there weren't too many possibilities. It had to be Henry...or Joey. I never did find out for certain, though I had my suspicions.

At the very bottom of that same column, I added a line that would change my life. It was a spur-of-the-moment decision, and I was taking a chance, but it led to some great times.

"Anyone interested in discussing books over brunch? I'll be at Judy's Cafe at 3rd and Bainbridge Streets with my copy of *Tales of the City* by Armistead Maupin. Bring your copy and meet me at 1 PM this Sunday. Let's talk!"

Ever the optimist, I had arranged two tables together, allowing for a seating of ten. Rising to greet each new arrival, I wasn't surprised that I looked up at each guy, since I topped out at 5 feet 5 inches.

"What a lovely piece you have there!" exclaimed the first one to arrive, lightly touching the Star of David that I always wore with my gold necklace. Giggling, I shook his hand, as he introduced himself as Aristotle.

"I know, I always read your reviews in *Philadelphia Magazine,"* I gushed.

Holy shit, I can't believe Aristotle is here. I wonder what he thinks of my book selection. I guess I'll find out soon enough, I thought.

Ari, dressed to impress in black slacks and a gold lamé shirt, exposing his smooth chest, adorned with at least a dozen necklaces, imperiously sat at the head of the table.

I didn't give myself time to think about the possible consequences from people who had actual power.

"Oh darling, I'm very sorry. That's my seat. Those seats are for my guests," I stated firmly, indicating towards the other chairs.

"But of course, Harvé, how rude of me!"

Oh my god, he pronounced my name correctly!

"Please make yourself comfortable," I assured him. "The others will be arriving shortly. Order a drink, if you like," I told him, as a young man I'd never seen before approached the table.

"Is this the Book Brunch?" he asked, in a perfectly lovely, lilting voice. "I'm Zed." As I reached for his hand, I ended up almost knocking his book to the floor. Quickly placing his book on the table, we greeted each other properly, with Ari standing to extend his greeting as well.

"I don't mean to be rude, but where have you been all my life?" Ari asked him, clearly interested in the young man, casually but impeccably dressed for the occasion. Zed laughed in response, taking the seat next to Aristotle.

He's probably only been living for half your lifetime, I thought, hoping my smile hid my less-than-charitable thoughts. *And can you believe he's wearing that Furberry scarf?* A fake Burberry. I could spot them a mile away.

In reality, I couldn't blame Ari for being attracted. Zed was one of those young men who oozed sexuality, without any effort on his part. Among his best features were his naturally blonde, thick hair, green eyes, thick red lips contrasting with his flawless skin, and his perfect jawline and cheekbones. If I cared about physical beauty, I might have been just a tad jealous!

Barely having time to finish my thoughts, my next guest walked in, adding his commanding appearance to our quickly-growing group.

"You must be Harvey!" his voice boomed, reaching around me and embracing me in a bear hug.

"Actually, it's pronounced Arvay" I quickly corrected him.

"Ohh, I'm so sorry, Harvé," he corrected himself. "I'm Giff, short for Gifford. So pleased to meet all of you," as everyone exchanged names and greetings.

Giff sat across from Zed, and I was struck by their differences. Zed looked 16 at best. Giff had to be at least 45. Zed, smooth face, might not even have to shave yet. Giff, bushy hair, bushy brows, with a long, bushy beard. Zed, thin as a wisp. Giff, big, burly, beefy. And Black.

As we chatted, placing our orders and getting to know one another, I was beyond pleased with the assembled group. I was the up-and-coming reporter at PGN. Ari was the veteran critic at Philadelphia Magazine, known for his insightful reviews of theatre, books and movies. Zed was an art student, enrolled at The Art Institute.

I have a tiny confession to make here. I sometimes jump to conclusions about people based solely on their appearance. Therefore, I was expecting Giff to say he worked in a warehouse or factory. I know, I know. I should know better than that.

It was a pleasant surprise when Giff informed us that he was a music producer, working with Teddy Pendergrass on both his albums and music videos, even after Teddy's notorious car crash that left him paralyzed. Of course, it was the hottest gossip in Philly when Teddy was found to have a transgender nightclub performer riding in the car with him the night of the accident.

I was finishing my first Bloody Mary as the waiter was bringing our meals. In advance, everyone had agreed to separate checks. I couldn't wait to start on my lox and bagels, with a side of khachapuri, a boat-shaped bread filled with eggs, butter and three types of cheese. Delicious! But can you spell cholesterol?

Before I could even get started, my final guests arrived, fashionably late. I was a little annoyed, but just a little. After all, I know very well how certain gays like to be.

I never thought that the ultimate party boys, Joey and Henry, the owners of Club Sanctuary, would be joining us.

Didn't I include that blind item about the backroom blowjob given to a bartender at a club in the same column as the invitation to the Book Brunch?

I quickly recovered from that thought as the two introduced themselves, bringing the total number of gay men seated at our table to six.

The food was delicious, as was the company. The conversation, specifically our different interpretations and responses to the book, was lively and friendly. I was truly impressed with this group of men whom I hoped would all become friends.

The discussions ranged from serious thoughts about whether a novel needed a strong structure or whether secondary characters needed depth, to more lightweight fare such as whether the names of characters really meant anything.

I found the different opinions thought-provoking and interesting. With one exception. Although he was certainly friendly and engaging, it was Joey who seemed to lack any real understanding or insights into the book we were discussing. It seemed that he was happy to just repeat whatever his partner, Henry, had to say. I wondered if Joey had even read the book.

After 90 minutes at the table, I was sure the waiter was ready for us to depart. While finishing our coffees and thanking everyone for attending, I suggested meeting again soon.

"I'm in," Giff said, with everyone nodding in agreement.

"Is weekly too often?" I asked tentatively.

"Not for me," Aristotle replied. "This was just the kind of group I've been looking for. But let's not pressure ourselves to read a new book every week. Let's read maybe one new book each month, and sometimes we can talk about a book that maybe we've all read before."

"And what do we think about this place?" I ventured. "It has a nice atmosphere, especially with the natural light and the jazz station playing in the background."

"It's a cool spot for sure," Zed agreed. "But honestly, it's a little pricey for me," he confessed.

"Don't worry, babe. I can take care of the bill for the two of us," Ari said, stretching his arm around Zed's slender shoulders and pulling him close.

"I don't know if we can make it every week," Joey said.

Placing his strong hand over Joey's, Henry corrected him. "Of course, we can make it. Every single week. And we won't be late again, I can promise you that. I just gotta make sure Joey here has his panties all picked out in advance so he doesn't take forever figuring out what color to wear."

Everybody laughed at that, but I had a feeling it wasn't just a joke.

"All right, let me see if we can agree on some future plans. First, although this place is very cool, how about we move our meeting up to the Gayborhood instead of Queen Village? That might be more convenient for all of us, and my friend Andy owns that new spot called Wednesdays.

Anybody try it yet? The food's good and Andy won't mind if we spend an hour or two there."

"Sounds like a plan," Henry said, as each of the Book Brunch crew agreed to the change of venue.

"And let's talk about a different genre next week. Has everyone read *Interview with the Vampire* by Anne Rice? Bring a copy if you have it, or I'll be happy to read a few passages to get the conversation started, if we need some reminders," I joked.

"I see my partner's out there with the car. He's always on time to pick me up," Giff said, winking at Henry.

As the host, I waited for all of the guests to leave. Ari and Zed walked off together, with Ari's arm around Zed's waist. *Nice catch*, I thought to myself, thinking that both of them had lucked out today.

Just before they turned the corner, it seemed that Henry was angry at Joey, as he was gesturing at him, not in a threatening manner, but clearly displeased about something. I wondered if it was about being late. Or maybe it had something to do with what I had written. Trouble in Paradise?

After brunch, I was feeling good about myself. Boosting my self-esteem was one of my core principles. I wasn't born into wealth, fame, power, or even beauty. But I had a strong core and a mission. I was going to make a mark in the world. I wasn't going to be easily forgotten.

I had decided early in life not to settle. Average things bored me. Cheapness repulsed me. Ugliness horrified me. Trivial and shallow thoughts were the epitome of stupidity. Tolerate any of that? Why, I'd rather die!

Though I was still at a point where I was living in a studio apartment, in the center of the Gayborhood, I had begun collecting items I considered to be of value. First editions of notable books. Sophisticated works by new artists, ones I considered to be up-and-coming. My collection of vinyl records, consisting mostly of classical and jazz, was small but growing. A special section was reserved for my beloved albums of Broadway musicals.

Later that afternoon, I found myself at Tea Dance, a Sunday ritual at Club Sanctuary. When I arrived, the sea of people didn't part for me in reverence. Not yet. But I wasn't exactly an outsider, either. Every week, it seemed that more and more people recognized me. A few of the A-Listers already knew me, valuing me as a source for keeping them in the public eye, if that was their goal.

Progress was being made. Success was at my feet.

My plan was to become a star in this town, come hell or high water, no matter who stood in my path or tried to pull me down.

High water. The calm surface of the sea lulls me into a sense of security, confident in my ability to navigate the tricky, subversive currents.

A sea filled with creatures pulling me in all directions, confusing me, surprising me, ready to swallow me. I reach for the sunlight above, a futile attempt to grasp onto reality, my fingers outstretched, finding nothing.

Where is my lifeguard? Will I ever find him?

CHAPTER FOUR

JOEY

I woke up late, as usual, but I was cold and sore. That wasn't usual. The grogginess in my brain was still dominant as I laid there, finding myself on the bedroom floor, unsure of what happened. Also unusual, my dick wasn't hard and I always woke up with a burning case of morning wood.

I resisted opening my eyes as the memories of last night slowly returned through the fog. I became aware of Henry, still snoring, but above me rather than beside me. *What the fuck?* I thought.

Stretching instinctively, I felt a tightness around my neck and heard a strange sound. Opening my eyes, I was astonished to find that there was a collar around my neck, with a leash attached, which in turn had been secured to the foot of the bed.

When did all this happen? I don't remember anything.

"Is the dog awake now?" I heard Henry ask, as my stirrings disturbed his rest.

"Yes Sir" was my meek reply.

"In the middle of the night, I woke up and it occurred to me you might run out around the neighborhood like a bitch in heat, fucking anything with a dick. So I decided to take some precautions," he explained, swinging his legs over the side of the bed, sitting up so I could see his face, still a little puffy from sleep. Even from this angle, his morning hardness was clearly visible.

"Oh, come on, Henry! You're being a little dramatic, aren't you?"

"Am I?" he sneered.

"We're going to talk later. But right now, I just want you to watch. Look and see what you're missing out on for at least the next three months."

Standing, fully erect, his engorged dick looking massive, even in his huge hands, Henry stood in front of me, stroking his manhood close enough to my face that I could smell his masculinity, but far enough that his beautiful maleness was beyond my reach.

Quickly stroking, he brought himself to the point of grunting, as I watched his cock lengthen to its limit, his balls tightening quickly, and with a few short thrusts into the air, he squirted his juicy goodness onto the sheets of the bed.

Still panting, looking me squarely in the eye, he stated matter-of-factly, "That coulda been yours. Coulda. Shoulda. But that ain't gonna happen anytime soon."

Henry turned and walked away from me, leaving me on the floor, chained to the bed, my cock still caged, unable to even express my desire for this man by getting my dick hard.

"Henry, don't do this to me!" I cried.

"Bitch, I'm not doing anything to you. You did that to yourself."

An hour later, Henry returned to the bedroom, silently lifting the leg of the bed to release the leash that kept me bound there. I dared not speak. I had lost my confidence in myself, in our relationship, in everything I had previously thought of as the foundations of my life.

Taking hold of the leash, still attached to the collar tightly wound around my neck, I was pulled into the living room, where Henry gave a simple command, "Sit."

Taking a seat on the sofa, Henry glared at me like the fool that I was.

"Dog, sit," he repeated, pointing at the floor.

Earlier, I didn't think my heart could sink any deeper, but somehow, I had not yet reached the bottom, because now I felt my heart falling into the depths of hell.

I had always been mostly submissive to Henry, but in truth, it was a casual thing for us. It was my sexual role, almost always, but there were times when we switched. It just seemed to be us expressing our natural selves to each other. No spoken rules. Nothing formalized. Subject to change at any time. The same was true in our lives outside the bedroom. Yes, Henry made many decisions and we were usually on the same page, but we were equals. At least, that's how I thought it was between us.

Henry took a spot on the sofa, legs spread wide, wearing a black leather jock with a zippered front, a leather harness around his muscular chest, and big, black shiny leather boots.

"I have a confession to make," he said, while staring into the distance. I could see the sparkle in his eyes, as the sun in the room shone on him, almost like a god in the heavens. He was stunning, a sight that not only impressed me, but excited me, though I was cock-caged.

"I'm angry and hurt and I want you to know that." Now he was looking at me directly, with eyes that were both accusatory and somehow still a source of comfort.

"But the truth is," he continued, taking hold of my chin and turning my head up so I was looking into his eyes, "...the truth is I still love you."

My heart soared in an instant. Eyes filling with tears, I started to speak, but he stopped me immediately.

"Not a word outta you until I give permission."

I obeyed without question, without hesitation, without a doubt that my heart still belonged to Henry.

"But love means different things to different folks, I guess. Loving you used to mean trusting you. Confiding in you. Depending on you. Now, I have doubts about those things."

Looking away, I couldn't bear to hear those words. After years of building a wonderful relationship with a man that I adored, I was now thinking that I had made the mistake of taking him for granted, thinking that we'd always be together, no matter what. Spreading my legs and getting fucked bareback by Xander, without having Henry present and approving of my actions, had been a terrible mistake on my part. I knew it before, but now I was truly understanding exactly what I had done.

"Clearly, you made a mistake," Henry said, once again turning my head, not allowing me to gaze elsewhere, insisting that I own my shame and my betrayal.

"When I think of my future without you, without us together, it's like peering into an endless black hole. Just thinking about it makes me uncomfortable and to be honest, scared. I've never even considered being without you before."

I couldn't possibly feel any worse, but I sat in stony silence, allowing the hurt to wash over me, almost drowning me, understanding more with each word from Henry just how badly I had wounded him.

"When I think of life with you, at least it gives me hope. I know that none of us are perfect, and maybe we can grow stronger as a couple, but I think we've made some poor choices in the past, and we might think about a new path forward."

"Wh...What?" I stammered.

Henry pulled me towards him, so I was sitting on the floor between his legs, but facing away from him. He began to stroke my buzzed head, in a gentle way that reminded me of his usual firm but calm demeanor.

"You acting out like a street cunt made me think about our life."

I winced as the words cut ever deeper into my wounds.

"Maybe we were approaching our relationship the wrong way. I think we were maybe trying to act too much like straight people. You know, the whole getting married, moving out of the Gayborhood, trying to follow a model that I really think wasn't made for us."

"You don't wanna be married to me anymore?"

Immediately, I was smacked in the head, with Henry pulling my leash more tightly around my neck, reminding me that silence had been requested. No, not requested. Demanded.

"Sorry Sir," I offered my apologies.

"Can't you follow even simple directions like when I tell you to shut the fuck up?"

My reply was to nod very slightly, meekly, with humility. No pretense on my part. True humility. I was being taught a lesson and I wanted to learn. I wanted to be trained. I wanted Henry to be in charge.

"And then there's our lazy approach to this whole Dom/sub relationship. I thought we could develop something new. Something beyond what we see in the leather community. I thought maybe you were strong enough, or had the balls to be obedient without me demanding to be in control all the time. I think I miscalculated there. I think you need discipline, strong discipline. Every day and every night, non-stop, 24/7 discipline."

Henry paused, continuing to rub my head gently, then wrapping his hands around my neck, tightening, them, constricting my breathing, wrapping his muscular legs around my head, enveloping me in a tightness that was both breath-taking and comforting.

Then he let go of me completely.

"I want you to decide, dog. Right here, right now. Do you want to be choked with my discipline, or let go? You can

53

have freedom or you can give in to me totally. It's one way or the other. What's it gonna be?"

I started to answer, but Henry once more told me to be silent.

"No discussion. No explanation. No compromise. I don't want to hear your opinion or your reasons. You may only state your decision in one word. You either say 'Discipline' or you say 'Freedom'. There are no alternatives. No middle-ground. Choose now."

There was no hesitation on my part at all.

"Discipline." The choice had been made.

***

"I just have one more question for you," Henry said, moving in front of me while dropping his jockstrap to the floor. Watching his swinging manhood, while mine remained encased like a caged beast, I tried to avoid direct eye contact. That's when Henry reached for his jock, holding it tightly against my face, forcing me to inhale his scent. This would normally be a pleasant experience, but now it only enhanced my frustration at being unable to achieve a hard-on.

Henry wrapped the leg straps of the jock behind my ears, keeping the pouch firmly against my mouth and nose.

Squatting down, Henry's dick, much larger and thicker than average and often the object of my lustful desires, hung so low that the tip was against the floor.

"Was that the only time? When you got fucked by that kid, Xander. Was that the only time you ever cheated on me? This is the time for honesty. Tell me, cuntboy. If you have anything to confess, do it right here, right now."

This was a moment I had dreaded for a long time, ever since our bartender Billy had sucked my dick in the back office of Club Sanctuary when he was begging me for a job. Long ago, I had decided to never tell Henry, fearful that I might lose him.

I looked Henry directly in the eyes, knowing what I had to do.

"I swear to god, Henry, I have never cheated on you before.

He looked back at me.

"Are you sure about that, boy?"

"Yes Sir, I am absolutely certain about that. Except for that one time with the skateboarder, I never ever cheated on you."

I said it with such sincerity that I almost believed it myself. All I could do was hope that I had made the right decision, hope that Henry would never find out, and that the subject would never be brought up again.

But on the inside, a small part of me died that day. I had had the opportunity to confess my sin, to make things right, and I didn't take it.

Please, please, please, make it be that Henry doesn't know. I don't want to lose him!

"Ok, boy, I see. It's time for me to grant you forgiveness. For everything you've confessed. I know I'm mixing up these sacraments, but in my personal church, with you worshipping me as your holy Master, I baptize you with my holy milk. Do you accept me as your one true Master?"

"Yes Sir." I was elated, believing that Henry didn't know about my other "sin" and now he never would know.

Towering above his loyal servant, Henry baptized me by milking himself and covering me with what he referred to as his holy cum. It was the most religious experience of my life.

CHAPTER FIVE

HENRY

I was taking a chance, but I knew Joey well enough to feel fairly confident that he'd choose a life under my discipline rather than break up with me. He isn't really the independent type, not very good at making decisions. Yes, he might chafe at the idea of me being in complete control. If that were to be the case, then I'd have to live with the consequences. Because I had to give him the choice. I wasn't going to keep him a prisoner against his will. But I will be in charge, if we stay together as a couple. I can't continue with our wishy-washy relationship that's based on a model developed by straight people, basically an attempt to keep family units together. The hell with that! If he agrees to my demands, we'll make a family that I design. Fuck straight society and what they think. And why bother to be like people who hate us anyway?

I like to be in control, and that's exactly what I'm gonna do. My plan is to put Joey into a position where he's forced into making a choice. To put him in a bind, as it were. Yes, a bind. That's a great idea!

By the time Joey was sitting meekly beneath me, wearing a leash and collar like a domesticated animal, I was very confident about our future. When I embraced him with my legs and squeezed his neck tightly with my hands, his body language already gave him away. There was no attempt at escape, no resistance whatsoever. He was now my property. I knew it before I ever allowed him to speak a word.

Still, I gasped when he stated his choice.

"Discipline."

That was his decision, freely made, and clearly, it was the correct choice for him to make. That boy really couldn't survive out there in the world without me taking care of him. Now, I'll be able to protect both of us, because he would never be given the freedom to cheat on me again.

"So you chose the tight leash," I stated, not allowing him to hear my gasp of relief at his decision. "That's what you want. That's what I want to give you. And now, there's no going back."

By the time I finished with Joey that morning, he was kneeling in front of me, sniffing the pouch of my dirty jock, with my cum juices dripping off the top of his head, acting like some medieval peasant who had just experienced religion for the first time. He now knew what it meant to worship a Superior Being, a Protector, a King.

Too bad I had to cage up his dick, I thought. *I would've enjoyed seeing him pleasure himself and make him eat his own cum after slurping mine. But that boy does have to be taught a lesson.*

I always say that no one is perfect. I have my faults, like everyone else. To demand perfection from anyone is pointless and will only lead to disappointment. I have high standards, for myself and others, but I'm also realistic.

Joey, of course, has plenty of faults. He requires support and structure, even discipline, from me. He makes up for his weaknesses, of course, with his love for me and loyalty to me. During this time, after I caught him cheating on me, he accepted the discipline and penance I gave him. Best of all, he agreed to accept even more discipline. That had been my goal for a long time now.

I had been feeling a little restless, and I sensed that we were drifting a bit. Maybe it was a good thing that he had gone astray. That gave me a reason to impose a new, more strict lifestyle on him. In my heart, I believed he wanted it and needed it. So did I. But of course, I'd be the one in charge, making all the decisions, having all the power and authority. That, I believed, was my right. I had earned it, I deserved it and I was going to take it.

My only disappointment was that Joey hadn't completely confessed his sins. I gave him the chance, but he didn't take it. Maybe he had convinced himself that Billy had never sucked his dick.

I knew about it almost as soon as Joey was cleaning his cum from the floor of the back office. Billy was even weaker than Joey. As soon as he saw me that day, he looked away with such a guilty look on his face that I confronted him, thinking maybe he'd already stolen something from the club, even before starting his first shift.

But no, that wasn't the case. He told me sheepishly that he really wanted to work at Sanctuary, that he was desperate for a job so he could stay with his boyfriend William (one of the 4 Williams we had met from Joey's hometown), and that he had given Joey a blowjob in the back office.

I never gave Joey a hint of what I knew. I thought he might tell me himself someday, since we were open about experiences with other dudes, with the only rule being that we'd always play together. Joey broke the rule, and I wasn't happy, but for me, it wasn't a deal-breaker.

By hiding the truth, I knew that even though I loved Joey, I could never trust him totally. That's one of the reasons I thought he needed more discipline, to be kept on a very tight leash. With HIV running rampant in the community, neither of us could afford to let Joey get too careless.

In reality, it's what we both wanted. I knew I could handle him and maybe another guy too. I was up for a challenge.

The day after Joey accepted a life of discipline, a life under my strict rule, I wanted to explain to him some of the changes that would be taking place. After another night spent sleeping on the floor, it was time for Joey to understand more of my plans for us.

"First, let me tell you about sex," I started, looking at Joey's disheveled appearance, including the pigtails I'd left when I buzzed his head. "Your dick is staying in that cage till I know whether or not you got turned poz, but that isn't because I'm scared of getting infected from you. It's your punishment, plain and simple. A well-deserved punishment and you know it," I began.

"Whenever we're out in public, and I mean anytime and anyplace, it's going to be clear to everyone that you are my servant, my slave, my sub. Whether it's because I call you my dog or my bitch, or whether you're serving me like a peasant serves a King, there'll be no question in anyone's mind about what role I play. I'm the King, got it?"

Joey yawned absent-mindedly, like he wasn't really paying attention. There I was, explaining his role in life, and he's acting so nonchalantly. I was beyond annoyed, but I remained in control of my actions and my emotions.

"Make the coffee, dog. You need to be paying attention. And if the coffee doesn't do it for you, maybe my leather paddle will wake you the fuck up."

I gave my permission for Joey to join me at the table, as we got our morning doses of caffeine.

"Have you taken a good look at yourself yet? Since I buzzed you, I mean."

"No Sir."

"I'm not asking your opinion, but I want you to see your hair," I told him, pulling on his leash to position him in front of the bathroom mirror. The look on his face, when he saw what I'd done to his beautifully maintained hair was unforgettable. Ultimate shock. Horror. Humiliation. Pleading with his eyes for his beauty to be restored.

"I like to be seen with a pretty boy. One reason I kept you around," I said teasingly, though he never realized I was just kidding.

Of course, Joey's good looks were what attracted me from the beginning, but I also enjoyed his submissive personality and usually pleasant manner.

"If you don't improve your attitude, and I mean immediately, you're gonna find yourself at the club tonight looking more like Dorothy from Oz than anything else, with those pretty little pigtails. I bet they'll look real nice if I let them grow out like that for a month or two."

"Sir, I'm awake now and ready to listen to your plans," he told me, as I led him back to the kitchen. It might take some time, but this boy was going to be trained in a new way of thinking and acting. The training had already started and Joey now realized it more clearly.

Returning to our coffees, I told the boy more about my plans.

"I wanna sell the house and move back up to the Gayborhood. This area was nice for a while," I said, referring to our Queen Street address in the heart of Queen Village. But I miss being up where we belong. Queen Village is too quiet, too boring, and to be honest, I think we're around too many straight people."

"May I speak, Sir?" Joey asked me.

"I'm not finished yet," I replied, but feeling a surge of satisfaction that he was already adapting to the new rules, understanding that my permission was now required for just about any action, including speaking.

"But you're a good boy for asking," I encouraged him, patting him gently on his unshaven cheek.

"We should make a helluva profit on the house sale and we're gonna get a condo in Center City. I've been hearing about some really good deals and I like the idea of a condo."

"Now what were you going to say?" I asked, giving him permission to state his mind.

"What about Zumi? I really wanna keep him and I think he'll be fine up in the Gayborhood."

"Of course, we keep Zumi," I assured him, referring to the Boston Terrier we had recently welcomed into our home. "One of your responsibilities is to take care of him."

"Your other responsibility is to take care of me and my needs," I told him, my thoughts going right to my dick. Ever since I was a boy, I had an extraordinary sexual desire, living in a nearly-constant state of horniness.

"Of course, Sir, just use me as you wish."

"Nice try, pussyboy. I don't want your permission. Remember, you chose discipline when you could have chosen freedom. So don't think I'm gonna be asking you if it's okay for me to stick my dick into you anytime I want."

With that, I felt my cock already expanding rapidly, just thinking about the ultimate power I now had. To be honest, the power wasn't really new, but now we were both openly embracing it as a true part of our chosen lifestyle.

"Stand up and bend over the chair," I told him.

My excitement grew as I watched my obedient boy assume the fuckboy position, as he had been ordered. I spit into the top of his ass crack twice, waiting for the saliva to drip down towards its intended target, my boy's tight little butthole. I grabbed a condom, then I thought about it for a second before I slid a second condom onto my pulsing erection. *Better to be safer than usual this time*, I thought.

Joey's moans during that quick fuck session were louder than usual, since his ass was being pleasured while his dick was tightly encased in a cage with no way to achieve any release. I reached around, tugging at his nipples and biting his neck, pumping and thrusting into his tight ass. I tried to hold back, wanting to extend my moment of pleasure, but I was too excited, too pent-up, too horny to delay, squirting jet after jet of cum into the tip of the condom, still buried deep inside my boy.

Barely finished shooting, I withdrew from his boyhole, went and retrieved the razor, and finished buzzing Joey's head to a uniform length. Although it would have been embarrassing for him to be seen in public with those pigtails, I didn't personally care for the look. I wanted people to be impressed with my good-looking conquest, not to be seen with someone looking like he had been groomed by a beauty school reject.

"Oh, we're also gonna add a new boy to the family. You'll be the main boy, but I need more than one ass to fuck."

Joey didn't say a word. I hoped he understood that I was sending a message that he alone couldn't satisfy me. It was also a message that Joey's days playing with other guys might have reached an end. He had to pay a high price for what he had done. Although I didn't want to go so far as to drive him away, I was determined that he wouldn't easily forget how he had betrayed me.

"Of course, you'll never fuck the new boy, though I might let him fuck your ass while I watch. I'll see what I decide later."

***

The next night, I walked into the house with my arm around Xander, the beautiful young skateboarder who had been the one boning my boy without my knowledge or permission.

As soon as Joey saw him, I noticed a look of fear and confusion in his eyes.

"What's he doing here?" Joey shouted.

"You better watch your tone, boy," I chastised him. "Greet our guest properly. I call him Xander. You will say hello to this man that you will only refer to as Mister."

Joey's features betrayed him. I knew he didn't want to do this. But I have to show this boy who's in charge and see how he reacts in different situations.

Joey reached out his hand in greeting, but Xander did as I had instructed him earlier and refused to take Joey's hand.

"Hello, Mister and welcome to our home," Joey said quietly, almost in a whisper.

"No! That isn't how you do it. Act properly and respectfully. Xander is my guest and you will not disrespect him. Try it again," I ordered.

"Hello, Mister, welcome to the home of my Master. I'm here to serve both of you," Joey stated in a loud, clear voice that surprised me.

"Hey there, tramp," was Xander's curt reply.

"Yeah tramp, make yourself useful and go get some drinks for the men in the room That means two drinks will be needed," I said, setting the tone for the evening.

By the time Joey had returned with our beers, both Xander and I were stripped down, with me wearing my leather jockstrap and Xander in his well-worn boxers. I sighed with pleasure as I started drinking, anticipating a hot night of fucking Joey and watching Joey getting fucked by the skateboarder boy from the park, the very one who had instigated the changes that were now taking place in our lives. I also pictured myself digging my cock deep into Xander's tight ass, hopefully while he was busy thrusting into the one now being referred to as the tramp. This was going to be fun!

"Hey tramp, before we get started, show Mister what happened to your dick, how you got punished for being such a dirty slut."

Joey's lips tightened in frustration, realizing that he had to obey me and that his enforced chastity would no longer be a secret just between the two of us. I had allowed Joey to wear leather chaps over frayed jeans today, but made sure he was wearing bright red frilly ladies' panties underneath, just in case Xander had any thoughts that Joey was masculine. That facade would disappear the moment he dropped his pants in front of Xander.

Seeing the panties made Mister erupt in raucous laughter, almost dropping his beer bottle in surprised amusement.

"I never did get a real good look the last time I was here, since I was so busy dicking the tramp's ass. Is there an actual cock somewhere there between his legs? Or are they her legs? I guess I still can't tell."

Xander and I were both laughing so hard at Joey's humiliation, but that subsided as both of us were also getting excited at our chance to dominate Joey, especially in front of each other.

Having a witness watching as a Dominant subdues another man makes it even hotter, I thought.

"Holy fuck, take a look at that hot mess!" was Xander's reaction when Joey pulled down his panties as ordered, showing his dick still locked into the tightness of its cage. "Does that mean the tramp can't even get a hard-on? He can't even control his own dick?"

Xander turned to me, grinning widely, giving me a high-five. "You the man, man! I never even thought of treating a bitch like that!" With one quick tug, Xander's boxers dropped to the floor, his long fat cock swinging as he approached the bitch he wanted to use, his cock already oozing from the tip.

"Hold up, dude. You're forgetting this," Henry told him, handing a wrapped condom to Xander.

"No man, I don't use them things. Never have. Never will. It's only bare skin against bare skin for me."

"You ever get tested? You do know about HIV, right?" I asked.

"My man, how dumb do I look? Of course, I know about the virus. But I don't need a test and I don't need any rubbers. We all got it. It's already a done deal. I'm here to enjoy the ride and no one's gonna stop me."

"Hear that Joey? You hear what you brought into our house and you let him do your ass raw. Whatcha think about your Mister now?"

Xander continued moving towards Joey, ready to stick his dick inside him, with no protection, no thought, no care about the possible, even probable danger of passing along a deadly virus. Until I moved to stop him, of course. Knowing now that it was almost certain that Xander was infected with HIV, and could very well have infected Joey, I wasn't going to allow the beautiful blonde skater boy to invade the territory that belonged to me.

"Sorry, dude, as much as I wanted to have fun with you and the trampboy tonight, I can't allow it. We had an agreement to only play with other guys when we were together for this very reason, so we could look out for each other and make sure neither one of us took unnecessary and unsafe actions. We were trying to avoid dudes like you, with that careless attitude. So sorry, but I have to ask you to leave."

"You're kidding me, right? You do know that every faggot in Philly is carrying this virus. Can't you see that? Why don't we just enjoy the time we have, including tonight, using bitches for what they're good for, suckin' our dicks and us fuckin' their pussy asses. C'mon man!"

"Sorry, dude. Get dressed and get out."

Xander was angry, but did as he was told, storming out of the door, disappearing into the night.

As soon as the door closed, Henry turned to me in anger. "You see what you did? You let that guy do you raw! He shot in your ass! And he does the same thing with every dude he fucks! How the fuck could you be so fuckin' stupid?"

Joey buried his face in his hands, crying again. He had cried more in the last few days than I'd seen him cry in all the years we'd been together. Maybe, just maybe, he was beginning to truly understand the dangerous situation he had put us in.

"Put your panties back on. That ruined the night for me. I don't even want to fuck you tonight."

I went into the bedroom, crawling into bed, but I left the door open behind me. Joey, sensing an opportunity, followed me into the bedroom and very slowly got into bed with me. My back was turned to him, but I didn't push him away. I had missed having my partner, my love, in bed beside me at night, so I allowed him to remain there. Joey, the liar, the tramp, the slut. Even with all his faults, I had to admit to myself that I actually, really loved him.

CHAPTER SIX

MISTER GQ

I started going to Club Sanctuary when I was 18 years old. Quickly, it became my favorite spot. It seemed to me to be a microcosm of everything I loved about gay life. Now, I don't mean the dirty underbelly of the culture, where the hustlers, drug-users and wannabes linger, like rats swarming through the garbage bins in the back alleys of Chinatown.

No, I mean the glamorous life, the beauty, the grace, the refined people who I wanted to join, enjoying their luxurious lifestyles. You question whether those types gathered at a gay disco. Are you kidding me? The place was crawling with them!

Back then, in my newbie days, that crew didn't exactly welcome me with open arms. However, I was not to be deterred. Their air of invincibility wouldn't protect them from my encroachment. I was invisible, like a gaseous substance, infiltrating their once-impenetrable defenses without them even acknowledging my existence.

I observed carefully. Their mannerisms, affectations, the accoutrements used to enhance their air of superiority. That was my aspiration.

I already had a multi-faceted plan. My gossip column at the paper was only Part One. The Book Brunch was Part Two. But I needed more, a way to get at the insides, with knowledge that could be used as leverage.

One night at Sanctuary, exact date unremembered, I was perched at one of the bars, sipping my Cosmopolitan, legs carefully crossed to better show off my newly-purchased Church's by Prada, recently featured prominently in what I referred to as "The other GQ", Gentleman's Quarterly.

"I feel like I should know those two," I mentioned casually to my friend Avery, who was busy playing with his drink, scanning the dance floor for a potential conquest.

"That's Percy and his twin brother. Mercy, I think. Yes, Percy and Mercy, I remember now."

"Hmmmm, they are the pretty ones, aren't they?"

I was thinking about a way to get the inside scoop on the lives of some of the Best Gays in Philly, potentially a new feature or at least a multi-part column. But I needed a mole. Tonight, it struck me that two moles just might be better than one.

I motioned for the two boys to come over to the bar, which they did without hesitation, both leaning into me, totally ignoring Avery. I liked them already.

"Order for yourselves, darlings," I instructed them, handing each a twenty-dollar bill pulled from my Hermes wallet, always kept safely inside my Coach shoulder bag. They had no problem getting the attention of the busy bartender, while I enjoyed being seen with these two boys, each clad only in a wrestling singlet, one in red, the other blue.

While they danced, both of them had removed the straps from over their shoulders, rolling the singlets down, revealing tight, washboard abs. Six packs? Eight packs? I didn't have time to count, but I knew what they had was impressive.

Just a bit below, encased in the tight, clingy fabric of their costumes, their prize packages swung as they danced to the beat of the music. Each time they turned their backs to me, it was hard not to stare, as their asses were split by the tight seams of the singlets into the most delicious looking man-buns. And I'm not talking hair, here, darling. I'm talking cheeks. Sweet, delicious, boyish cheeks just waiting to be doused with butter (or something) and eaten alive.

Once they had their drinks, I was ready to get to know more about them.

"Which one of you is Percy?" I asked.

They both giggled at that, a boyish chuckle I found so appealing. Their smiles could surely work their way into the bedrooms of more than a few of the rich gays who interested me.

"If you're asking which one of us is Paris, that would be me," answered the one on my left.

"And I'm Milano," added the one on my right.

"We're named after cities," they said in unison, clearly rehearsed and used often as an opening line.

Percy and Mercy, I thought. *That Avery can be such an asshole, sometimes!*

It crossed my mind that Avery might have misled me on purpose, but I had more important things to think about. Specifically, how to convince Paris and Milano to join me in my little detective game.

One thing I know for sure. Money always talks. My conversation with these two beautiful, blonde, green-eyed boys centered on that. How much would ensure them meeting, greeting, and then bedding a few Richie Riches and telling me all about it?

***

The first party at Sanctuary I ever covered for the paper was the 1985 Christmas Spectacular, the Snow Ball. The headline for the column was:

Royalty Rules at Snow Ball

I know, not exactly ready for a Pulitzer Prize, but it struck me as appropriate. My columns were a mix of covering events in the gay community along with tidbits of gossip about our local gay celebrities. Lesbian news, of course, was included, but I often found it difficult to get anything newsworthy about our local ladies.

The queens at the Snow Ball didn't disappoint. They never did. Part of my job was to dig into the chaos, describe some of the more outrageous looks and hopefully find information about someone acting out in a way that would entertain my readers. Of course, if a show was included as part of the evening, I would certainly cover that, hopefully with an interview.

The Snow Ball will not just be remembered because it was the first event I covered. When I look back at the clippings I've collected of my columns, the photos engulf me in a wave of nostalgia. Images from that first Snow Ball showed people expressing themselves in fabulous costumes, make-up, hair, and being totally open with their Queer identities.

There was a show at Sanctuary that night, featuring two legendary disco queens, performing their hits for the crowds at the club. The early show, that started just after 1 AM, would have been missed on an ordinary Saturday night, but this was the Snow Ball, so plenty of people arrived at the party earlier than usual for an after-hours club. Many dressed in elaborate costumes reflecting the snowy, wintry theme of the night. I wrote about them extensively in the column, including a few funny "snowboys," dressed in chubby styrofoam balls around their bodies, with carrot noses and very long, erect carrot cocks. Too funny!

Watching Nona Hendryx that night, being adored by her fans as she lip-synced to her recent hit song,

Transformation, was unforgettable. She had been part of the Philly group known as Patti LaBelle and the Bluebells, and now she was striking out on her own, making a name for herself. In 1985, she had already outed herself, so I hoped to get an exclusive interview about her experiences, though I wasn't successful.

A huge star in her own right, it was hard to believe that anyone could cause the crowd to become more frenzied, but it did happen that night. Carried in on a pallet by muscle men clad like slaveboys from ancient Rome, as glamorous as Cleopatra herself, the one and only Grace Jones also performed at Sanctuary that night. The vision she presented, in a white latex catsuit with a feathery headdress, a glittery white cat-like mask over her eyes and silver thigh-high boots, was ultimate Snow Ball. Her performance included two songs: *Pull Up to the Bumper* and the song that completely captivated everyone with its hypnotic beat and haunting lyrics, *La Vie en Rose*. I think I was just stunned by the performance, unable to move my eyes from her glory, wishing the song would never end.

After writing extensively about the performance by the two disco superstars, I devoted several paragraphs to a trio that I had christened as The Three Kings. They were the current members of the Board at Sanctuary, namely Joey, Henry and Alejandro aka Jando.

Joey, the actual owner, was clearly high that night. My sources informed me that he was heavily into the Quaalude scene, leading him to spend hours on the dance floor, floating the nights away. He struck me as a decent-looking blonde boy, with a nice athletic swimmers-build body. Clearly, a bottom boy, was my judgment.

Jando was heavenly, a delight to watch, with beautiful Latino features that struck me as exotic. I was unable to tell anything more specific about his heritage, though I later learned he was Puerto Rican. That particular night, he

71

seemed pre-occupied with managing the event, barking orders to the bartenders, stage-hands who were hired for the event, and others responsible for seeing that the customers were having fun and being served properly.

Henry! Oh my god, Henry! What can I say about him to truly express the excitement I felt when I looked at Henry. Self-confident, assured, clearly the man-in-charge, I pictured him using his muscular Black body to dominate me. At one point in the evening, his eyes met mine, just for a second, and I melted with desire. Despite his young age, he seemed mature, masculine, manly, and massively talented.

I was determined to meet The Three Kings someday. On that particular night, however, they weren't aware of my existence. I was nothing to them. By writing about them in my column, I hoped to change that.

Luckily, I kept the clipping in my scrapbook, so I can quote it in its entirety. The section about The Three Kings went like this:

Besides the obvious royalty present at the Snow Ball in the form of Ms. Nona Hendryx and Ms. Grace Jones, this reporter did not fail to recognize the importance of the event organizers, including club owner Joey, party planner Alejandro and a young man who struck this reporter as the true genius of the entire event, Henry. Gay Philly owes a debt of gratitude to these Three Kings for bringing stardom and a night of glitz, glamour and a bit of mayhem to Center City Philly. Club Sanctuary has earned a well-deserved reputation for the best gay parties in the Tri-state area, with the Snow Ball capping a year of fabulous gay extravaganzas. Hail to The Three Kings!

At the time I wrote the column, it didn't strike me as hyperbole; I was quite serious in my admiration. Today, when I re-read this and some of my other columns, I smile at my desperate attempts for attention and validation. However, the bottom line is that my plan worked. I did indeed get to know Henry, Joey and Jando, as well as countless others, as I earned my place as an observer, commentator and reporter about all things gay in Philly.

At the time of that first Snow Ball, however, I had no way to make a real impression on anyone, certainly not The Three Kings. Lacking funds for a glamorous costume, I did the best I could with an outfit that today would draw a yawn from someone with my impeccable taste. Comparing myself to those adorned in chic finery, I realized all I could afford was a one-way ticket to Cape Envy.

I shudder to think that I actually went to the club in such ordinary clothing as a blue shirt I found with a snowflake design, and my non-designer jeans. I took consolation in the pearl necklace draped carefully to maximum effect. Putting forward my best front, I tried to fake my confidence to mask my utter humiliation, but of course, I went totally unnoticed by the men I so desperately wanted to see me for the glamorous being that I truly was.

Someday I will be seen. I will be noticed. I will be important!

My friends (whom I actually consider to be mere acquaintances) think of me as unfeeling. I know that's what I project. It's also why, when I'm at home, totally alone, I often spend time pricking myself with a needle. At least, that's how it started. It wasn't long before I moved on to using other, sharper objects on myself. I want to feel something. Feeling pain reminds me that I am alive.

It's also why I visit the bath houses. I want to get pricked again, over and over, but here, I'm seeking something less sharp and more filling, if you get my meaning.

So that night, after the Ball, I found myself trying to be nonchalant as I pushed my money under the plate-glass window shielding the cashier at the bathhouse from any threats. I'm extremely picky and selective about any man that I might consider dating, but I have no such cares when surrounded by the blackness of the orgy room, eagerly reaching for any opportunity to be mated with an unseen, horny anybody. We all have weaknesses. Being penetrated by multiple partners, totally anonymous, is my way of providing comfort to myself, filling a need that wasn't being met in any "decent" settings.

Indecency, thy name is Harvé! But only in secrecy.

The day after the column ran, a bouquet was delivered to my desk, an assorted arrangement designed by Gilberto, the best florist in the city. The card simply read:

To Harvé,
We appreciate you.
From Henry and the other Kings

I still have that card, kept safely with my other treasured possessions, in a scrapbook, positioned next to a pressed pink carnation from the bouquet. Along with the physical items, my secret desire to have a future with Henry was securely and safely stored away, known only to me. I never let Henry know how I felt, though he may have figured it out. For some reason, Henry only had eyes for that boy Joey. I never saw any evidence that Henry had even the slightest real interest in any other guy.

***

Paris and Milano, those beautiful twin boys, were a godsend as far as providing information. They could work their way into any bedroom, providing an intimate eye into

74

the lives of some of Philly's most famous and powerful gay men.

I met with them on Wednesday nights, giving me time to turn their stories into written columns for the paper before my Thursday deadline. Friday was publication day, and I wanted my column to be the freshest, juiciest, most talked-about column for each week.

I thought about meeting them at Dewey's a popular hangout on 17th Street, but then decided I should be more discreet. With plenty of gay boys hanging out at Dewey's, my inside sources might be too easily recognized later.

Instead, the boys asked to meet at my apartment, but I had to decline. I'd be positively mortified to have those fine, yet gossipy young men see me in my home environment. In those days, I wasn't wealthy yet, and I preferred to keep that a secret from as many people as possible. Not that I was ashamed of my living quarters...check that, I was ashamed of my apartment. What's the point in denying it now?

It isn't like I was broke. Truthfully, all my money was being spent on clothing and accessories, in an attempt to make a good impression on the people who mattered to me. It was easier to impress those people with my appearance when I was out and about. Easy enough to never invite anyone to my apartment. I've come a long way since then, though for some reason, it's still a rare occasion for anyone to actually visit me at my home.

I suggested we all meet at Dirty Frank's, a real dive bar on Pine Street. Gay people just didn't go there. Personally, I despised the place, but I did believe we'd be safe enough to have a private conversation there, along with a few drinks. I figured that buying a round or two might loosen their luscious lips even more, spilling every gory detail of whatever they may have learned.

By the time I got there, Paris and Milano were waiting for me outside, on the corner. I had no idea which one was which. I mean, these hotties were identical. Clearly, they enjoyed coordinating their outfits. In the club, they'd been wearing identical wrestling singlets, except in different colors. Tonight, they were wearing milky-white jeans, with graphic tees that were cut off to once more show off those amazing abs. Paris wore a tee with a Madonna print and Milano's featured a different Madonna print. I mean, could these two possibly be any cuter?

My concerns that the straight crowd inside Frank's might be hostile were relieved when I saw the place was less than half-full, with just a few old white guys on the bar stools. Every table was vacant, so we chose the one farthest in the back, hopefully ensuring the privacy of our conversation.

Before they could even start, the waitress was at our table. She glanced at me coldly when I ordered a white wine, snickering at my apparently odd choice of beverage in this "fine" establishment. Perhaps sensing my lack of easy funds, both boys ordered a common brand of beer.

"Harvey, we got some good news for you," one of them said.

"It's Harvé," I corrected him with a stern look "The H is silent."

"Oh, my bad!"

"And which one are you?" I asked Madonna shirt Number One.

"I'm Milano, the older one. And the wiser one, I might add."

"Yeah, he's the old man!" Paris joked, reaching over and giving his brother's left nipple a hard pinch, causing Milano to pull away, faking pain, but clearly enjoying the playfulness.

They were both laughing at that, sitting across the counter from me, looking so boyishly fresh and delicious that I thought I might choke on the innocence that seemed to ooze from their very beings. But of course, in reality, they were anything but innocent. Quite naughty and mischievous was how I imagined them to be. But pretty baby faces can hide a lot.

Was it wrong of me to be seated in a booth at Dirty Frank's, across from a young, gorgeous set of twin boys, with a raging hardon? Many will probably think so, but that was exactly the position I found myself in.

Shifting my position in a vain effort to get comfortable, I asked, "What did you get for me?"

"Well, first, we met..."

Milano ribbed his brother with his elbow.

"Remember what we decided. Money first. If we tell everything, dude could walk out on us and leave us hangin'."

Though that stung a bit, I did understand. It occurred to me that they had probably already been through plenty, and most likely they had ripped off some guys and had been ripped off themselves. Or maybe that was just my preconceived bias about the lives of two guys whom I considered to be a couple of street urchins. Truly, I can be so judgmental, rendering my verdicts so quickly, and without any real evidence to support my conclusions.

"Ok, ten each upfront. Then another ten after I hear what you have to say."

"No," Milano told me, actually staring me down, daring me to defy him.

"Twenty each upfront. Plus at least three more beers while we spill the beans. Then twenty more for each of us when we're done. Otherwise, we take a walk right now."

Paris looked like he wasn't even aware of the conversation, allowing his older brother to be in charge.

Leaning in closer, Milano never moved his eyes from mine, whispering, "And if that ain't the deal, I'm gonna scream right here how you just propositioned us to suck your dick before we get up and run. Think about how these straights are gonna react to you when we do that."

Oh no! This wasn't at all how I wanted things to go between us, I thought.

I was the first to break eye contact. For the brothers, that was a signal that I had lost the battle of wills and they high-fived each other at their perceived victory.

Sighing, reaching for my Calvin Klein wallet, I tried to hide the bills inside from the boys' views. Pushing two twenties across the table, I whispered, "It doesn't have to be like this, guys. I'm not your enemy."

"Maybe," replied Milano. "But you gotta prove that to us first. Till you do that, we're gonna treat you like we treat everybody. We only trust each other, 'cause really, we ain't got nothing except each other."

I noticed that Paris didn't even reach for his share. Milano took both twenties and stuffed them into his socks. As he did that, Paris hollered across the room, ordering two more beers to the table.

Though the meeting at the bar cost more than I had wanted or expected, the information provided by the twins provided enough intel for a month of columns.

I had zero regrets handing Milano the second pair of twenties before we left Dirty Frank's Bar and went our separate ways.

CHAPTER SEVEN

JOEY

Things have been different ever since Henry came back home, after storming out of the house that day he caught me getting barebacked by Xander. Previously, our relationship had been strong, based on love, mutual respect and trust. Now, not so much trust, I guess. I mean, I can't blame him. We had promised to only play with others when we were together. I was the guilty party. We both knew it. I was getting what I deserved.

Occasionally, we dabbled in kink play. It wasn't the main thing with us. Our sex was fun, or at least, that's what I thought. It was rare for me to take the dominant, active role, but it wasn't unheard of.

Although we hadn't discussed it in detail, I did accept Henry's offer to provide discipline. I'm not sure I knew at the time exactly what that meant; what I was getting myself into. But my trust in Henry was boundless, so I felt safe entering into this agreement.

A week had gone by, and I was getting used to sleeping in bed at Henry's side again.

"Not tonight, boy," he growled when I approached the bed this evening.

"Sit on the floor, cross your legs, and pull your knees as close to your chin as you can."

Yanking my hair, he pushed me closer to the wall, deciding he didn't like my current position.

"Hands behind your back and keep 'em there. You fuckin' cuntboy. Fuckin' pussy. Fuckin' asshole. Look up here at me, boy."

Moving my eyes skyward, all I could see was a hard, throbbing, dripping-wet Black cock swinging in front of my face. Henry spat on his dick, continuing to slowly move his hips, his hardness slick with spit, which eventually dripped down onto my encased manhood. I was being forced into chastity as punishment and Henry showed no signs of relenting on my three-month sentence of being cock-caged.

Taking hold of himself, Henry stretched his muscular man-meat, slowly stroking himself. Grabbing hold, he struck me in the face with the slippery sausage, stinging my face with the force of the blow. Squatting in front of me, I was cock-slapped on the left side of my face, then the right. Rising a bit, another cock blow to the top of my head. Again. Again. Again.

Continuing to tease me, cock-slapping me on the top of my head, then taking aim at my face, over and over and over. He let himself get soft, just a bit, not enough to lose his erection, but just enough to keep him from flying over the edge in manly ecstasy.

Not once did he enter my waiting, open mouth. He never reached for the tight hole between my legs, waiting, yearning for the invasion I was sure would soon come. I needed to be entered, to be invaded, penetrated. But no. Nothing. Just denial. Knowing that he had the right equipment to satisfy my hunger, I was left with drool dripping down the side of my mouth and even more drool spilling out of my forcibly limp, flaccid tool. A drool tool.

Still slapping me with his cock, Henry approached his orgasm again, then slowed down, his breathing softening from gasps to quiet, rhythmic, controlled breaths against my cheeks, into my eyes, my ears, my mouth. Only his breath entered me. Now I was beginning to understand the pain of torture, of being denied, of being controlled.

Henry leaned very close and whispered into my ear, "You dirty boy. Say it. Say 'I'm a dirty boy.'"

My voice choked out the words. I was so upset about Henry denying me the pleasure of invading my spaces, I would say anything, follow any order, if it meant being satisfied with some much-needed, even forceful penetration. Anywhere. Everywhere.

Dick-slapping me out of my thoughts, Henry insisted, "Say it, pussy. What are you?"

"I'm a dirty boy," I whispered.

"Again, say it again. Say it every time I bitch slap you."

I got hit with his cock hard in my face just then.

"I'm a dirty boy."

"Louder, bitch." SLAP!

"I'm a dirty boy."

SLAP! On the top of my head.

"I'm a dirty boy."

SLAP! on my right cheek.

"I'm a dirty boy."

SLAP! Left cheek.

A dozen more times. Twenty more times. Both of us breathing heavily, grunting, with Henry showing no signs of slowing down, faster, and faster the cock slaps came.

"I'M A DIRTY BOY!"

I was screaming, heaving in passion.

That's when Henry turned his dick, aiming it away from me, squirting jets of creamy man milk onto the floor, without a drop touching me. I wanted to cry.

"I don't share my bed with dirty boys," he sneered. "Not tonight anyway. Sleep right where you are."

Stretching his legs, tight from squatting in front of me for so long, I watched Henry walk away from me, climb into bed alone, falling asleep almost immediately.

As much as I wanted to eat his cum off the floor, I knew he'd be furious if I did so without his permission. I felt extremely frustrated while being trained, but I had to show I could follow his directions. I didn't want to lose him. I had to succeed in this. I had to submit to his training.

The next day would be our first time returning to the club together. Henry went in early, which we normally did together, to get the club ready for the night-time crowd.

"You stay inside the house today. No going out. Not even with Zumi. I'm having a dog walker come over today to take care of him. You just wait here for me to come home. I want you to be properly rested because I'm putting you to work in the club tonight."

Not knowing what he meant, I did as ordered. To be honest, I thought just being at the club was my work. I mean, I didn't really do anything there except drink, dance, take some drugs, and have fun with my friends. That was my role, or so I thought.

That night, Henry told me what I was going to wear to the club. It was my first time back after what I would describe as my "little indiscretion." Many others wouldn't describe it so kindly.

I balked when I saw what he wanted me to wear. An old pair of jeans that looked like they'd been picked up from the closet floor. Black leather boots that were okay, but out of style. Black leather chaps. Those I liked, because they hugged my ass so tightly, and I liked how my buns looked in them. A plain-jane white tee shirt. Not even a designer label. Black leather suspenders and a black leather vest completed the look.

"Really? That tee shirt?" I sniffed.

The stern look on Henry's face made me quickly realize my mistake.

"One more word of complaint outta your mouth and every piece of pretty-boy clothing you own is going right out in the trash. You understand me?"

Biting my lower lip in frustration, I meekly obeyed. And though there were certain things that I felt rebellious about, there was no denying that my dick felt a surge of desire. It was struggling to escape, to expand, to grow, and most of all, to shoot a huge load, but there was no escaping its tight jail cell.

Henry, with his back to me the entire time, dressed in full leather gear. Damn, he did look fine, all dressed to impress the biker crowd. Any submissive would be proud to walk with this man.

"One more thing," he told me as we prepared to leave the house. "Just remember, you told me you wanted discipline. I'm done fuckin' around with you. I wanted to control you totally for a long time, but I held back. Then you proved I was wrong to give you freedom. I was completely wrong. You never deserved it."

"Every time we walk to the club, everybody's gonna know who your Master is. You're gonna be wearing this," he said in his calm, stern voice, wrapping a studded leather dog collar around my neck.

I hung my head in silent submission.

"And I'm gonna be leading you with this."

My heart sank when I saw the leash he was holding, attaching it to my collar.

Private humiliation was one thing. I had no doubts about that kind of discipline. I never even considered a situation where Henry would not only restrict me, but maybe take it so far as to constrict my freedom.

Am I ready for this? I thought. *Total restriction? Complete constriction?*

Henry wasn't in any mood to give me time to consider any of this. Clearly, he was now getting what he had wanted all this time. It was only later that I'd even think about how he had sacrificed his wants to take mine into consideration.

Though my mind was reeling with confusion, my body kept telling me that Henry was right. I was sexually excited by everything being done to me. The collar. The leash. The public outing of me as a subordinate. My balls ached and my dick was oozing.

Yes, this is what I always wanted too, I decided.

The walk to the club seemed like it took longer than usual. One reason might be that I was aware of every person, wondering what they thought when they saw a Black man in full leather gear, leading me by a leash, which he kept tight so I was forced into close proximity, though never permitted by his side and always in the rear. I could hear the laughs, the snickers.

"Don't look down in shame, boy. Unless you're ashamed to be my bitch. Is that the problem?"

"No Sir," I answered, raising my eyes while trying to accept this new position as a true subordinate, a total submissive.

"You're damn lucky I don't make you pee on that hydrant like the dog you are. But maybe I'll just save that for next time," he warned me as we passed the corner of 12th and Walnut Streets. We were in the heart of the Gayborhood, and with those words, Henry was letting me know that even if I was feeling humiliated, he could take it to even greater degrees if he wanted to.

I was already feeling more comfortable by the time we reached the club. I automatically headed to the main entrance, expecting to spend the night in the disco section, like I almost always did.

"Whoa boy! Where you think you're goin'?"

I stopped in my tracks, confused at first.

"I'll be checking in on the disco and Aphrodite's Lounge later on," Henry told me, referring to the lesbian lounge upstairs from the main disco. "But you, you fuckin' dirty dog, you're spending the whole night in The Hole."

"Master Henry, hello!" the young man at the door greeted us. "Is this a fresh recruit?" he asked, obviously referring to me.

Henry's laugh made me realize I hadn't seen him smile since the day he caught me red-handed, or should I say, red-assed, shamefully breaking our vow.

As Henry talked a bit with the bouncer, I glanced inside, realizing that I hadn't stepped foot in The Hole for a long time, maybe a few years. All the staff members were dressed in a uniform consisting of a red jockstrap, black boots with red socks, and a red bandana around the neck. A few had further adorned themselves with black leather bracelets or a set of tit clamps, but the basic uniform identified them as staff members.

Henry pulled my leash back so I was facing the bouncer. "You don't have to tell everybody, but I want you to know this is actually your boss, the owner. But tonight, he isn't being given the boss treatment. As a matter of fact, he'll be working at Station Number Three."

Scrunching up my face, I wondered what Henry was even talking about. *A station? What station? And Station Three? Shouldn't I at least be at Station Number One?* I wondered.

The bar was filling up quickly with club members. My members. My customers. They walked right past, ignoring me, as I realized I had no status here. No one recognized me. However, everyone knew Henry and clearly, everyone liked him and respected him. For the very first time, I felt disconnected from his life. While I was partying it up like a dizzy queen over at the disco, Henry had been making contacts and connections in the disco and in The Hole. If I had given it any thought, I would have realized that he probably also knew every lesbian up in the lounge.

"What's his name?" the bouncer asked.

"Just call him 'dog,'" Henry replied simply, then tugged at me, leading me by the leash to the back of the club.

Against the back wall were very large, wooden chairs with seats and backs padded in black leather. The seats were up on stands, with footrests in the front.

I knew what they were. I'd seen them in 30th Street Station, the Amtrak Station in Philly. Guys would get their shoes shined there.

Oh no! was my first thought.

A man I'd never seen walked over casually. He was dressed in the staff uniform, but he also wore a vest, adorned with chains, with a number of keys hanging from the chains.

"Vinnie!" Henry greeted him. "This is your new bootblack boy for tonight. I thought Station Three might be a good spot for him?"

Vinnie looked me up and down. "You think he got what it takes? It's hard work and you know my customers are used to getting good service over here."

"Dog, say hello to Vinnie. He took over as the manager here after Cap'n Clyde decided to move to Key West, where he can wear his jockstrap at the bar all year without worryin' about his balls gettin' cold in the winter."

I laughed politely, realizing that I didn't even know that Clyde had left. I was getting embarrassed that I knew so little about what went on in my own club.

"I'll take care of the dog from here. I know you got plenty to do, managing every part of the club," Vinnie said to Henry. I wasn't sure if Vinnie knew who I was. Henry made no effort to explain.

I mean, shouldn't I get some sort of special treatment? Feelings of entitlement are hard to break, but Henry was now in a position to teach me to look at life from a different perspective.

"Take a seat on the stoop at your station, dog" I was instructed. "Watch how the other boot sniffers treat their customers. If you want any tips, you should follow their example."

Before walking away, Vinnie held me for a moment, turning me to face away from him, and I felt him rubbing the back of my tee shirt. The strong odor from the boot polish seemed to follow me everywhere after that point. It was only later that I discovered that Vinnie had marked me as a bootblack by writing the number 3 on the back of my tee, using black boot polish to make the mark.

Feeling humbled, I watched the work being done by the boys at the first two stations. Seeing the love, the passion, the care that they put into their tasks, polishing the boots of other men, I started thinking that maybe my perspective on life was upside-down.

I should be looking up at men, not looking down on them.

Watching the bootblacks, I was impressed with their efficiency and their dedication to the task at hand. Then, I noticed the men whose boots were being polished. One was totally ignoring the boy beneath him as he puffed on a cigar, casually blowing smoke rings into the air.

The man seated at Station One watched the boy beneath him intently. I wasn't surprised to see him start to fondle himself through his jeans, and from what I could see, the term "Monster Cock" had probably been invented for this guy. Truly, he looked like he was even more hung than Henry.

The bootblack worked up a sweat, while his client was working up a different kind of sweat. Stretching his legs, he opened the buttons of his leather pants, reaching inside and pulling out what looked like a 12-incher to me. Uncut. Prime white meat. I noticed the bootblack pause for just a moment, until the man spat right on the boy's head, chastising him for stopping his task.

"You know the rules, boy. Work it or you won't be getting paid. And yes, you can use some of my spit on my boots."

Fascinated, I watched as the boy scooped up some of the man's spit from the top of his head, mixing it into the polish being applied to shine the boots. My gaze moved back to the customer, who was now casually stroking his semi-erect manhood, when I noticed that a crowd was gathering.

Before I realized what was happening, a boot was kicking me in the back. "You here to work or to watch the show, boy?"

A tall man had seated himself at my station, legs splayed wide, boots in the stirrups, ready to be served. I tore my eyes from the masturbating man with the monster meat and set myself to work.

With only a vague idea of what I was doing, I kept glancing sideways to get clues from the other boys. Station Two was just about finished, I thought, when his client thrust the bottom of his boots at the boy there. Seeing that boy lick the bottom of his client's boots clean was honestly one of the most beautiful signs of submission I had ever seen, one that I never would have imagined. If my cock hadn't been caged, I know I would have creamed my pants at that moment in time.

As I began working, I felt myself being drawn into the task. The odor of the polish, the general atmosphere in the club, the knowledge that I was openly being submissive to a total stranger, in a non-sexual but somehow very sensual manner, all contributed to the feelings swirling inside me. Soon, I was polishing the boots in front of me with enthusiasm, enjoying the excitement of being placed into this role.

"Do it, bro! Get him wet, yeah!" The man whose boots I was polishing was calling over to the guy at Station One, Mister Mega Meat, who was grunting loudly, stroking furiously and about to let loose. "Look over there, boy!' my customer commanded me. "That's some kinda service over there!"

The bootblack at Station One remained in his place, but raised his eyes to face the cock aimed directly at him. Murmurs, moans and groans were coming from the group of men now surrounding Station One, enjoying the show.

The squirts of jizz hit the boy's face with splats that could be heard on the other side of the room. The sub knew what was expected of him and the crowd watched as the boy, apparently with a big stiffy in his pants, licked his lips and swallowed what he could of the man's creamy release. Anything he couldn't reach with his tongue was scooped up, mixed in with polish and applied with a fresh coat onto the man's boots.

Two or three minutes later, the job was finished and it could be said that Mega Meat had the creamiest, best-polished boots in the house. Though I was still busy, I could see that the bootblack had earned a cool twenty-dollar bill for a tip.

My client didn't get hard, didn't pull out his dick, didn't seem to appreciate my service. When I finished, the man reached into his jeans pocket, pulled out a one-dollar bill, and handed it to me.

I wondered if I was really that bad at shining boots or if I had been set up for humiliation by Henry. I never knew the answer to that, because I knew it would be disrespectful to ask Henry.

This was exhausting work, as I discovered as the night went on, with more and more customers wanting to be serviced. However, there were breaks when I wasn't busy. Even the more popular boys at Stations One and Two got occasional breaks and I found it was fun just to chat and pal around with them. Turns out that the three of us had at least one thing in common. Submissive, submissive and submissive.

During one of the few times the boy at Station One was free, he walked over to my station, two beers in his hand.

"Hey Three, I'm One," he greeted me. "Did you already meet Two?" he asked as he offered me a beer, which I accepted gladly. Hearing his name, Two looked up from his work, grinning broadly and nodding his acknowledgment of me.

"But what's your real name?" I asked One.

The look on his face showed his surprise at my question.

"In here, I'm One. I could get fired if I gave out any more information. Not without permission from Sir over there," he said, nodding in the direction of Vinnie.

Taking a long swig from my beer, I pondered that, deciding it was better for me to follow the rules. I thought to myself: *What would Henry want me to do?* And the answer was clear. He'd expect me, he would order me, to comply, to give up my identity and just be known to anyone in The Hole as Three, the boy who worked as a bootblack at Station Three.

Later on, Henry came into The Hole, making his usual rounds of the various sections in Club Sanctuary. I watched from the corner of my eye as he had a conversation with Vinnie. Then Henry walked over to Station One and took a seat.

"You say One is at the top of his game tonight, right Vinnie? He's the best boy you got working tonight?"

"Yep, it's One, as usual. He got a real talent for it, so if you want a real shine, One is the boy you gotta use."

"You heard him, boy. Gimme the best shine you can. I wanna be able to see myself reflected in my boots by the time you're done."

After being so proud of myself for obeying the rules, and doing what I expected Henry would want me to do, I had to contain my anger and resentment that Henry wouldn't make me shine his boots in public, a sign of my submission to him. Instead, he chose a different boy to do that job.

Henry was strong, proud and dominant. But even with his strength, he couldn't help himself. He kept his eyes directly on Three, on me, the entire time that One was working on him.

In reality, I felt like I belonged to him more at that moment than ever before.

It was his privilege to have me. It was also his privilege to deny me. I couldn't imagine my life as anything other than devoted to him. I was finally learning and accepting my place.

CHAPTER EIGHT

HENRY

I love Joey, I really do, I was thinking. *I've loved him since even before I met him in Rittenhouse Square that first night. But if we don't make some changes, I don't know what'll happen. I feel like I always have to hold myself back. I try to act like we're equal, but it's so clear that we are not equal. I'm the Dominant. I'm Superior. And I'm fuckin' sick and tired of pretending otherwise.*

I knew that if I just talked to Joey about this, he'd probably agree with me, but he wouldn't really get it. I decided that I had to show him, to demonstrate what it means to serve me the way I deserve to be treated. I don't just want him to repeat words that I put into his mouth. A parrot could do that. I want him to actually feel it, to experience submission, degradation, humiliation. And if I'm being honest with myself, that's the only way that I'll ever be fulfilled in this relationship.

Just imagine, that little bitch thought he could betray me behind my back. If I hadn't come home early unexpectedly that day, we might have continued down the same path, with me growing more frustrated every day that I was supposed to act like we were partners, that we were always on the same page, that I respected him as my equal. I do love him, but I don't consider him to be at my level. No way!

I also had to be sure that Joey was not only interested in being my sub for life, but also that he was ready. He had to

92

be tested. If he failed, well, even though we already had put a lot into our relationship, I thought that I might just have to move on. That isn't what I want, but I feel that it's what I might have to do. This relationship has to move on to the next level, or I'll be forced to start all over again with a new boy.

So far, he's showing me that he might be worthy. He walked home from the Chinatown restaurant in bare feet. He slept on the floor like a dog. He sat still while I shaved his head into a buzzcut. His cock is now caged like a bitch. He even spent a night working as a bootblack in The Hole.

I wasn't sure he could do it. That boy isn't exactly known for working hard, and he didn't say a word when I humiliated him by having One shine my boots instead of him.

There are a few more tests he needs to pass before I make my final decision, but there's one other change I need to make in my life, in our lives, because if I don't, I know I'm gonna suffocate.

Grabbing a drink, I called Joey into the living room.

"We gotta have a man-to..."

I stopped myself. I almost told him we had to talk man-to-man. I changed direction quickly.

"I got something to tell you, dog," I continued. "I mentioned this before, but I never finished saying what I had to say."

Joey sat quietly in front of me, listening. At least, I hoped he was paying attention. I had learned long ago that he had a short attention span.

"There was a time when I thought I wanted to live here, in a neighborhood that's close to Center City, but feels more like a suburb. I thought I wanted to settle down into an upper-middle-class lifestyle and act like the straights do. You understand?"

"Yes Sir. I moved here because I wanted to be with you."

"Well, it ends up that I don't like it here anymore. It's too fuckin' quiet. It's too fuckin' straight. It's fucking boring!"

Joey was staring down at the floor. I used the toe of my boot to lift his chin, so he'd be looking at me.

"I'm moving back to the Gayborhood. I don't want this house. I don't want this life." And just to add a little cruelty, I added, "I don't wanna sleep in that bedroom where you betrayed me."

I knew that hurt him. I said it anyway. I felt no pity when I saw him starting to cry.

The truth is, he deserved to be confronted, to be reminded of his guilt. Because in fact, he did betray me. And he had potentially harmed me. We still don't know if he got infected and he might have passed that virus right onto me.

"The question is, do you wanna come with me or not? This is the time for you to make one more decision. If you say 'Yes,' then you're not just agreeing for us to keep on living together. You're also agreeing to continue to be under my discipline. You know a little of what that's like. But I mean complete, total discipline and control. Me over you. And if you say 'No,' then that's it. We'll be finished and I'll start looking for a new boy. I'll walk out that door and never look back."

"I..." Joey started to answer.

"No, dog. Not a word. Not yet. I don't want you to decide in an instant what will be a life-long decision. Sit there and think about it. I'll come back in an hour. Tell me then."

Joey's eyes reflected a mix of terror and confusion. I wondered if he had ever thought about us separating. He never looked very far ahead about anything. I was fairly certain that, in his day-to-day existence, he didn't plan for anything. But just going along with the flow wasn't good enough anymore.

An hour later, I returned. Joey was asleep on the floor. I was amused by the sight, but also knew that it could mean that Joey hadn't thought through my proposal, or maybe it meant he just didn't need much time to decide.

Kicking his side to awaken him, he looked up, startled. "I'll give you a minute to wake up," I told him. "I assume you made up your mind about this."

Joey never woke up quickly, so I knew that I needed to give him some time, or I'd never know if he truly meant what he said. I continued with instructions as he slowly came to his senses.

"I don't wanna hear any explanation. All I want is a one-word answer. Either Yes or No. If the answer's Yes, I continue with your training. If it's No, I walk out right now."

Positioning myself directly in front of him, I gave permission for him to speak. "What's it gonna be, dog?"

As I expected, the answer was immediate and spoken with certainty. No quavering voice indicative of doubt. A firm, solid, heartfelt reply.

"Yes."

With that, the deal was sealed. Finally, I'm going to have things the way I always wanted them. No more pussy-footing around.

***

Before I made the changes to our lifestyle, back when Joey and I were supposed to be equal partners and I was playing the part of the suburban house-husband, I started researching life in the gay leather community. Some of the research was done via books and magazines. I also had plenty of local authorities, including leaders and members of the gay motorcycle clubs in the area.

A few had their club headquarters outside of Philly; some were even located over in Jersey. Those didn't appeal to me, since I had already decided to reject that suburban aura. One was in South Philly, so I gave them careful consideration. But only one was headquartered right in the Gayborhood, with their clubhouse in a small, garage-like space on Camac Street, right next door to the Camac Street Baths. Club members were known to head straight for the bathhouse after a ride, and that was one of the deciding factors for me. Leather-clad men, riding their bikes, partying back at their clubhouse, and then letting off some manly steam at the baths sounded like a great way to spend a weekend.

I also needed the camaraderie of men like me. Other strong, dominant gay men. I was still searching for my community. Club Sanctuary was a gathering spot and a safe place for a huge segment of the gay community, and that was our intention when Joey and I started the club.

As time went on, I found that it was overwhelming to try to find a sense of belonging in a community that literally included thousands of individuals, many of whom, if not all, were vying for attention. Sometimes, too much is too much.

Becoming a card-carrying member of The Camac Malez Motorcycle Club (CMMC) would keep me within the large, inclusive community while still allowing me to focus on a smaller universe contained within the larger group of gays. I'd be a full-fledged member. Joey would only be permitted to join as an associate member, due to his lower status as my submissive. I found that rule to be very much to my liking.

May 7, 1992, was the date when the dog called Joey betrayed me, acting out some weird fantasy like a common street whore. Three months later, after having his dick under my total control, wrapped in a tight chastity device, I was ready to take him to the clinic for a test to determine his HIV status.

Once the test was done, we had to wait another week for the results. The weekend when we'd find out if the slutty whore had gotten himself infected was going to be a busy one.

Sometimes I think I shouldn't refer to him as a slutty whore. But isn't that just stating the truth? Should I try to sugarcoat it and if so, why? To protect his feelings? Was he thinking about my feelings when he opened his legs for a skaterboy? We all know the answer to that one.

But then, I do still love him. However, my love has changed, evolved. I want to love him and accept him for everything he is, even if part of him is a slut. Because while I'm accepting that, I'm also rejecting the preconceived notions of love and marriage that have been inflicted on us by the straights. I hate to think how I was indoctrinated and how long it took me to figure out what I really wanted.

I knew that at least two of our events that weekend would be fun. First, the CMMC Bike Ride for AIDS would be taking place, a fundraiser for those who needed help during these horrible times. Club members could take associate members along as guests, which sometimes turned into "dates," but could also be a way to invite guys who could get more people to pledge donations.

Joey, the slutboy, had already been told to make a sizeable donation to the cause. I know he would have done it anyway, but I turned it into an order so that we'd both understand how things were going to be from that point forward. I'm going to be in charge of everything.

This meets both of our needs, so I never hesitated in making known what he was going to do under my orders. I enjoyed giving the orders. He enjoyed taking them.

The ride itself was glorious. A pack of gay motorcyclists, all decked out in full leather gear, speeding up I-95, heading towards New Hope, PA. There was a gay carnival in town that day, so we had plenty of entertainment once we reached our destination.

For me, however, the thrill of the day was the ride itself. Feeling the awesome power of my brand new 1992 Harley Davidson Fatboy between my legs, enjoying the freedom of the ride and the envy of the straight men driving their suburban-style sedans with their wives and kids in tow. Plus, I had my Number One Bitch clinging tightly to my waist, occasionally nudging his face into the back of my leather jacket, placing his full faith in my ability to assure his safety and security as we sped along. I just knew his dick would get hard if I'd uncaged him, but that would be held back for later.

As I thought about all this, especially thinking about his dick under my total control, my cock grew hard and strong, right there on I-95. If this wasn't living the good life, then I don't know what heaven is. I could ride like this forever, especially with Joey right in back of me, exactly where he belonged. A man and his cuntboy. Perfect!

As I was spending more time with the Alphas at the Camac Malez clubhouse, I was finding a new community, one that seemed a better fit for me. Yes, Club Sanctuary was definitely a community, and as a matter of fact, Joey and I had that idea when we first conceived of the club. But it was a community with thousands of members, with plenty of cliques and sub-groups. And I always thought of the disco as being more like Joey's community. He fit in so much better with the glamour queens than I ever did. Or ever wanted to.

But with this small group of men, dominant, masculine men, I felt at home. I could talk about my bitch, what I did to him, what I wanted to do to him, knowing that they understood exactly what I meant. They were just like me. Gay Alpha males, open to new experiences, unbound by societal conventions.

Many of these men were regulars at The Hole, but I had failed to take advantage of the connections there. I think I was just too busy managing all the different bars and activities at the club, letting the opportunities in the leather bar pass me by. Joining CMMC made things much more clear to me. I recognized my purpose as well as the purpose of the boy I wanted to bring along with me.

The other big event for us that weekend was the first Wet Briefs Contest at the club. Alejandro always came up with new and exciting events to draw in the crowds. And like many events we held, Jando turned it into a fundraiser. We could never forget that as we partied, there were many of us in desperate need. We might have fun; we were determined to have fun, but the raging epidemic showed no signs of abating.

It was almost time for me to unleash my boy's dick from its enclosure, but I had one more idea first. I had this almost compulsive desire to see him humiliated in public. A Wet Briefs Contest could provide a perfect opportunity to do just that.

Four guys entered the contest, including Joey. Of course, he didn't enter on his own. I wouldn't allow such arrogant behavior on his part. Before going out on the stage, I took him to the club's back office.

"Clothes off!" I ordered.

Joey obeyed me, of course. I still admired his body and my cock had an immediate reaction to seeing him naked and submissive.

"You know the other guys in the contest are gonna be wearing their best briefs, hoping to be judged the winner, and the customers are probably gonna be cheering for whichever guy has the biggest dick, you know?"

"Yes Sir, but how am I supposed to win if I can't show off my dick?"

I was so amused by that statement I could barely stop laughing.

"You think your dick's that impressive that you might win? I'm letting them see how tiny yours is. And how it's in a little cage, like a little birdie with no escape."

I could see Joey wince as he realized his predicament. Then he said something that surprised and delighted me.

"Sir, I'm gonna go out there and put on a show, just for you. I know other dudes will be watchin', but I dedicate myself to you. There's nothing I want more than to give you pleasure, Sir."

My cock almost exploded just hearing Joey tell me, in all sincerity, that he was willing to be publicly humiliated just to please me.

But I didn't tell him that. The satisfaction was my private pride in myself for training this boy to be so humble and obedient.

"Put these on," I told him, handing him bright red, lacy, frilly, see-through women's panties. His chastity cage could be seen if you looked closely. Once the panties got wet, everyone would know.

All the guys in the contest, including Joey, would enter the stage wearing basketball shorts. Very short shorts, like the old style. The white satin of the shorts had a translucent look, so I could already see that Joey was wearing red underneath. Shirtless, with a nicely-developed chest and muscular arms, Joey walked out onto the stage to join the other boys.

The DJ played some striptease music as the four boys dropped their shorts. The club was packed, and guys were clapping, cheering, laughing, screaming, all in good fun.

I heard someone yell, "Look at the panty boy!" which gave me a great deal of pleasure.

The four guys on stage had been instructed to start with their hands folded over their packages, and then to slowly

100

raise their arms and fold their hands behind their heads. That's when the real show would start.

Any audience member could make a donation, grab a spray water bottle, and shoot a few squirts of warm water on the boy they chose. Of course, the water was warm for a reason. Unlike a wet tee shirt contest, with cold water used so the nipples would tighten, we didn't want to see these boys' dicks shrivel up.

Ok, I admit, I would have liked to see their dicks get shriveled in the cold. But a big dick never did impress me. One reason I liked Joey so much. To hear him tell it, he thinks his dick is bigger than average. I'm here to set that record straight. That boy's dick is NOT big. Never was. Never will be. Why would I lie?

The entire show amused me, and it was clear the crowd loved it too. Lots of squirters, using their water bottles on their favorite boy. The briefs were soon dripping wet, and since each of the contestants wore various styles of briefs to best show off their packages, it was soon apparent just what each one had to offer.

Of course, this being a gay club, one of the contestants lost control and became rigid as a young twink knelt in front of him, squirting the bottle in his hand while he rubbed his own dick with his other hand. I let it go on for a bit before sending over a bouncer to guide the squirter off the stage.

I just barely paid attention to the guys in briefs. My attention was squarely on Joey, who got plenty of squirts, slowly but surely being exposed as a caged, celibate boy. Some squirters even went back for seconds. I made note of anyone interested in squirting Joey's panties more than once, thinking we might have something in common. I was always planning, always looking forward to new adventures and new connections.

When Joey saw one guy approach him with a squirt bottle for the third time, he turned around, spread his legs wide and bent forward, giving the guy a clear shot at squirting his wiggling ass clad in tight, bright red panties.

All I could think was: *That's my boy! That's my very good boy!*

After we'd collected plenty of cash to donate to a charity, the contest drew to a close. By way of applause, a winner was chosen.

Ronaldo, the beautiful dark-haired Latino boy who got hard during the contest, won first place, and deservedly so. His cock was enormous and the crowd clearly approved. He was given $100 in cash and an automatic renewal to the club for next year.

Second place went to Jeffrey, a brown-haired, green-eyed pretty boy who pumped his fist high in the air and pranced around the stage like he had just won a WWE tournament. He was jumping up and down as he joined his crowd of friends, clutching his $50 in prize money.

Dickie looked a little nervous at being left on the stage, next to a boy in dripping-wet panties. I understood. That could be embarrassing to lose to Joey, so I was pleased to see a huge smile of relief on Dickie's face when he was announced the third-place winner. He strutted off the stage, rubbing his cock into the wetness of his purple mesh briefs, claiming a sense of superiority. His friends joined him in celebrating, ready to get treated at the bar with his $25 in prize money.

A few people clapped when Joey walked solemnly off the stage, alone, with nothing to show for his efforts. Alejandro met him as he stepped off the stage, wrapping an arm around his shoulders as if to console him.

Ten minutes later, I found Joey, still with Jando, in the back office. Joey was in his chair, one foot up on the seat, still clad in wet panties, talking with our friend.

"Leave us," I told Jando, who knew better than to object. Everyone at Sanctuary knew I was the boss.

Walking over to Joey, I took him by the hand, guiding him up from his seat. He started to speak, probably about to say something stupid, so I pressed my finger against his adorable, wet lips, shaking my head in a silent "No," so he couldn't break the mood.

"Wait right here, slut."

I moved quickly to open the sofa bed we had in the office, just for moments like this. I motioned for my boy to join me, and I positioned him on his back, pushing his legs open and quickly pulling down his panties, tossing them on the floor.

I heard his sighs as I removed my necklace, where I kept the key to his dick cage safely secured so I was the only one with access. With a sharp click, the lock was loosened, and Joey's prick lay limply on his belly, seeming not to realize the sudden freedom now available. His balls were shrunk to the size of small grapes, and I had to suppress the urge to laugh.

Joey didn't move. Unsure of what he was supposed to do, He waited for instructions, breathing heavily.

"Don't say a word, dog. Not one word. Just feel the experience. You're never gonna forget this feeling, slutboy," I whispered.

Moving so my face was between his legs, I spread his cheeks far apart, looking at his little pink hole. *How beautiful you are,* I thought, never losing my sense of wonder at the sheer beauty of this particular piece of the male anatomy. I spit right at the hole of wonder, now watching the wetness drip along the side of his cheeks. I spit again, watching as the moisture penetrated the opening, like a small stream making its way towards an ocean of paradise.

Then I touched it. Gently, oh so very gently, not pushing inside, just slowly rubbing the opening, feeling the hole trying to suck my finger inside. I refused its invitation, gently rubbing in circles around the wrinkly ridges of manliness. But this wasn't a strong, macho manliness. This was a man, but one submissive and obedient to my commands. I'm the man in command of men, and particularly in command of the one now spread open in front of me. My breathing turned to moans as these thoughts floated in my mind.

I wanted to fuck him hard and fast. But I didn't. I wanted to control not only him, but also myself. My finger continued to encircle his tightness, until I switched the position of my hand, cupping his balls and using my thumb to apply pressure against him.

I could see that Joey's dick was coming back to life, perhaps now with the muscle memory of past orgasmic experiences. I watched as this wonder of creation, a dick growing with desire, tried but failed to reach up to his belly button. I applied more pressure against his hole with my thumb, feeling it gently pop open. This time, I accepted the invitation to enter, feeling the grip of his ass muscles, hearing his moans of almost unspeakable pleasure.

"Play with your little stick, there, boy," I instructed quietly. "Just one finger and your thumb. Your little thing doesn't need a whole fist around it."

"I wanna watch you play with it, but slow. No quick stroke off, boy, not now, not today."

I could barely keep my hands off my cock; I was so turned on by this scene. Joey using two fingers, following my orders, writhing in pleasure in front of me, his dick straining to release the pent-up desires and the three months of cum just desperate to shoot off into a milky mess of madness.

Pulling my thumb out of his tight hole, which hadn't been stretched open by man cock in months, I pushed the digit against Joey's lips, forcing them open, as he tasted his masculinity. Taking my hand back, spitting into my palm, I rubbed the wetness into his back hole.

Almost without warning, Joey arched his back, curling his toes, reaching a sudden moment of sheer rapture, lightly touching the most sensitive point just under the head of his dick as he exploded.

There was a tsunami of sperm, spilling onto and spreading over his body, wave after wave, as I watched in utter fascination. Little rivers of his babies, swimming with the tide, pooled into the recesses of his belly button.

Multiple waves of milkiness swept over him as his body released the sexual energy that had been denied him. Cum washed over his abs, past his nipples and into the nesting pools of his neck.

His heaving breaths betrayed him, leaving no doubt as to his state of complete ecstasy.

He didn't get soft immediately. He continued to ooze, his cock still emitting sperms, though with much less force than the first ocean waves. As he slowly softened, a small stream of cum continued to spill onto his belly.

Looking back now, I wish I had thought to make a video of it.

Once his labored breathing stopped, I tossed his panties to him.

"The cock crowed once. Now clean up your mess," I said in my coldest voice. Honestly, I enjoyed that show, but I didn't want to give him too much credit for pleasing me.

Once he was dry, I laid directly on top of him, pressing my body into his with all my strength. I had a need to pin him beneath me. I had to make him understand that none of this was a joke. When he tried to speak, I signaled that he was to remain silent for now. Grabbing hold of the mattress, I pulled myself even deeper against him, wanting to drown him in my masculine superiority.

Then grasping and pulling his hair, I started to kiss him, deep, wet, sloppy, passionate kisses, my tongue probing his mouth, caressing and biting his lips, as my cock lengthened and strengthened between us.

I moved my hands under his ass, grabbing, pulling, spanking his meaty cheeks. I was bouncing on top of him, flopping like a fish just pulled from the water, gyrating against his hot, sexy body.

He didn't just lay there like a dead log, instead meeting my thrusts with body movements in sync with mine, catching my rhythm and dancing along with me, our choreography as beautiful as any ballet, with the Dominant one leading his submissive into sexual bliss. I felt his hardness against me again, signaling its readiness, after finally being freed from its enclosure. It needed multiple sessions to release months of denied pleasure.

Reluctantly, I pulled my body from his, wanting to enjoy the pleasure of holding his body captive with mine, but knowing I needed to reach for his rosebud.

Getting on my knees, I lifted him and flipped him over, watching his buns quiver with desire, seeing him humping against the mattress.

"Don't move like that, you dirty dog," I growled, using my hand to spank my bad, disobedient boy.

"No one told you to grind your little girly dick into anything!"

He forced himself to remain still, as I once more took control, again spreading his legs open and spitting into his private cave, his tight pussy, his hole that belonged only to me. Again, I used a gentle touch to excite him, my finger barely touching his entrance. My eyes widened with desire as I saw the way he opened himself up to me, inviting me to probe deeper. Using only my spit for lube, I slid two

106

fingers inside, as he gasped for breath. I knew just how badly he needed to be penetrated fully, so I took my time, withholding from him what he wanted more than anything, which was to be stretched wide and pounded lustily by my swinging rod. Instead, I withdrew my fingers, watching his ass trying to maintain its grip, but my slippery digits made their escape.

I was enjoying the squishy sounds my fingers made, almost as much as the moans of pleasure escaping from Joey as he pushed himself against the ever-increasing strength of my probes. I wanted to see more, so on the next thrust, his pucker opened to three fingers, increasing the volume of his moans accordingly.

"Please Sir, let me stroke off. I need it so bad!"

"Do it, but keep it slow. I want you to shoot off, but not too soon. Are you still my dirty boy?" I whispered.

"I'm your dirty pig boy," he told me, making my cock throb with desire. "Your dirty obedient pig boy."

Joey started to slap his dick against his belly, moving his body back and forth, still trying to get even more of his Master inside him. I gave him what he needed, moving my fingers faster and faster into his tightness. His little cunt was like heaven, tight as fuck, having gone without being stretched for months. Just how I like boy ass. Fresh, wet, pink, tight.

Joey's second orgasm almost matched the first in his passionate, volcanic release of sperms shooting through the air, splattering his body with slippery sperms. I was close to joining him, but I had to hold back, as I watched his eyes roll back, arching his back, cumming for the second time in just a few minutes.

"Aahhh, now the cock crowed twice," I whispered into his ear.

I don't know why I was thinking about that verse from the King James Bible.

107

And Jesus saith unto him, Verily I say unto thee, That this day, even in this night, before the cock crow twice, thou shalt deny me thrice.

I had forgiven him for his sins. First, betraying me. Then lying about it. Yet, watching his "cock crow," as it were, made me think of this quote from my Bible study days.

It's weird, but none of us can control our thoughts completely. This is what was going through my mind as I decided I had to see Joey's cock crow thrice.

Once his oozing cock softened a bit, I laid back down on top of him, without being cleaned up first. Pressing my full weight on top of him, our bodies slid against each other, his cum juices lubing us both.

Reaching between us and scooping up Joey's cum, I then reached between his legs and used his own cum to provide a slick entrance for my raging hardon. I wanted to wait a bit longer, but my passions overcame me.

Both of us dripping in his orgasmic juices, I had to pleasure myself, so I left him lying and panting on his back while my manhood took aim at his dripping hole, pushing the tip of my cock where it belonged. In the ass of my dirty pig boy. My obedient dirty pig boy.

I used my dick like the pro I am. My feelings of superiority, of authority, of control, fueled my passions. It wasn't just a man's dick pummeling another man's ass. It was the idea of having a man submit to me, recognizing my mastery over him, knowing that I would train him, degrade him, use him, all for my masculine pleasures.

I kept a slow pace at first, enjoying the sights and sounds of my thick Black erection stretching that willing and eager boyhole open, forcing myself inside, then out, then in, then out. Spanking his ass, harder and harder with every thrust inside. Pulling his hair, grabbing his throat in a chokehold, pushing his back downward so his ass was even more accessible to my desires.

Without asking permission, he was already stroking himself again, but I was too out of control to care, carried away by my desires, my pleasure, my thoughts of sexual and personal domination.

Just as I was nearing my peak, spanking that fat white ass so hard to be sure he knew it was my property, I saw his squirting dick achieve his third nut since his degrading show at the wet briefs contest, losing to every other guy, now known to all as the submissive boy in panties and cock cage, forever a boy, never to be a real man like me.

"I see the cock crowed thrice. That's my boy!" I told him, as I beamed with a wave of satisfaction.

That thought, combined with the sight of him cumming beneath me drove me over the edge. With a feral howl, I released the essence of my manhood, my hot jets of creamy cum, directly into him, shooting again and again until my squirting subsided. A wave of satisfaction washed over me, as I held myself inside my boy, gripping his waist firmly, not wanting to pull out. Once I finally did, I collapsed on top of him, feeling like I had finally achieved what I had wanted from our very first night together. Total domination.

I knew that Joey probably didn't even hear my biblical references to the cock crowing. He had no religious background, and I felt no real need to explain it to him. If I did, I could have hurt his feelings by explaining that the reference had to do with a prophecy of betrayal.

I'll get some good laughs about it when I tell the story to some of my Alpha buddies. They knew about making cocks crow. I relished the thought of sharing the story of my sub being so turned on that he showed me his pleasure three separate times in one session. The Alphas will be impressed and proud of me for my skills.

***

An hour later, I tossed an envelope to Joey. His test results. Luckily, negative. Yes, I knew the results before I fucked him raw. Because, of course, I did.

CHAPTER NINE

MISTER GQ

Looking back at my old columns for the Gay News, I have fond memories of those two boys who were the first of many moles I planted in the community, gathering gossipy items for a public hungry to know the dirty details.

Paris and Milano. Teen twins. Gay. And as they eagerly confessed to me, they were also lovers. They saw nothing wrong with that. Truthfully, neither did I.

I had always been taught that incestuous relationships were taboo due to the possibility of inbreeding leading to birth defects. If that's true, then what's the argument against gay incest? I don't know. You tell me, if there is one.

They described themselves as best friends for life. If anyone is going to be your best friend for life, wouldn't your twin make the perfect choice? Paris and Milano believed that to be true.

After I met them at Club Sanctuary and asked them to work collecting gossip for me, they shared some information during our first session, over drinks at Dirty Frank's Bar.

Closing my eyes, I can hear their young, eager voices, telling me about their experiences that week in 1986.

Scanning the text of my column, I laughed at how much detail I had to leave out of the story, trying to be gossipy enough to hook the readers, while simultaneously trying to avoid any lawsuits for libel.

"A little gay birdie (or two) wonders if their rich businessman friend from the Merry-Go-Round will be buying stock in a candle-manufacturing company. Seems like a lot of hot wax was used to satisfy his devious desires."

That fun little tidbit was the first blind item in that week's column. The second said:

"Is someone seeing double? Double trouble in their bed? Two identical blondes, one in the front and one in the back? At the same time? Mister GQ heard this for a fact. And it all happened inside the bedroom of one of the most famous TV personalities in Philly. And yes, he got his start doing summer stock in New Hope. Oh my!"

Even now, as I'm recognized as the reigning Queen of Gossip in Philly, with plenty of boys eager to tell their tales, I get hard thinking about those twins and their joint encounters with some of Philly's Finest. Those columns back in the day led me to a life of writing celebrity columns for some of the biggest magazine titles in the world. It wasn't long after those items started appearing in my column when I was suddenly greeted with warmth, affection, and yes, I'm quite sure a little envy was also involved, every time I set foot in Club Sanctuary. The former lonely boy had transformed himself into a glittering, gossiping STAR!

Though I'm glamorous, fabulous, and gay, gay, gay, I will admit that actual gay sex has little appeal for me. I'm more about the lifestyle, the glitz, the glitter, the glam. I find gay sex to be a little...well, it's so messy. I'd rather dine at the finest table at the best restaurant than remove my fashionable clothing and expose myself to some wretched creature with an erection pointed at me. Not that I'm a virgin. I had sex a few times. As few times as possible, that is!

Of course, I'm talking about romantic sex here. You know, sex with someone you have feelings for. That's rare for me, or, if I'm being totally honest, it's non-existent.

Dirty, disgusting, wet, anonymous sex in the orgy rooms at the baths? That's different. That's what I do when I'm trying to have feelings, physical feelings. Emotional attachments have nothing to do with those purely physical acts.

You disagree with me? Ask me if I care about what you think. Better people than you have already judged me.

And the scenes described by the twins hold little appeal for me. Obviously, they enjoyed their experiences, the weirder the better, it seemed. I have no need for those kinky scenes when other individuals are involved. Actually, they scare me. I can't trust anyone enough to let them tie me down, for example, or to drip hot wax on my private parts. Once they start on me, I don't know where that scene might lead.

Though I could never trust a man to perform those acts on me, I do trust myself. The night after the twins told me about their hot wax encounter, I couldn't get the scene out of my mind.

I always burn scented candles during my nightly, luxurious bubble baths. Tonight, I'm immersed in the scent of cherry and vanilla as it floats from the candle, filling my safe area, my security blanket, with the most pleasing aromas.

As I soak, my eyes are closed, totally relaxed, my thoughts wandering, now remembering the words from Paris and Milano. Sitting upright, I'm suddenly aware of the melted wax collecting at the tops of the multiple candles surrounding me. bright, shiny, dare I say...attractive? With fingers slightly trembling, I touch the steaming melted wax, quickly withdrawing my finger from the heat.

I'm slightly surprised at my body's reaction, feeling myself suddenly growing rigid.

Why? It's because I can feel something, an increasingly rare occurrence for me.

Picking up the candle, seeing my reflection in the deepening pool, I'm reminded of the sauna at the baths. The heat. The prying eyes. Watching myself as I slowly lift the candle, like a Catholic priest lifting a holy chalice during their worship services, I tilt the candle in my direction. I think of a priest, ready to take a sip from that holy vessel.

And then I feel it. The heat. The sudden jarring feeling of searing heat on my left nipple. Now on my right. I'm groaning as I feel the burning sensation, and my cock releases itself into the water, as I experience the sensual, sexual sensations on my erect, stinging nipples.

Collapsing back into the tub, total relaxation clears my mind.

I'm taken back to a date with a potential suitor. A church date, for god's sake. That should have been enough of a warning, but his dreamy hazel eyes captivated me into agreeing to attend a worship service at a Catholic church.

It was only then that I realized how beautiful the stained-glass windows appeared from the inside of the building. But then, the service began. Some strange rituals, strange to me, at least. When he told me what the "Communion" was all about, well, that ended my thoughts of him as a suitor.

I wrote about the experience in one of my most infamous columns. The backlash was fierce. I learned my lesson. Better to keep my opinions about the religious practices of others to myself. Lesson learned. I have no more to say about the topic here.

Discovering the effect that drippings of hot wax could have on my body and my libido provided an alternative to using my small knife, making cuts in places where no one will ever see them. Those incisions sometimes leave scars, and at times, it brings me pleasure to look at them, to touch them, to caress them. Reminders that I do have feelings. I am human. I do exist. Even in my current circumstances, rich, well-known, and respected, there are still times when that inner voice whispers to me:

You're not worthy of this. You didn't earn this. They don't like you. They never did, never will.

My readers, my loyal little pixies, lived for the gossip, looking forward each week to hearing about the scandals, the cheating, the lying, the drug use and alcoholic binges. Did I ever think that writing about the lives of others was somehow a way for me to fill the void in my life?

Yes, of course. But I don't think that makes me any different than my readers. We all have a need, I think, to know about the social lives of others. It isn't like I only wrote about scandals. I was also happy to write about success stories. Those are important to know, too.

But my top-rated columns? Scandalous, of course! You already knew that.

Would I want to read about my exploits at the baths in the paper? Would it surprise you to know that I sometimes planted blind items in the paper about myself?

Here's a secret. It's exciting to think that some young hottie might spend the night beating off to something I'd written about myself.

But if the stories were told in a public fashion, with real names, real dates, real details about my nights of nastiness? Please Judy, never, never, never!

I don't know if my gay lifestyle is unique, but I do know that I'm exclusive and very picky. I want a partner who not only knows which fork to use at which serving, but who also shares in my enthusiasm for such knowledge. Like, if Martha Stewart were a man, I think we'd get along famously. Now don't get me wrong, I love Martha exactly as she is, but I want a life partner of her caliber. Just with a penis. Hopefully, one that he doesn't want to use too often. Understand?

My problem in a nutshell? Intimate, romantic sex scares the life out of me. Anonymous sex with multiple partners using me at their will? I'm all for it.

Does it make any sense? All I know is that this is what I do. I'll leave it to my therapist to explain it in some academic paper that no one will ever read.

The funny thing is, I know that all those guys want me. Even the twins. During our meetings, when they would describe in detail their sexual exploits, I could tell by the way they looked at me that they wanted to do all those nasty things to me, too. They tried to hide it, but a guy like me can tell. It's so obvious.

Even at Club Sanctuary. Everybody there wants a piece of me. They just pretend they don't. But I notice all the invisible signals. Like when a guy turns his back to me, I know he wants me to look at his ass. He's probably fantasizing that I'm eating his ass, and then he gets excited thinking about me thrusting inside him. But in reality, I ignore that ass that he's so clearly offering to me. I don't want it. He can keep on dreaming, but I wouldn't even invite that street trash into my home, let alone into my bed. But, I have to let the little people have their dreams. That's my responsibility as the one they worship.

Sometimes I wonder how it is that every gay guy finds me so attractive. I mean, I don't have muscles. I'm not the prettiest or the most handsome. I guess it's just my sex appeal. The vibes I give off. Yes, that must be the reason they all want me.

I saw the signs of the effect I had on gay men from my earliest days at the club. They'd put on airs, teasing me with their coquettish behaviors, toying with my affections as they relentlessly cruised me, but never having the confidence to approach me.

At a Sanctuary party in 1990, after I hadn't seen them in over a year, I spotted Paris and Milano on the dance floor. Looking like they hadn't aged a day, dancing with the energy of lustful teens, having eyes only for each other, I reminded myself of how much those boys used to like me.

Of course, I had already moved on to other sources for my gossip information, because I had a constant need for new material. My taste in men had also become more refined, as I moved into apartments that were ever more fabulous, dined at restaurants with the most fabulous experimental cuisines, dressed impeccably, read only the finest literature, and only gave my attention to men with similar vanities.

Feeling a little sorry for the twins, who seemed to be stuck in time rather than successfully progressing through life as I was, I could see that their tight outfits seemed just a bit...well, let's be nice and I'll use the word "shabby." Just a bit. No one else seemed to notice, but I had a definite eye for details like that.

By the time the DJ's remix of the current hit "Gonna Make You Sweat (Everybody Dance Now)" by C&C Music Factory caused a swarm of dancing queens to flock to the dance floor, I was in the mood to dance myself. I didn't need an invitation from anyone. My confidence allowed me to dance with or without a partner, though I did find myself dancing right next to the twins.

Making my best moves, I smiled warmly at them. Their puzzled looks made me wonder if I had transformed myself into such a glamour queen that I was now completely unrecognizable.

"It's me, Harve´," I shouted in their direction. One of them, I think it was Milano, shrugged his shoulders and rolled his eyes at me. The twins, arms embracing one another, moving as one as they were grinding their hips suggestively to the blasting beat, slipped out of my view into the middle of the crowd.

I knew it, I thought. *Those stupid fools have the memory of a goldfish.*

Honestly, I pitied them. They probably still live together, sleeping in the same bed in some run-down studio apartment, maybe even outside the Gayborhood. Why was I even bothering to give them a second thought? Clearly, they were not deserving of my time.

Looking through the various scrapbooks of my columns allows me to travel through time. As I look back at more than 15 years of writing columns, carefully placing my current 2001 columns in chronological order, I take a moment to review what I wrote during one of my favorite years: 1994.

That was the year I fell in love. I know, you might be thinking I'm not capable of such an emotion, but this was true love, I can promise you that. It was made all the more glorious because he loved me back; I could tell by the special way he looked at me.

Everything about him was beautiful. His face, his body, even his name. They called him Pedro. Pedro Zamora. Yes, you probably know him as the first openly-gay man to appear on the reality TV series called The Real World. Season Three was his season. For me, no one else on the show really mattered. They could have been anyone.

And yes, as I sat at home, by myself, watching him interact with the other people on the show, and as I read about him in places like People Magazine, I heard the stories that he had a boyfriend. Of course, that's what they would say. I should know. I'm a gossip columnist myself.

I know how to present a celebrity to the public, so I ignored those publicity pieces. I could see by the way he looked at me through the TV screen, that he was interested in me.

I was sworn to secrecy, so I dared not reveal his secret...our secret. I wrote secret letters to him, intimate letters, and though I never mailed them, I know that he was aware of my love.

Sometimes, I would wonder why others just couldn't see the reality. I mean, the show is called The Real World, right? But then I'd remind myself that even reality TV isn't as real as viewers believe.

I wrote about the show for the paper, with a focus on Pedro, since our goal was to inform our gay readers. Of course, I never mentioned my special relationship with Pedro in my columns. I simply described events as they happened on the show, not wanting to inject my personal, intimate relationship with Pedro into my musings.

When he announced that he was HIV-positive, I was devastated, along with so many others around the country. I wanted to fly to San Francisco to comfort him, but that wouldn't be appropriate.

I did learn about his AIDS activism that started even before he was on The Real World, and I happily shared that with my readers. And though the episode where Pedro had a commitment ceremony with his boyfriend cut me deeply, I also wrote about that.

Pedro Zamora died on November 11, 1994, at the age of 22, shortly after the final episode of Season 3 of The Real World had aired. I know that I wrote something about it in my column, but I never look at that part of the scrapbook. I don't remember what I wrote in tribute to him. I'll never know. I can't bear to read it.

***

My thoughts are disturbed when the phone rings. Surprisingly, it's Joey, the owner of Club Sanctuary. He asks if I'm available to meet with him, his lover Henry, and the rest of the Board of Directors from the club. It seems they have a big announcement to make.

I check my calendar. Tomorrow, September 10, 2001, is open. I tell Joey I'll meet them tomorrow.

CHAPTER TEN

STRETCH
TUYEN
BILLY

Stretch:

I'm a gaymer. I'm gay, and I excel at games, of all types. Video games, board games, even athletic games. And I'm gay.

When I was in school, my coach told me I could throw a baseball "like a rocket." "Accurately." "With precision." Those were his exact words. I remember words exactly as they are spoken. Always.

He also told me I could catch just as well. I could easily see where the ball was going, so if I'm in the outfield, I can see the spot where I should be in order to catch the ball. I never drop it.

Those are some of my talents.

Along with my talents, I also have...deficiencies. That's one of the terms my teachers used when describing me to my parents. Deficiencies.

I don't excel at socializing. I have problems meeting people, making connections. Even casual conversations can be a struggle for me. Eye-contact? Forget about it.

Deficiencies.

That word is so negative. I don't like that word very much. But, as the teachers explained to my parents, that would be one of my "labels." That's another word I don't care for. It sounds like I'm a can on a shelf or a package in the mail. I don't want to wear a label.

I met Henry when we were both playing on the same team in the Gay Softball League. People call me Stretch for the obvious reason. I'm tall. I look even taller than I am, because I'm also skinny. Like, super skinny. But I'm strong enough to throw a wicked strike over the plate or get the ball from the outfield to first or third base when I'm not pitching.

When I'm not playing ball, it can be hard for me to sit still. I fidget. I constantly play with my fingers, always moving them in some manner. I don't know why. That's just how it's always been for me.

I've seen some changes in my time. The biggest change, of course, is the disappearance of so many of the guys, not just from the area, but also from the teams. You know why. AIDS. Even today, the very word gives me a case of PTSD.

I've also seen the changes in Joey and Henry. At first, they were young, carefree, fun-loving guys who brought joy to the field when we played our Spring tournaments. Now I see them, and while they've matured somewhat physically, they also seemed to go through some fundamental changes, in the way they interact, and the way they treat each other.

I think what I'm trying to say is that I always thought of them as equal partners. Now, at least from my perspective, Henry's taken over and treats Joey like...well, I hate to say this, but he treats Joey like chattel. Like property. Like a slave.

I know part of our community is into that stuff. Not me.

I was a little surprised when Henry invited me over to their new home in the Gayborhood. This was the first time they ever invited me to anything. I wonder what this is all about.

Henry extended the invitation, as Joey stood silently at his side. I took my tiny notebook out of my pocket to write down the address. The pencil I was using to write was barely a stub, which drew an odd look from Henry. That made me feel a little embarrassed, so I used my larger than average hand to try to hide that little stub.

In letters so small that most people might feel the need to use a magnifying glass to read, I wrote down the address.

I don't know why I write in tiny letters on tiny pieces of paper. My friend...the one true friend I have outside of the guys on the softball team, doesn't see anything wrong with this. He likes to come over to visit me in my room.

Yes, I live in a tiny room. It isn't even really an apartment; it's more like one big room. Anyway, he likes to come over to suck my dick.

He calls what I have between my legs a "whopper." All I know is that he has to stretch his mouth wide open to take me. If he tries to back away, I just hold the back of his head and hold him really tight against me as I move my "whopper" in and out of his mouth.

It's the same every time he comes over. I play the scene as if it's a game, because that's my style. I'm a gaymer.

He wants my whopper in his mouth, then he screams something about how his mouth hurts and his throat hurts and how my dick is just too much. That's when I hold his head really tight against me, so he can't move. And I push into him over and over till I nutt down his throat.

Then he pulls his dick out of his pants. His dick is not a whopper. No, sir. But he plays with it and I watch him stroke till his cum covers his belly. Then he fixes his clothes and goes home. He doesn't even wipe the cum off his body. He just leaves it there, zips up and walks out of my room.

I think he's a little weird.

The night I went to Henry and Joey's condo, I took my tackle box with me. That's nothing unusual. I take it everywhere. Even to the softball games. I have everything in there that I might need, so I can't really go anywhere without my tackle box.

The first thing I asked Henry when I walked into their place was where I should place my box. Maybe I could put it with theirs? I'm pretty sure everyone has a tackle box like mine. I mean, why wouldn't they? It really just makes sense. I like all the little compartments where I can place all my stuff, in the exact place where each one belongs. That's called organization. My life, just like my tackle box, is very organized.

"Dog, take Stretch's tackle box and go put it with yours...I mean, with ours," Henry told Joey.

That's a relief, I thought. *I know my box will be safe if they just keep it in the same place as theirs.*

As Joey, who I guess now has a new name of Dog, started to take my box into a different room, I had a small panic attack. It was always better if I kept my box in my line of sight. That was the only way I could be sure it would be really safe.

I interrupted Joey, saying, "Hey Dog, I want you to leave the box here instead."

That made Henry laugh and smile. "You heard the man, Dog. Do what he says and leave the box right there where he can keep an eye on it."

"You know, Stretch, I like your style," Henry told me, as I smiled at him.

Henry and Joey talked for a few minutes. I wasn't paying enough attention to the words as all the objects in the room caught my attention. They had so many things! Beautiful things that I couldn't even imagine owning. Honestly, I had no use for so much stuff. For me, everything important was placed carefully into its compartment in my tackle box.

"I want to watch you fuck his ass," I heard Henry say.

The word "fuck" caught my attention and suddenly I was looking at Henry again.

"Wh...what?" I stammered.

"We know you got a giant cock. I want to watch you fuck Joey's ass. Right here, Right now. I'm trying to find a third guy to join us in our relationship. This is like a test for the position. You know, like a job interview."

"Bitch, get into the position," Henry said to Joey, who now seemed to suddenly have a new name. Changes like that sometimes confused me, but I had learned to not make my discomfort too obvious when I was around new people. And though I'd known both Henry and Joey for years, this was a new situation and I was trying to be adaptable.

Joey took off all his clothes, standing naked in front of us. I already had my whopper hard in my pants when I saw that. Then Joey went over to a sofa, laid on his back, grabbing hold of his legs and pulling them back, way far back, and I could see his asshole and everything.

"Henry got up and stood close by the dog, the bitch, or whatever his new name might be.

"You wanna be inside this hole, right, Stretch? I know I wanna watch you stretch him open. That's what you do, right? I heard that's how you got your name 'Stretch', right?"

"But that isn't how we play the game," I protested. "First, you try to fit my whopper in your mouth. Then you try to pull away and scream. That's when I hold your head tight and make sure you keep me in your mouth, even if I hear those choking sounds you make."

In my mind, I was reliving every sexual experience I had ever had. It was always the same.

"Then after I finish and you swallow what I give you, that's when you open your pants and play with your little dick. I like to watch that part. Then you get yourself wet and messy and zip up and go home. That's the game. That's the only game I know."

"Hmmm," Henry said, thinking about this unexpected development. "Do you wanna play a new game tonight and get your whopper inside the boy's pussy?"

Staring at Joey, spread-eagled in front of me, ready to get pounded at Henry's command, I explained the best I could.

"Well, no," I said those words slowly, deliberately. I didn't want to make a social error. I'd been taught to be careful in new situations like this.

"I really like the game my way. If that's okay with you."

It felt good when Henry placed his strong arm around me, though I pulled away just a little when I thought his grip was getting a little too strong for my comfort.

"I like you, Stretch. And Dog, you can get up and put your clothes back on. Run down the street and get us a couple pizzas."

"While we wait for you, I'm gonna ask Stretch to show me what he keeps in his box."

That night was fun for me. We ate pizza, and I opened my box so they could see the important things I always carried.

But I only showed them the things in the top layer. The more important things, my secret things, were kept hidden from view by the sliding sections at the top.

Henry seemed to like my troll doll, the one with the orange hair. And my miniature matchbox car. And my collection of buttons, though I had to stop him when Henry tried to reach inside the box to handle a button. He didn't get all huffy and snooty like some people do when I have to tell them not to touch anything.

Before I left, Henry asked for one favor. "Can we see it? Can we see the whopper?"

No problem, I thought, opening my pants, pulling down the zipper, reaching inside and grabbing hold of myself.

"Holy shit!" Henry said.

I knew he liked it. I knew he was in awe of it. Everybody was. They always told me when I showed it.

Then I was on my way back home.

I hope we play the game tonight, I thought, as I walked quickly back to my room, hoping my friend will visit.

Once the game is finished for the night, and I have that feeling of deep satisfaction calming my mind, I'll be ready for my favorite game of all. That's when I play with my toy soldiers. You know, the little green plastic ones that come in bags that always seem too big to me. I like smaller bags.

I guess I have a few thousand toy soldiers and I admit that my mind is at ease when I'm manipulating their movements with attacks and counter-attacks.

Maybe I should join the army someday. I know a lot about battle strategies. And in my mind, I can picture myself playing my special nighttime game with some of the other soldiers. That might be fun.

***

"That was interesting," Henry commented to Joey.

"What's your verdict?" Joey asked.

"I like him. He's a cool dude, but a little eccentric. And clearly, Stretch won't make a good second boy for me to play with. I need someone who'll fuck you and let me fuck him. And he doesn't play the game that way. I'll keep looking, though. No worries there. Our third man is out there somewhere, just waiting to be discovered."

***

127

Tuyen:

My eyes were drawn to Joey the first time I saw him walking past my restaurant. He was on the other side of the street, walking his dog on their way to Franklin Square, which at the time was a rundown, under-used, mostly deserted park at 6th and Race Streets. To more accurately describe the scene, the dog was walking the man.

I found that interesting. A man being led by a dog seemed like not much of a man to me. Perhaps Joey was the type of man I was looking for. One incapable of training, but most likely easily trained.

That's how I treated men. I still do. I train them and bend them to my will. I treat them like trash. And white trash is my favorite flavor.

Although I'm fairly new to this country, I've learned and adapted quickly. My family moved from VietNam to Philadelphia, with my parents arriving here a number of years ago. I was left in VietNam, being raised by my strict grandparents. My grandfather ruled his family with an iron fist. His word was the law in his home.

I admired my grandfather greatly. He taught me everything I know about being a strong ruler of the house. For that, I am most grateful.

When I arrived in the USA at the age of 18, I moved in with my parents. This has caused some problems for me, as I want to be the boss of the house. My father, like his father, is already the boss. That leaves me in a difficult situation.

When I visit men in their homes, I become their boss. They submit to me because I am stronger than they are. I know how to rule. These American men had no such training. They were mostly raised by females, it seems, and they act like they must obey, rather than give the orders. Very strange customs these Americans have.

It soon became apparent to me that Joey had a routine, being walked by his dog at the same time, passing by my restaurant twice each day, going to and then returning from the park.

Being short in stature doesn't prevent me from having a commanding presence, so I had no difficulty attracting Joey's attention.

His eyes showed me that he craved discipline. I knew I could provide him with exactly what he needed.

On the third day of his passing by, I stood at the door of my Chinatown restaurant, named Viet. Our simple but hearty meals of authentic Vietnamese dishes drew large and loyal crowds for lunch and dinner. Standing by the door, in front of our large picture window decorated with a flaming red dragon, I simply let my presence be known, crossing my arms with my legs spread wide. I know what a pussy like Joey wants and my masculine posture demonstrated that I could give it to him.

It was no surprise to me when Joey crossed the street to be near me. Already, his posture showed that he would submit to me and be my white bitch.

His dog, a little Boston Terrier, jumped up on me as Joey tried to control him. Looking at the dog, I barked the command "Stay!" The dog sat immediately, obeying my command.

"Wow! Zumi never listens to me," were the first words that came out of Joey's beautiful pink-lipped mouth.

He even sounds like a girl, were my first thoughts when I heard him. His soft, feminine voice was intoxicating.

"I know how to control dogs," I replied, knowing that Joey already realized that I was referring to him, not to the cute canine now sitting patiently on the sidewalk.

Both of our dicks were already hard. I could see his. He could see mine. Through our clothes, of course.

He has a little dick, I noticed. *And a hot ass. Perfect!*

I was sure that Joey could tell that my dick was bigger than his. Of course, it is. I am clearly superior in every way to this person.

I know that Joey will not be providing any pleasure for me today. Hopefully, that would come in time. For now, I dismissed him with a curt, "Enjoy your walk today." With that, I turned and went back into my restaurant.

It isn't like I need Joey. I already have a few white boys to service me the way I like it. The way I demand it. They are only too happy to obey, to be used, to be degraded.

Tonight, I walk a few blocks from Chinatown into the heart of the Gayborhood. I'm not well-known in this part of the city, though it's so close to my home. But I'm not a club-goer. I meet my boys out on the street, because I have a strong preference for street boys. They're the hungriest. Not for food. For attention. For control. For structure. For pain. That makes them feel alive.

Thinking about one of my favorite street boys, I find my way to Gregory's apartment, a tiny walk-up studio at 13th and Spruce Streets. He's one of my favorites, enjoying his role in my games as much as I did.

He was expecting me, and he had prepared himself as I instructed when I called him earlier today. He was beautiful, decked out in his Ao Dai, a silk tunic often worn with matching pants by my people. Though this dress can be acceptable when worn by either men or women, Gregory had been instructed to buy his tunic from the women's section of a nearby clothing shop and to wear it for me tonight. The white silk shimmered in the dim light of his bedroom, and I found the beautiful embroidery attractive and alluring.

The whiteness of his bare feet and bare legs, free of trousers, caused a surge of excitement through my body, with my hardness quickly increasing in intensity and the desire was already building within me.

I am a true Dominant Male, but I will admit to one problem. I use that word "problem" with caution, because it doesn't really describe the situation. To be more specific, I have to draw out the foreplay as long as possible, in order to extend my pleasure. Every scene ends with me thrusting my hardness into a hot, wet, waiting boyhole, and always with the same result. The pleasure for me is so intense, so overpowering, that I shoot off my sperm load after one or two thrusts of my hips, into and out of that delicate hiding place. I've tried many techniques, but nothing I do increases the time I can spend actually fucking my submissives.

I don't care what they think. They dare not criticize me. It's my problem because my pleasure doesn't last as long as I would like.

But I'm getting ahead of myself.

I want to enjoy the view of him, dressed in an Ao Dai that any Vietnamese woman would envy. He was already pitching a tent, excited at what he knew would be happening soon.

I paid no mind to his excitement, removing my shoes to enter his place, motioning at my feet for the boy to prostrate himself in a show of submission, placing my foot on top of his head and pushing him down, his face smashed against the floor as if to leave an imprint of the patterned tiles there.

"Fold my clothes properly, boy," I instructed him, shedding all my clothes for my servant to place carefully on the table in the foyer. I never wasted time getting naked, preferring to parade around, showing off my tightly muscled body, smooth and hairless save for the thick bush

131

surrounding my erection. That quickly, I was already oozing. Though it felt good, I knew it also meant another very quick orgasm for me.

I grabbed Gregory by his hair and pulled him into the bedroom, tossing him onto the queen-sized bed that dominated the tiny area. He was on his back and I lifted his tunic to peer at him.

Smiling with satisfaction that his entire body was hairless, I told him, "Good to see you obeyed my directions. You know I don't like hairy dogs. But last time I was here, you disrespected me by not shaving yourself, especially down here," I said, now pulling and stretching his balls. They felt good and heavy in my hand.

Full of cum, I thought.

"Take your dress off, woman!"

I was close to nutting already, just seeing him so smooth and naked in front of me.

With both hands, I reached for his nipples. Hard and pointy and already stretched out longer than a "normal" man. That was my doing. Taking hold of his hands, I spit into each one, telling him, "Rub that into your titties, woman. Make yourself feel good."

He knew how I liked it. He didn't actually rub those nips, but instead started pinching and twisting them with his lubed-up fingertips.

I took hold of his hair again, pulling it with enough force that I knew it would hurt. His face contorted with pain, as I started slapping him in his face, then taking aim at his balls, slapping them with the palms of my hands, and then moving my attention to the beautiful mounds of flesh at his backside, which was left beet-red the last time I had visited him.

"You wanna get pinned, woman?"

Though I asked the question, we both knew he had no choice. He was going to get pinned no matter what he said.

"Go get them," I gave the order.

When he returned., I placed him in a kneeling position on top of the mattress, forcing his legs wide open. "Hands behind your back. Don't act stupid," I admonished him, because he knew the correct position for him to get pinned.

The look of pure desire in his eyes was enough to make me shoot without even touching him. I looked straight into his eyes as I opened the first clothespin and clamped it onto his right titty, quickly followed by another clothespin clamped on the left. That's when I started flicking them with my fingers, hearing the snap of the small wooden device against his skin.

"I see you like that, my little doggie," I whispered, flicking my fingers against his dripping hardness.

I removed one of the pins, admiring the way the it had smashed his nipple into a squashed mess of flesh. I pinched and twisted that little mound as my submissive moaned with a mix of intense pleasure and pain. My cock was dripping, a long string of my pearly manliness hanging from the tip.

Ritualistically, I moved my attention to the other hard nipple, repeating the process, playing with his man tits till I saw his cock gleaming with wetness and desire.

"Look down. Eyes off me. Look down at yourself. You call yourself a man?" I teased him, once again flicking his erection so it swung wildly through the air, slapping up against his belly.

He was panting as he saw me reach for his balls with a clothespin ready to be clamped on the bottom part of his egg. One by one, clothespins were attached to his hanging balls, which eventually moved tightly into his body, with ten pins digging their wooden teeth into his sensitive flesh, five hanging from each delicate sac.

I took my time moving from playing with the pins on his nipples and those clinging tightly to his balls.

His moans were met with more punishment, as I took a wooden ruler from the clothespin bag and began tapping out a beat, wooden instrument against wooden instrument.

I could barely contain my excitement at the sights and sounds of this quivering person reacting to every touch from me in a mix of rapture and pain.

"So nicely decorated!" I complimented him. "Just need something at the top. Like the top of a tree for the holidays," I said, laughing.

Neatly arranging a semi-circle of six clothespins clamped on the area just above his throbbing meat pointing directly upward, I felt a surge within me that had to be fulfilled. If only I could hold off for just another minute or two.

Pulling him from the bed, I took hold of his arms behind his back, forcing him into an awkward waddle across the room as the pain from the clacking clothespins made walking a difficult task. We walked the short distance out to his kitchen, then back into the bedroom. Forcing him face-down on the bed, his ass in the air, I knew the pins would be causing more than a bit of discomfort. That's when my desire totally overpowered me. I couldn't wait. I forced his legs open wide and quickly grabbed two condoms, hoping that a double dose would decrease the sensation and maybe give me at least a minute or two to enjoy the pleasure of his ass clasping my dick.

I pushed myself into his eager hole. One, two pushes inside him and then it happened, the inevitable explosion of intense pleasure as my cock erupted with spurt after spurt of my sperms into my willing boy.

Of course, it was pleasurable. I loved being inside a submissive boy, especially if his skin was white. I leaned against him, grunting my pleasure, just wishing that it didn't always end so quickly.

For me, the most beautiful sight in the world was when I was watching my dick being pushed into the hot hole of a whiteboy.

The second most beautiful sight was to watch a submissive boy enjoy his pain, realizing that he's under my total control, being forced to endure a hardship, but still being sexually excited to the point of losing control.

Switching my position, I sat on the bed so I could rub my bare feet in his face. "Do it, boy. I wanna see you squirt."

The click-clacking sounds of the clothespins still clinging to the boys nips, balls and cock were as sweet as the sounds of a wind chime to me. Sniffing my feet and stroking himself, he quickly made a wet mess on his belly.

I reached towards the stickiness with my feet, then held them right at the boy's mouth.

"You know you want it. Eat your own cum right off my feet, you dirty fag."

And he did it. He enjoyed it. I liked it too, but I wasn't being humiliated. These subs. So dirty. So needy. They were lucky to have me give them what they deserved.

***

My plan was to get Joey into a similar position, serving for my pleasure. I'm not the type to hesitate, but I did have a plan to have a little fun with him before making him mine.

The next time I saw him, smiling as warmly as the bright morning sun, I greeted him with a simple "Hello."

"Hello there," came his soft reply.

"Actually, I prefer to be greeted in my language," I told him. "Say 'hello' in Vietnamese."

"What? I don't know any Vietnamese," he protested.

"Of course, you don't," I chided him. "Americans only want us to learn English, but they don't take the time to learn a second language themselves."

I could see the boy thinking about my words.

"Maybe you could teach me," he suggested, falling right into my trap.

"I'd be happy to," I replied. "My English isn't perfect, but it's better than your Vietnamese, right?"

"How do I say 'hello' in your language?"

"Xin chảo."

Joey clumsily repeated the words after me. To me, it sounded like he said "Ching jowl."

"No," I told him. "Try it again. Xin chảo."

"Ching jowl. Chang jang. Shang hang."

I sighed. This would be more difficult than I had originally thought.

The next day, Joey stopped at the door of my restaurant, waiting for his lesson in speaking my language. I made him wait for a few minutes before I came out to see him. *It's a good lesson for him to learn not to expect me to be waiting for him,* I thought.

"Hello," was my first word to him this morning. He started to repeat his horrid rendition of my language as he struggled to remember the lesson from the previous day. I held my hand up to silence him.

"No. Let me teach you a more proper greeting. In VietNam, you would not greet me with 'Hello'" I informed him.

"What should I say instead?"

"Listen closely. I'll say it slowly."

"tôi là con chó của bạn." He started to speak and I once more raised my hand to keep him silent.

Then I repeated the phrase. "tôi là con chó của bạn."

Joey stumbled through the lesson as we repeated the phrase together, at least 10 times. Oh god, my dick was straining with desire as I heard him say the words to me.

"tôi là con chó của bạn."

Joey had no idea what he was saying. In English, those words meant "I am your dog."

Two days later, Joey was proudly greeting me loudly from across the street.

"tôi là con chó của bạn."

I would come out of the restaurant, smiling at my stupid little student. Others on my block who also spoke Vietnamese would laugh and smile knowingly at the trick I was playing on the young white man, who was walked by his dog, looking like a homosexual in his weird-looking outfits and bowing to his Master, proclaiming himself to be my dog. I was very pleased with the results of my lesson.

I was sure it wouldn't be long before I'd be showing him just what it meant to be my dog. I had many more tricks to teach this one.

I think it was the fifth day after I first spoke to Joey, when I was watching from the window of my restaurant, eagerly awaiting his arrival. I saw him as he crossed the street onto my block, and while I loved the way his body looked in the tight latex shorts he was wearing that day, I didn't like the fact that he wasn't alone. A man was walking with him. A Black man.

In my neighborhood, many of the residents were afraid of Black men. Many of us had stories of problems we had. I was no exception. I was very cautious with people whose ways I didn't understand. And I had been a victim. Three Black men had surrounded me one night, tearing my gold chain with the emerald dragon charm, and running quickly away into the night.

Maybe Joey was bringing one of those very same Black men to me, to harass me for humiliating his white friend.

Still, I went outside, feeling brave in my own neighborhood, where I could count on neighbors for protection if it was needed.

Joey called out his usual greeting, with friendliness that made me feel comfortable that I was in no danger.

"Hello," I greeted both of them.

Joey introduced his friend as Henry, whom I had never seen before.

"You speak English, right?" Henry asked me, eyes blazing, a look completely different than the respect that Joey always showed me.

"I don't know what you've been teaching my boy," Henry barked, "But I'm here to tell you that this is my boy. MY boy. Get it?"

I wasn't expecting this, so I answered innocently, "What do you mean?"

"I know who you are. I know how you treat your boys. You and me got a lot in common. But we are not going to have this boy in common. He is mine. He will always be mine. And as of right now, this boy is forbidden to walk on this block. You will not see him again."

Directing his commands at Joey, Henry continued, pulling Joey's hair right there in public, commanding him, "Boy, you will not walk this block. Never! No questions, no comments, no pleading, nothing. This is forbidden territory for you."

With that, Henry pulled Joey's arm, leading him away from me.

I don't know how Henry knew about me. But clearly, he was threatened by my presence. That made me a little proud, though I was sorry that I had lost the chance to add a new dog to my collection. Still, I knew that others were out there, ready to be trained.

It would be a long time before I'd see Joey again.

***

Billy:

My eyes were on Henry from Day One, when I met him and his boyfriend Joey at the club, along with my friends Willie, William and Bill. Yes, we were the Four Williams, partying in Philly after a trip from Joey's home town in Northeastern PA.

Though Henry was my goal, I can't deny that I approached Joey, begging for a job at Sanctuary, while blowing Joey in the backroom of the club. Sworn to secrecy, since Joey was afraid of losing Henry if he ever found out that Joey had betrayed him, I actually couldn't wait to tell Henry every juicy detail. How I crawled in submission, how I sucked Joey's dick and balls, how I kissed his feet.

Henry didn't seem to mind it too much. After all, he and Joey were still together.

But I never told Joey that Henry knew all about it. It seemed that each of us knew part of the story, with no one really seeing the big picture. Just like the famous question, "Who knew what and when."

After all four of us Williams had been living together in Philly for a few years, Willie, the first one of us to move here, was getting tired of my antics. Yes, he was the one in charge. The one we worshiped as The Master and the one who had given me the name PigBoy.

That didn't bother me. I wore that name as a badge of honor. I was a pig. I was a boy. No one, including myself would ever deny my PigBoy credentials.

When four young, horny gay guys live together, there are bound to be some conflicts. The fact that I was a bartender at Sanctuary just made things worse.

139

I was popular there. One of the best bartenders. I even created my own drink, the Sanctuary Sucker.

Perhaps "created" is too strong a word.

Joey told me he wanted the fruitiest drink I could make, so I poured him a rainbow cocktail. The combination of grenadine (red syrup), pineapple juice and blue curacao liqueur forms the basic layers of colors. Since Joey likes his drinks with a kick, I added several shots of vodka, and topped it off with cranberry/cherry juice. Adding one of those little paper cocktail umbrellas delighted Joey, who, after downing his third, loudly proclaimed me as the Original Sanctuary Sucker.

My cheeks turned red at that pronouncement, because my session with Joey in the backroom of the club had indeed turned me into a "Sanctuary Sucker."

My station at the club was always busy. Unless it was a special night when all the bartenders would dress in a certain way, I was always serving drinks in my briefs. Always showing my round ass and my full pouch for the customers to enjoy. Mesh, cotton, whatever. Always sexy, often colorful, but always in briefs. Never boxers or those horrid boxerbriefs which struck me as an odd fashion compromise. And never, never, never anything feminine. I'm a PigBoy. Emphasis on the word 'boy.'

The night I saw Joey being forced by Henry to enter a wet briefs contest, watching when Joey dropped his shorts to let the world know he was wearing panties...well, I knew it had to be Henry's idea. I swore if I ever got the chance to please Henry, I'd do almost anything. But not that. There was no way I would ever squeeze myself into some dainty pair of lacey women's panties.

Willie was threatening to kick me out of our house. "Can you believe after all this time, he'd treat me like that?" I asked, as I handed Henry and Joey their glasses. They were taste-testing the Sanctuary Suckers, nodding their approval as they enjoyed the strong drinks.

An hour later, I was at the new home in the Gayborhood where Henry and Joey, my bosses, had recently moved.

"I'm looking for a second boytoy for me," Henry explained,

He looks so hot in all that leather gear, I was thinking, my excitement growing at the thought of serving them both. Though for me, Joey was an afterthought. I had already tasted what Joey had to offer. Yes, I enjoyed it, but Henry was the one who drew me in, as I thought about his offer.

Henry leaned back as he watched me obey his command to strip naked. Inspecting me like I was a dog at the National Dog Show, he reached between my legs, fondling my balls, and commenting, "I feel one. Yes, I feel two. So far, so good."

Joey laughed, while Henry was stroking me till I reached my full length.

"Any problem with being watched? Sometimes I like to see my bitch gettin' bred, so you can't be a total sub. Sometimes you gotta be able to dominate his cunt. Can you do that?"

I had plenty of experience being versatile so it was no lie when I said, "Yes Sir."

"But you will always be submissive and obedient to me. Understand? If you ever try to act like you're the Master, you'll be out on the street in 5 minutes. Got that?"

I nodded.

"Tell me," Henry commanded. Will you always submit to me as your Master?"

Yes Sir," I replied with no hesitation.

"Both of you are my good boys," Henry told us, rubbing our heads with glee, thinking that his search for a new sub in the house had finally ended.

"Let's seal the deal then," Henry said. I want each one of you to be licking and kissing my ass while I fuck the other one, and tell me how much you worship me while your tongue is licking my hole."

"You get the dick first," he told Joey, pushing him down on the floor. "And you, show me how much you worship my Black ass. But before you start, I wanna be sure you know how to obey, so go get a pretty pair of panties outta Joey's lingerie drawer, and come back to show me how pretty you look dressed like a CuntBoy."

Damn! I thought. *What'm I gonna do now? I was just tellin' myself I'd never get dressed in panties. Never. Not even for Henry.*

Then I came to my senses, realizing that I couldn't pass up the opportunity to join Henry as part of his family of subs. Henry pointed at the drawer I was permitted to open, and then I reached inside and selected a beautiful pair of purple lace panties, sliding them up my legs till my cock and balls were tucked inside the tightness of the pouchless panties. I knew what to do next. Crouching behind Henry, I moved my head to match his thrusts into Joey's ass, showing my devotion as I had been instructed.

I'm happy to report that I'll be moving in with Henry and Joey on Friday.

CHAPTER ELEVEN

HENRY

My life was moving exactly in the direction I wanted. Two hot subs ready to serve me sexually at home. From my perspective, things seem to be moving smoothly.

At the dinner table, we were enjoying the results of their collaboration in the kitchen. Billy and Joey both liked to cook, or at least, to prepare and serve the meals. I enjoyed watching them work and then serving me.

The aroma of roasted chicken filled the room while we ate our salads.

"We have some unfinished business," I announced, looking at no one in particular.

"Me?" Joey asked.

"Or is it with me?" Billy inquired.

"Everybody put your hands on the table," I told the boys, doing the same with my hands. "Anything look funny to anyone?"

Joey shrugged. "Looks normal to me."

I think Billy knew what I was talking about, but I also understood his hesitation to say anything. He was the newbie in the family, still learning how to navigate without hurting anyone's feelings, or getting punished for stupidity or arrogance.

"Billy, why are you looking at Joey's hands?"

"No reason. His hands are fine. Nothing wrong there," Billy lied.

"Joey, look at your hands. Then look at mine. Then look at Billy's. What's different?"

I know I was being cruel. I saw the flash of recognition in Joey's sad eyes. He was already starting to cry.

Instead of answering, Joey moved his hand from the table and placed it in his lap, his fist closed tightly.

The look on my face let everyone know that I strongly disapproved of that move. But Joey wouldn't budge, silently refusing to return his hand to the tabletop.

"Don't make me smack you," I warned him.

Still, no movement.

"Boy, I'm warning you."

Joey's lips trembled as he pondered his choices. The hand that remained on the table shook visibly.

"No! Don't do this. Please. I'm begging you. I never ask for anything. But I'm asking you now," he pleaded with me.

My mind was already made up.

"Billy, go in the bedroom and wait. I have to talk to this one."

"Can I get some chicken first? I'll eat it in there."

"Don't aggravate me," I scolded him. "Go sit in the fuckin' bedroom till I finish talkin' to Joey. And be glad you don't go completely without supper for mouthin' off to me. Now go."

Once we were alone, Joey visibly relaxed. He felt safer when it was just the two of us. I understood. We had a long history together.

Looking to be sure that Billy had closed the bedroom door, I took hold of Joey's hands, firmly but gently. I was going to hurt his feelings. I knew that, but I also believe this step had to be taken. I felt I should at least explain my reasoning to Joey.

Stroking his beautiful hands, freshly-manicured with his nails polished with a clear shine, I hesitated for a moment.

Squaring my shoulders and straightening my back, I said the words that needed to be spoken.

"Joey, listen to me. I know how much this means to you," I whispered, gently touching the ring on his finger.

His quiet sobs broke my heart.

"We tried to do it their way. The straight way. That isn't for us."

I wanted to hug him, to take his heaving shoulders and comfort him. But no. I simply held tightly to his hands.

"You're always gonna be my Number One. My Number One boy. But I want us to make a new kind of life. To avoid the problems we ran into before. You're still mine. You always will be. And I'll always be yours."

Joey's body was getting more limp with every word I said.

"Take it off. Now."

He sobbed, without making any movement.

Finally, he looked at me directly. "Please Sir, this means so much to me. I don't wanna lose this symbol. I don't wanna lose you."

"Understand one thing, Joey. That ring is a symbol, but it's the wrong symbol for us. Trust me, I have everything planned. But this is the first step. You gotta give it up."

His body tensed up again. "I don't wanna lose you," he pleaded.

"If there's one thing I'm certain about, is that you will never, ever lose me. And I will never, ever lose you. I promise you that with my life. But you have to trust me."

I gave him time. More time than I wanted, but I also knew just how much this hurt.

"You take it off me," he said. "I can't do it."

"You can and you will. I'm waiting."

A piece of my heart was melting. I remembered going with Joey to buy our wedding rings, when the merchants on Jeweler's Row refused service to us, just because we were gay. Our joy at finding Bernard, who gladly helped us make our selections and who did the inscriptions as his

145

wedding gift to us. How Bernard then walked Joey down the aisle to give him away...to give him to me.

It was a beautiful, emotional ceremony. But it was all based on a lie. Not about us or our devotion. We had proven our devotion to each other through years of being together. Enjoying so much of life as a couple.

All of that was overshadowed by my growing discontent with mimicking the example fed to us by straight society. I wanted to rebel against that. No, I had to rebel. It was killing me slowly, day by day, as I felt my gayness, my queerness, being denied.

That's why I had insisted on us changing our lifestyle. I might not be sure exactly what I wanted, but I was 100% certain of what I didn't want.

Joey's beautiful eyes, swollen with tears, looked deeply into mine. Finally, he said what I wanted to hear.

"I do trust you, Sir. You're the only man I trust completely. But even more than that, I love you. I adore you. I worship you. And to show just how much I trust you, I'm going to do what I have to do. I have to obey you."

With that, he twisted the ring, pulling and tugging until it was free from his finger, and he placed it in the waiting palm of my hand.

Looking at his now ringless finger, I was surprised to see the whiteness of the area that had been covered by the ring, though I should have expected it.

I blinked away the tears that were forming in my eyes.

"One more thing. I need mine back too. I know you have it hidden somewhere."

No matter what outfit he was wearing, Joey always wore a special gold necklace I had given him years before. It was solid gold, with a golden dog tag that showed the symbol of our shared zodiac sign, Gemini.

I had almost forgotten that the dog tag was actually a locket. Reaching for his prized possession, Joey unlatched the locket, showing my wedding ring safely hidden inside.

"I never let it go. I couldn't it. I kept it next to my heart ever since that night when you left it on your pillow."

I gulped, feeling a tinge of regret. *These damn symbols,* I thought. *Why don't we have our own? Our own symbols. Our own rituals and ceremonies? Why do the straights have to control every fucking thing?*

A week later, the three of us were back at the dinner table. One of them was broiling salmon and roasting asparagus. It mattered little to me which boy did the cooking. They were both good at it, and I was good at eating what they prepared.

It was one of our regular meals together. None of us worked at the club on Monday or Tuesday, the slowest nights of the week. We knew we could count on the rest of the crew to be sure things ran smoothly, though we could always be called on in case of emergency.

"Let's enjoy the meal," I said, "Then I got a little trip for us planned this evening."

That's how we found ourselves on South Street, where I eventually led my two boys into a tattoo parlor. I'd been thinking about a different way for us to show our commitment to each other. I knew Joey was ready to get inked with my design. He had proven his loyalty to me countless times.

"Billy, my boy, I know you're slowly proving yourself to be a worthy member of our family," I said, winking in Joey's direction. "But Joey here is gonna get marked permanently. You, my little baby boy, you're gonna get marked, but just a temporary one. We need more time before we mark you up as one of my boys."

I knew that Billy would get over his disappointment, and maybe he would one day become a permanent member of our gay tribe. That's how I thought of our group. I was the chief, of course. And I liked the idea of having a tribe of boys under my command.

We sat in the lobby of the shop, and Billy started flipping through the books of sample tattoos. Joey sat by my side, attentive as always.

"I had Gio make a design just for us," I told Joey, pulling a folded paper from my pocket.

Gio was our friend, with his own art studio just two blocks away on South Street, who had designed our body-paint Halloween costume a few years ago.

One thing about Joey. That bitch is a sentimental one. That's one of the major things I love about him. He can't hide what he's feeling. Not from me, anyway.

"This is gonna go on both of our arms. We're gonna match. This is the mark of our tribe," I told him proudly, revealing a stunning design.

Joey took the paper, caressing it, looking at me with adoring eyes.

"I can't believe it. It's stunning!"

I didn't have to tell Joey that I agreed with him, but I did.

"Gio is amazing, isn't he?" I asked, watching Joey inspect the design. The centerpiece was a heart, and inside the heart design were the stripes of the Gay Pride flag, in those 6 glorious colors. Surrounding the heart was an Infinity symbol, assuring that the love within our tribe, and right now between me and Joey, would endure forever.

Billy had been given permission to select a design for his temporary tattoo. He checked with me to be sure his cartoon of Bugs Bunny in drag was acceptable. Laughing, I gave him the okay and Billy went to the tattoo area to get the work done. Completing a design using hentai wasn't going to take long.

"Actually, we're both getting two tattoos today," I whispered to Joey.

Joey gasped audibly when I showed him the second design. Two hearts, melded together into one, with the initial "H" inside the first heart and "J" inside the second. Henry and Joey. The same design that Joey had inscribed inside our wedding rings.

"If you agree to it, I want this symbol tattooed on our ring fingers. I'm asking you, like I did a long time ago, will you be my Number One boy and the first member of my tribe forever?"

Joey's tears of joy were all the answer I needed.

"Yes, Sir. Yes, Henry. I will be your Number One boy forever."

"You're making me a happy man, boy. I just have one more thing to give you."

I handed Joey a small box, and even I was on the verge of losing my emotions.

"I had them melt down our rings to make this. I want you to wear it forever. Please."

It wasn't like me to say "Please" to anyone, let alone one of my subs. But this was a special occasion.

Taking the golden locket, in the shape of an erect phallus, out of the box, I waited as Joey opened it, revealing our wedding date inscribed inside:

12/25/80

Hearing his soft gasp as he saw the reminder of our love, our commitment to each other, made me feel romantic. But our lives were changed now, and I had to remind myself that I was no longer going to recognize Joey as an equal partner. Yes, he would be my Number One, but he would also always be my sub.

I watched as he removed his favorite necklace so I could attach the locket.

"It looks perfect on you," I whispered.

"I love you, Sir," he replied. "My love for you lasts through Infinity and beyond."

When Jorge, the tattoo artist, was ready to begin working on us, he commented, "I'm loving the Pride colors inside the heart, but I have to tell you, there's no way I can do that second design on your ring fingers. There just isn't enough room to do all the details."

That was an unexpected setback.

Jorge continued, "I can do the hearts, or I can do the initials. Just can't do both," he said, slowly shaking his head, trying to picture a way to accomplish what I wanted.

"It'll just look like a blob of ink on your fingers, really."

Joey started to say something, as if he was about to offer his opinion. "Be quiet, dog, I'm thinking," I admonished him, reminding him publicly of his lowly position.

Jorge laughed, then quickly caught himself and looked away, as if he was embarrassed for Joey.

"Don't feel sorry for him," I told Jorge. "He's in the exact position in life that he wants and deserves. Ain't that right, little doggy?"

Joey did exactly as I'd trained him, nodding and smiling obediently.

"I want the initials. The 'H' comes first, since that's my initial. And I want the 'H' to be bigger than the 'J'. As a matter of fact, can you make the 'H' a capital letter and the 'J' a small letter. I think that'll be perfect," I told Jorge.

"You're gonna like it that way, right boy?" I asked Joey, rubbing his head affectionately.

This was one of the happiest days of my life.

When we walked out of the shop, our bodies tattooed, marked as members of our own little tribe, I could not have been more proud.

CHAPTER TWELVE

YANDI

"Yo, you goin' to Flaco's party tonight? You know he always gets the best bitches to show up. I'm thinkin' I'm ready for a good BJ tonight, ya know?"

That's my bro, Blanco, always thinking and talking about getting his dick sucked.

"Imma be there," I replied, grinning and grabbing my crotch, pulling at my maleness, knowin' I be BIGGER than most of my dudes. "Some lucky mami gonna be gaggin' on all this," I bragged.

I talked a big game, 'cause that's what was expected. Everybody in the gang did it. We bragged, we smoked, we drank, we partied, we basically did anything we wanted. Life was about havin' a good time.

Kensington was our home turf. North Philly. We owned the streets and everybody knew it. If we wanted something, we took it. If somebody crossed our turf, we let 'em know not to try that again.

But the parties were the best. Hangin' with the guys, gettin' high and drunk, fuckin' with the ladies.

It really don't get no better than that. At least, that was true for all my homies. I wasn't all that sure, to be honest.

There was something wrong with me. I knew it. The guys never noticed. But I had this feeling that I just couldn't shake. I wasn't right. I had strange thoughts that I just couldn't get outta my head.

When a lady was suckin' my dick, and I mean, we had very pretty ladies who wanted to hang with us, and gave us what we wanted, but it was like she wasn't even there. I mean, I felt her as she did her thing. I always popped one off in her mouth. When she was slobbin' my knob, and I was watchin her bouncin' titties and she all up in my bizness, that was supposed to be all that, right?

But...

I felt like I was livin' in crazy town. A hot ass bitch, suckin' and slobberin' all over me, and I'm thinking about...guys?! I mean, holy fuck! Who does that? I should be thinkin' 'bout fingerin' her up...turnin' her 'round and doin' the pound action on her...

I swear to god, I ain't no fag. Sometimes I see some of them in the hood. Guys dressin' all queer, wearin' these faggy crop tops, shakin' their asses like they some kinda hoe, even wearin' makeup and shit. Hell no, that is not me. And ain't never gonna be me either. Fuckin' dumbass fags.

I can't control my thoughts...my mind keeps jumpin' from images of pussy to...DAMN! I don't even wanna say it out loud!

As soon as my dick gets hard, no matter where, no matter when, no matter who's kneeling between my twitchin' legs...these weird ass thoughts keep jumpin' inside and fuckin' with my headspace.

A few years back, I spent some time in a shelter. Those were bad times, before I took on the colors. Being a runaway, needin' to escape my Moms and whatever man she was hookin' up with that week, I decided to never go back. No one there to give me a helpin' hand, nobody to look up to, no MAN to show me the ropes the right way, so I ain't gonna lie. I hung my hat at that shelter down in Center City for a minute.

That's where I met that kid. I wish I could forget his name, but sometimes, when I'm grabbin' my junk for a quick stroke, I kinda whisper his name out loud.

"Eloy."

Even hearin' my voice say it, I know it's fuckin' crazy. Why do I say that young boi's name, even after all this time went by? I don't never see him around. No idea what he's doing or if he's even still alive. But it happens every time. I say that name out loud, but quietly, like it's my private secret.

"Eloy."

Sometimes, when I'm sure no one is following me, I take a quick sneak down to Center City, and sometimes I find myself outside that club. The one called Sanctuary. Not to see the faggots. But I always think maybe I'll see him. That boy. Eloy.

I wrote a poem once. We both did. Me and Eloy. His was about the coquis. Mine was about...well, I said something in that classroom that I never shoulda said out loud. Part of my poem, the part at the end, went like this:

Avoidin his gaze
Cause he'll never be mine
He like the bitches
I think they witches
Castin a spell
To make him forget
I could be his
You wanna bet

He think I don't like him
That ain't the truth
Better he think that
Cause...

This ain't no gag
I think he gon' kill me
If he know I'm a fag

I still can't believe I was crazy enough to read my poem in front of the class. Not that anyone paid it no mind. But I said the words. And then, I spent some time with Eloy. You know, foolin' around. Kid stuff. That don't mean nothin'. Right?

CHAPTER THIRTEEN

MISTER GQ

At this point in my life, I seem to spend more time looking backwards than I do looking ahead. I gloat about my successes, even as I sit alone in my huge apartment on the Benjamin Franklin Parkway, lounging on my balcony with the magnificent view of the Philadelphia Museum of Art. There's no question that I'm a success.

Still, I've made sacrifices. I can't even count the number of men I've rejected. Who can blame them for wanting me? I'm rich, well-educated, well-informed and I know everybody worth knowing in our little metropolis here. Who could ask for anything more?

The times have changed, though. Maybe that's why I think about the past as much as I do. The grand parties. The balls. The shows. The after-parties. And of course, the men. Fabulous, funny, and flawed. All of them. But then, they disappeared so suddenly. I call it the scourge. The terrible fates of so many, and I had to report about them as part of my work in journalism.

Relaxing at home, my mind has a tendency to wander. Often, the topic that occupies the space between my ears would be the beautiful members of the male species. Sometimes, a fantasy. Other times, real, actual memories.

Right now, another former suitor, a young, classically handsome young man named Todd, amuses my thoughts. He had class, just like me. It's a pleasure to be in the company of a man who actually has an appreciation for the finer things. Like art. Todd was an expert in art appreciation.

On one of our dates, we wandered the treasures of the Philadelphia Museum of Art. The building itself is a treasure, but my true adoration was for the objects enclosed within the structure.

A special exhibition of Italian Renaissance art was the main attraction during our date. My heart was fluttering as we approached the exhibit hall, anticipating an afternoon of delight with Todd, seeing these masterpieces on display right here in Philly.

Approaching one of my favorite paintings of all time, Saint Sebastian by Pietro Perugino, I was overcome with emotions at seeing the actual work by the artist.

My breathing became labored, my heart was pounding, and the room began to spin. Todd later told me that I fainted right there, collapsing to the floor of the gallery.

When I awoke, I was in a bed at Jefferson Hospital.

"Ahh, good to see you awake. You had an art attack," the man in the white coat told me.

"Oh my god, am I gonna die? Do you have to operate right away?" I asked, scared to death that my young heart had already given up on me.

Todd interrupted, explaining, "No, babe, not a heart attack. You had an art attack. The doctor here was explaining it to me. Some people, when in the presence of true beauty, experience what's known as Stendhal Syndrome. They get so excited by the beauty of what they're seeing, that they have a physical reaction."

That actually made sense to me. I absolutely adored the image of Saint Sebastian created by Perugino, so I wouldn't doubt that the sight of it caused me to faint.

Here's how I described the experience in my column:

This reporter, while visiting the Renaissance exhibit at the Museum of Art with my beau, had a rare and exotic reaction upon seeing the Saint Sebastian by Perugino for the first time. Only the most sensitive and intellectual individuals are prone to Stendhal Syndrome, where the mere sight of extreme beauty causes a physical reaction. May I encourage all my readers to visit the exhibit? I'm quite sure that it'll be an unforgettable experience.

Okay, maybe I exaggerated the part about intellectuals, and I left out the part about me crumpling to the floor, but nobody fact-checked me. However, Todd objected to being called my "beau," and he ended the relationship right after he read that. I guess I spoke too soon.

I adore my collection of classical music CDs, though of course, I really prefer to actually attend the performances of the Philadelphia Orchestra at the Academy of Music.

On this particular day, however, I'm listening to pop music. Shhhh! It's my guilty pleasure. But it is indeed a pleasure.

A song that captures the essence of the 1990s for me is one that I listen to repeatedly. Have you ever heard "What is Love (Baby Don't Hurt Me)" by Haddaway? It was released in 1993, becoming an instant hit and a song that I still love to this very day.

When I look back through my scrapbooks, re-reading my columns, I like to play music that reflects the times that I'm remembering. That song, for me, captures the 90s. Questioning love, what does it really mean, how do we express it properly, while also hoping to not be hurt. How exquisite! Those lyrics haunt me.

But I don't always get hung up on the lyrics. Music to just make me feel good is also appreciated, I'm thinking, as "Dancing Queen" by ABBA bounces through the air for me, transitioning then to the classic hit "Never Gonna Give You Up" by Rick Astley.

I find myself dancing, all alone, in my apartment, when my choreography is interrupted by the phone.

"Hello," I answer, sullenly.

"Hey, it's me, Joey. Got a minute?"

"Honey, for you, of course. What's up, sweetie?"

"Henry wants to know if you'll meet us for dinner tomorrow. We have a reservation at Trust. An outdoor table. Every member of the Board from the club will be there. Henry says he has some big announcement and that the press will probably be interested."

"What's it about? Any trouble at the club?"

"No trouble, but I don't know what he wants to announce. Can I tell him you'll join us at 6 PM?"

"Absolutely, count me in! Looking forward to seeing all of you tomorrow."

I still have the page from my datebook in one of my scrapbooks.

I tremble when I see it.

"Meet Henry and Sanctuary Board at Trust. 6 PM. The date at the top of the page states:

Monday, September 10, 2001

I put the date out of my mind, turning back to thinking about the 90s, leading up to the new millennium, the 2000s.

Though the clippings help me to remember specific details, I'm struck by how clearly I remember some events, even while the entire decade seems like a blur. Maybe that's how memory works. I don't know. But that's how it is for me.

Smiling, I read the headline for the column I wrote about the Leather and Lace Ball at Club Sanctuary. which seemed to attract every leather queen in the tri-state area. I never smelled so much leather and frankly, my dear, it gave me a major headache.

Then there were the annual Q-Balls, with so many dancing Queens and Queers, wearing a kaleidoscope of outfits, trying to be crowned Miss Q, the reigning Queen of the Year.

Without a doubt, the party of the year, really the party of the century, was the Y2K Ball.

"You never heard of Y2K? Why you silly thing!"

Oh lord, here I go, talking to the scrapbooks again. But there's no one else here to listen to my stories.

Y2K referred to an error in computer programming in the early days of computing. Dates were entered as mm/dd/yy, leaving only 2 digits available for the year. Eventually, some nerd decided that might cause a problem when the year turned to 2000. The rumor was that when the computers saw "00" as the date, they might think the year was 1900 instead of 2000, and apparently that would cause mass confusion, massive outages, all leading to robots taking over the world. Or nothing in the world working. Or...something like that.

Anyway, for those of us non-scientific types, we saw it as a chance to party. Maybe the last chance to party before the whole world crashed down around us. So, the Y2K party was born.

What I remember the most about the Y2K party was the countdown to midnight. Supposedly, that's when the world would disintegrate and with computes becoming confused, nothing would work.

Sanctuary was packed. I was a little nervous, not being sure what to expect. The warnings on the news had been ominous, even though thousands of computer programmers had work tirelessly for months, trying to rewrite every line of code that contained a date to accommodate 4 digits.

The DJ stopped the music for the countdown. The crowd chanted:

10-9-8-7-6-5-4-3-2-1

At the stroke of midnight, one person shouted out "Happy New Year!" That person may have been me. I can neither confirm nor deny that nasty rumor.

No one else said a word as the club went silent. I had never witnessed anything like it.

Someone screamed. Some nasty queen accused me of being the offender. As if!

After 30 seconds had passed, with the club in total darkness and silence, people began to get worried. Time seemed to move incredibly slowly. As if the clocks had actually stopped.

45 seconds. Still nothing.

People began to head for the exits. A few were running. (Not me, I swear on my mother's grave, it was not me.)

Those motherfuckers at the club played us for fools for an entire 90 seconds, during which time my life passed before my eyes.

Then, as if by magic, the club roared back to life. The music was louder than ever, the lights brighter, all bringing the crowd to a cheer as they realized the joke was on them. That crowd partied as hard as they could for the rest of the night.

My mind jolts from that memory as my eyes move to the bottom of the column, to the thick black box with the dreaded words "In Memoriam" boldly announcing more bad news for the readers. Not long after starting the column, I began to document names of those taken by the virus. Not a task to be taken lightly, my focus was on remembering the names of local community members, as well as those of national interest.

I could list a thousand names or more from these memorial sections, but what would be the purpose in that? Is the quantity of names something that would impress anyone with the horror of the times? Or is it more about the quality of what was lost?

The irony is that I am a failure when it comes to telling the stories of these lives. Selecting a name at random, I read the words:

Scott Johnson, retail merchandiser, Strawbridge & Clothier, deceased June 18, 1995.

My wrinkled brow betrays my scattered thoughts. Did I know Scott Johnson? I don't know. Suddenly, that thought scares me, my heartbeat increasing as my anxiety level rises.

Will I be forgotten so easily? Does anyone remember Scott Johnson? Is he mourned by someone who cared for him? With no way to answer these questions, my mind makes the leap to the terrifying questions that I try not to consider.

Will I be remembered?
Will I be mourned?
Will anyone know my name?

Other stories capture my attention as I try to forget Scott Johnson, whose name is now a memory that I can't forget. I take some small comfort in the fact that someone cared enough to provide his name and some small amount of information about him so his name would be included in the memorial section. My breathing comes a bit easier as I find a sliver of consolation in that thought.

"Oh!" I gasp, though there's no one here to hear me, as I come upon a name that will never be forgotten. I had written a number of stories about the tragedy that befell Matthew Shepard. Fairly or not, his story defines the state of Wyoming for me, since I can honestly say that I know nothing else about that state other than Matthew's story.

"You know about him, don't you?" I say to the air surrounding me. Perhaps the plants on the sill hear my words. Join me in my mourning. Witness my tears as they fall silently, just at the very thought.

I've read each of the articles countless times. I could quote them verbatim. I transport myself to that mysterious state, Wyoming, as certain words attack me from the pages.

"beaten"
"tortured"
"left to die"
"age 21"
"targeted and teased as a child"
"beaten and raped during a high school trip"
"depression and panic attacks"
"October 6, 1998"
"tied to a barbed wire fence"
"coma"
"pistol-whipped"
"fractured skull"
"October 12, 1998"
"dead"

The words "Wyoming" and "Matthew Shepard" will also be joined together in my mind. I know it doesn't make sense to blame an entire state for the horrific actions of two individuals, but that's how it is for me. May your heart be more forgiving than mine.

I skip over stories of parties, carnivals, gossip about kings, queens, and in-betweens, drowning in my state of sorrow. During days like this, I cannot distinguish myself from the horrors that I wrote about, trying to distance myself so the words won't surround me, suffocate me, kill me.

"You argue that words can't hurt," I say to the plant across the room.

"I know you can hear me!" I'm shouting now, sorrow turning to rage.

The plant looks at me impassively, refusing to share in my emotional rants of despair. Frantically, I'm searching through various books, flipping pages, searching for the story of...

Brad Davis.

I fell in love with Brad the first time I laid eyes on him, in the 1978 film "Midnight Express." Besides Brad's riveting performance, the musical score by Giorgio Moroder, widely known as the "Father of Disco," added a dimension that made the film even more impressive to me.

Brad's performance in the film captivated me. His beauty came through the screen, and I could see us together in the theatre, watching that film, with me gently holding his hand as he caressed my leg. I gasp as I remember, a memory that's so private, so intimate, that I can never share it with anyone. I keep the secret from the spider plant, *Chlorophytum comosum*, who is now eyeing me suspiciously.

"No! I will not tell you what happened. Only Brad and I will ever know the truth!" I shout. I look away to avoid the prying eyes of the spider.

I was lucky enough to see Brad onstage, in New York City, paying the lead in the Off-Broadway production of

164

"The Normal Heart", written by Larry Kramer. That was in 1985. Unknown to anyone at the time, that was the same year when Brad received his HIV diagnosis.

After the performance, I gathered with others at the theatre's exit, hoping for a private moment with Brad. Unfortunately, he was distracted by all those others crowding around him, as I seemed to be the only one willing to give him some private space.

His eyes met mine, for a brief moment, and he gave me a slight nod. I got the message. He didn't want anyone to know about us. I winked at him as I backed away, understanding the importance of keeping our private lives away from prying eyes and ears.

Back at my hotel, I even refused to tell the potted plant about what had happened that night. Secrets must be kept!

Saving my favorite memory of Brad Davis for last, I lean back and dream of "Querelle," a ground-breaking work in the field of gay cinema, based on the novel by Jean Genet. I don't even have to look through my scrapbooks to find my article/review. I still have that magnificent movie poster, with Brad in his sailor outfit, leaning against a structure, a guard tower at a prison, clearly phallic and constructed of brick, to reignite my memories.

The framed poster has a signature. It says, "With Love, from Brad." I try to ignore that section. The script resembles mine and the ink, while it could have come from any writing instrument, bears a strong resemblance to one of my favorite markers. I don't remember signing it myself. Why would I do that? Maybe Brad signed it that night outside of the theatre. The truth is, I just can't remember. That seems to be happening more often, though I can't even be sure of that.

My thoughts of dear Brad always conclude with the knowledge that he felt compelled to hide his HIV status, fearing that he would be denied roles. I have no doubt that he was correct about that. He died at age 41 on September 8, 1991, having committed assisted suicide by drug overdose, according to his widow Susan.

Proudly hanging right next to that poster is the Andy Warhol (Blue) version of the movie poster, featuring two young men, both beautiful, with a bright red tongue in stark contrast to the black and white drawing. Yes, it is personally autographed by the artist and is one of my most prized possessions.

Oh, if only I had been cast in the part of Nono, the man who penetrates the character Querelle, instead of Günther Kaufmann! To have our affair come to life, Brad and I, right there on the screen for everyone to see, instead of hiding our love as if we had to own our shame.

"Damn, look at the time. You're making me late for brunch!" I holler at the assemblage of houseplants. They ignore me as I rush to leave, making a mental note that I also agreed to meet Henry tomorrow, to cover his big announcement.

CHAPTER FOURTEEN

JOEY

My mixed emotions are betrayed by my erratic behavior. I find it difficult to concentrate as I think about my situation. A situation of my own making, which just makes it worse. It didn't have to be this way.

I couldn't object when Henry brought Billy into our home. He had no idea that Billy was a source of my guilt and shame. Billy knows what I did, allowing him to blow me in return for a job offer. Unless Billy told him, there's no way that Henry could know. And not too long ago, I looked Henry in the eye and swore that I had never betrayed his trust, except for the time he caught me red-handed, or more accurately, bare-assed, in bed with Xander.

Now Henry has marked me as the Number One boy in his tribe, getting me tattooed with our family insignia, the rainbow flag colors within a heart, surrounded with the Infinity symbol. As a further gesture of our commitment to each other, we now had our initials tattooed on our ring fingers.

Billy was left out, a second-class citizen of the tribe. The symbolism wasn't lost on me. Henry was telling me with certainty that I belonged to him and we belonged together.

I like Billy, but I can't trust him. If he tells Henry about the blowjob first, he could ruin everything. I've made up my mind. I have to confess my sin to Henry, hoping he'll understand and forgive.

I want to go kneel before him, confess and beg for forgiveness, and maybe even do my penance. Right now. But Henry had given strict orders that he is not to be disturbed. He's busy preparing some sort of announcement for tomorrow. Don't ask me what it's about. I don't have a clue.

I set my resolve, determined that I'll confess everything right after the meeting. In my more youthful days, I might have made a dramatic announcement at the meeting, in front of everyone. This time, I had the chance to consider the consequences if I did it that way. First, it would make the confession less personal. It would also make the meeting more about me, when I knew Henry was expecting everyone's attention to be on him. I congratulated myself on my wise decision. *I'm so much more mature now!* I thought.

The night before the meeting, the one where Henry plans to make his major announcement, I wander from my usual hangout, on the dance floor of the main club, to the upstairs lesbian lounge. Sunday night and the place was packed!

A far cry from the scene a scant three months ago. Back then, the lounge, then called Aphrodite's, resembled one of those bars in some deserted Western town that you'd often see on TV. A few crusty old gals at the bar, with a singer dressed in some outlandish outfit walking around, belting out tunes, while an even older and crustier gal pounded out some tunes on the old piano in the corner.

OK, I'm exaggerating, but not by much. Ever since our beloved Georgie had passed away from a bout with breast cancer, Aphrodite's seemed to have the life sucked out of it as well. In a word, it was depressing.

Of course, no one ever wanted to forget Georgie, but we also wanted a spot for the local lesbians to gather, network, dance, party and pretty much just be themselves.

168

Jando, our resident party planner, summed it all up when he scanned the damage, assessed the situation and declared, "Burn it all down! Burn it to the ground and start all over!"

The lounge was closed for 4 weeks, as everything was removed. Stripped down to the bare walls, it was even more desolate, but now it had a quality it lacked earlier: potential.

Jando, known for his love of the unusual and the unexpected, didn't hire a seasoned veteran designer to re-do the room. Instead, he found a young, enthusiastic student and gave her the opportunity of a lifetime, to design a new lesbian club from scratch.

"Joey, Henry, this is Fantasy. She's agreed to develop an entirely new lounge for the club. You're gonna love her ideas!"

Fantasy, who couldn't have been any older than 19, eagerly shook our hands and breathlessly threw out her ideas.

Confident, competent, and completely charming, I thought, as I admired her stylish outfit and stunning hair. She reminded me of a walking and talking sunset, wearing clothes combining white, yellow and gold, accentuating her gleaming, long, red hair.

Henry seemed pre-occupied, so he came off as aloof, but I knew better. First, he trusted Jando with this decision. But more importantly, he had recently been consumed with thoughts that went beyond Sanctuary.

Fantasy explained her overall concepts for the re-design of the lounge.

"I want a combination of the old and the new," she told us. "You know, Aphrodite's Lounge was a very cool concept to start with, but some of these lesbians today have no idea who Aphrodite is."

Intelligent and funny! I thought.

169

"How do you want to create that combo of old and new?" Jando asked. We could always count on him to be sure to get the details. That's why he excelled at planning events.

"First, I want to change the name of the lounge, of course," Fantasy continued. "An homage to the person who actually invented the disco concept."

"You're going to call it Joey's, after me?" I teased, and we all burst out laughing.

"Well, that was my second choice," Fantasy shot back.

I was having fun, just acting silly and being around people who could joke around with me. It reminded me that life had been a little too heavy for my tastes recently.

"Actually, I was thinking about Regine. People call her the Queen of the Night. How cool is that? She's an icon already."

My face crinkled up, as it often did when I was confused.

"A lady named Regine invented disco? Seriously? I thought it was the Bee Gees or John Travolta or somebody like that."

I was only half-serious. I knew it wasn't those guys, but I also never heard of Regine before.

"It all started back at the Whisky a Gogo in Paris. Regine was the first one to replace those old jukeboxes with DJs spinning records," Fantasy explained.

"So I want to call it Regina's. Not only to honor Regine, but the word 'Regina' actually means 'Queen,'" she continued. "Now, I don't want to disrespect the Queens in the main disco, but the real Queens are gonna be right up in here!" She was laughing; all three of us were laughing.

"And of course, if you pronounce it a different way, the wrong way, it rhymes with a certain female body part," Jando added. I almost spit out my drink at that one!

Opening night at Regina's was a smash hit. Fantasy knew what she was doing, and this place appealed to the female

170

crowd. Photos of female icons adorned the walls, varying in size from tiny portraits to larger-than-life full body photos of other queens of glamour.

Most striking to me was that Fantasy didn't just adorn the walls of the club with white females. I think that might have been the case with most designers. But no, Fantasy went beyond what was expected, producing a gallery of gorgeous, glamorous Queens showcasing the universal appeal of feminine beauty. Truly a sign that all types of women were welcome here. Men too, if they chose to hang out here, of course.

It could have been an exhibition at an art gallery. It was seriously that well done. And though no one would expect customers to actually study the decor, Fantasy included a small description next to each photo, providing the name and a brief write-up of her accomplishments to explain every photo.

"I love the off-balance look," I told Fantasy, as we walked along the gallery of images.

The pictures were hung in a manner that some might have thought of as haphazard, but I recognized the artistic arrangement, and it struck me as whimsical in design. While some pictures were hung straight, others were at odd angles. Some were quite large, while others were minuscule.

"The layout just screams 'Queer' at me, which is why I just adore it!" I exclaimed, bringing an appreciative smile to Fantasy's face.

She took my hand, guiding me, pointing out some of her favorite pieces.

"Look at how we honored this one!" she said, pointing excitedly at one of the photos in the exhibit.

"Never expected to see her in a lesbian lounge!" I screamed, catching sight of the image of Nancy Reagan, in one of her supposedly elegant poses, just oozing an air of

171

superiority. But the image had been altered, with a word bubble quoting her as saying "Just Say Snow" instead of her of "Just Say No" slogan, as she sat behind a table with lines of cocaine carefully positioned in front of her.

Giggling like a couple of schoolgirls sharing some dark secret that would only be funny to pre-teens, we walked along, as I admired the images of so many significant women, including:

Frida Kahlo
Grace Jones
Bette Midler
Diana Ross
Shirley Chisholm
Rachel Harlow
Eleanor Roosevelt
Yoko Ono
Gia Carangi
Madonna
Toni Morrison
Gertrude Stein
Sylvia Plath
Georgia O'Keeffe
Angela Davis
Patti LaBelle
Mia Farrow

And seriously, the list goes on and on. Now I wish I had actually kept a list, but trust me, Fantasy had created an amazing display of women who made a difference.

The rest of the decor enhances the feeling of being in a feminine paradise. Beautiful pastels everywhere, a comfortable dining area where bar snacks could be ordered and devoured, and bar stations designed to draw the customers in.

Our profits soared as soon as Regina's opened, helping us to make up some of the lost income from the other sections of the club.

I won't lie, as beautiful, exciting and fun that Regina's was, I felt a tinge of regret each time I saw it. For Georgie, of course. If you know anything about grief, you understand that it never really goes away. We do our best to cope and, in my case, my heart tried its best to contain my feelings. I didn't want my sorrow to consume me, but I also never wanted to let Georgie be forgotten. That's why I had asked Fantasy to include her photo in the gallery. Sometimes, I'd find myself standing there in front of her photo, remembering, crying on the inside, wishing that she was still here.

Everyone called the new lounge Regina's, and rightfully so. Only in my mind, I thought of the place as "Georgie's."

CHAPTER FIFTEEN

HENRY

I'm in my comfort zone, hanging out with my fellow Alpha males at the clubhouse. We're practicing how to make bondage knots properly. There's an art to it, you know. The wrong kind of knot could end up hurting a sub, I mean, not in a good way. We want to keep them subdued, submissive, under our control, but we don't want to cause real physical harm. That's how I feel, anyway.

"What's that one called?" I ask Toby, who's considered one of our resident experts. I was concentrating on my Burlington bowline, an essential skill when you don't want your knot to collapse.

With a knowing smile, Toby said, "This is a Struggler's knot. It's guaranteed to never come loose, as long as you tie it properly."

"Exactly what I need," I tell Toby. "My sub can be a squirmy little devil, always trying to figure out a way to get loose. I need a sure thing to keep that one right where I want him."

Moving closer, I watched the moves to make the Struggler's knot, then repeated them using my practice rope.

"You're a natural," Toby complimented me.

"I got needs and this is gonna help me meet those needs," I answered, laughing.

It's relaxing and enjoyable to spend time like this. I have the freedom to be myself. No one passes judgment on me here. No one has expectations for me to be perfect, or to always be the one in control. Sometimes. even a strict Dominant such as myself just needs to relax.

I have my private tribe at home. This was a different kind of tribe, a brotherhood, a group of men with common interests.

My life seems perfect in so many ways. I have almost everything I want.

My private little tribe is meeting my needs for intimacy, and the clubhouse is meeting my needs for a community. You might think I'd be content as a suckling pig.

But as the new millennium was getting underway, here in the late summer of 2001, I made a decision to expand my vision. I know this move might be disruptive. Maybe I won't have as much time to spend with my two subs, Joey and Billy.

I'm seeing a need for leadership, for men like me to get involved, and I want to help solve some of the problems that I see so clearly. I see myself in a position of leadership, and the time to make my move is now.

Ever since the start of the AIDS epidemic, I've seen the strength in our community as we've supported our own. I've also seen a steady rise in anti-gay rhetoric and actions, as people express their growing hatred in more visible ways.

It wasn't unusual for gay men to be harassed. People would sometimes throw things at us. Scream at us. Shamelessly confront us with their faces contorted with rage.

I knew all of this happened, but I'm alarmed at the growing intensity and openness. It's hard to understand exactly why we're hated so much, but I have to accept it as a fact of life in order to be able to combat it.

Not long ago, the City Council member for our district, which included the entire Gayborhood, was forced to resign due to some financial scandals. I always thought he did a piss poor job of representing the gay community, so I was happy to see him go. After thinking through all the issues, I decided to declare my candidacy for that City Council seat. I'd run on a platform of equality, but also to demand protections be put in place, to help our community with our struggles to live peaceful lives.

I need a lot of help and support if I'm going to win this election. First, I need to get the support of community leaders and the press. That's why I've invited the Board members of Sanctuary, including Fantasy, our newest Board member and a reporter from the Gay News to dinner tomorrow. I'm going to announce my candidacy and seek their support. Without their approval, my candidacy will be dead on arrival, so tomorrow is a big day for me.

I'm excited and I truly believe this will be a positive step for me and for my community. I'm taking the first step tomorrow at 6 PM.

This afternoon, I'm joining the other Alphas in the club, heading out for a ride. Being a city boy, I wasn't brought up to enjoy activities outside the urban environment. That made these trips even sweeter for me. And I was happy in the company of other men who shared my status.

Riding with them was a pleasure and I felt privileged, though I'd never admit that. Because in reality, I belonged here. These men were my buddies, and in my short time as a member of the club, our bonds had grown strong.

Feeling connected, within this community of men, gives me a feeling of power, combined with a sense of brotherhood. *I hope I'll never lose this connection*, I thought, as we sped along, creating a roar that broke the tranquility of our rural surroundings.

I could do this every day for the rest of my life.

CHAPTER SIXTEEN

MISTER GQ

My original idea for the Sunday Book Brunch was to gather a small group of gay men to discuss books every week. The dream was to engage with others in philosophical discussions about themes, characters, settings, etc., hopefully talking mostly about books centered around gay life and characters, though not exclusively.

It proved to be successful, though not always exactly as I had expected. Our first obstacle was the schedule. Meeting weekly proved to be difficult, since our members didn't always have enough time to read a book every week. One of the first changes we made was to set the schedule to monthly, agreeing to gather on the 2nd Sunday of each month.

This month, the group would gather on Sunday, September 9, 2001.

I live in the past, more than the present. My mind takes me places so far away, sometimes in a misty haze, other times as sharply as the haunting sounds of the Gay Christian Men's Choir singing at the services I occasionally attend. I know, I know, I'm betraying my Jewish heritage every time I enter one of those halls dedicated to the worship of the christian gods, but for me, beauty is as beauty does and I find the music, and the men singing those melodies, irresistibly drawing me inside.

But I digress. Looking back at the first brunch, which was a tentative affair at best, I clearly remember the attendees being Aristotle, Zed, Gifford, Henry and Joey. Oh, and me, of course.

I thought we might form a core group of friends and we'd all get to know each other, hang out, and well, who knows? Ari and Zed showed up a few more times, then they seemed to lose interest. Despite Henry's promise, neither he nor Joey ever attended again. Sigh. I would have enjoyed spending more time with Henry. Joey? Not so much.

My point really is that the group's members changed over time. Only Giff, the music producer, attended regularly. His keen interest in literature and his expertise with popular culture led to interesting observations.

Whether we were discussing *The Picture of Dorian Gray* by Oscar Wilde, *Goodbye to Berlin* by Christopher Isherwood (which provided the inspiration for *Cabaret*), *City of Night* by John Rechy, or *Giovanni's Room* by James Baldwin, Giff's insights into the themes, character development, settings, and any other details being discussed were thoughtful and on point.

I remember the intense sorrow and regret I felt when both Ari and Zed's names were listed in the "In Memoriam" section of my column. It's hard to explain the overwhelming sense of sorrow, of dread, even terror, that coursed through our community, as more and more names were added to the rapidly-expanding list. That was especially true through the 90s, as the numbers of young men dying prematurely skyrocketed.

Now, in 2001, the epidemic continued at an even more alarming rate. At the end of the year, more than 800,000 cases had been reported in the US, and over 450,000 had died. The death rate was an astounding 57%.

I struggle to think of the impact of losing hundreds of thousands of lives. My mind shuts down if I even try to really comprehend the depth of the losses.

Turning my attention to other matters, I feel comforted when I'm involved in the stories being told in the books I'm reading. Personally, I'm more emotionally involved while reading, but I won't deny the impact of other media, including film and, to a lesser degree, television.

During our last Book Brunch in August, Giff made a suggestion. But first, we thoroughly dissected the novel *B-Boy Blues*, written by James Earl Hardy and published in 1994, with our consensus being that this was an excellent, authentic portrayal of Black gay life, and that we should soon read and discuss the sequel, *2nd Time Around*.

"You wanted to make a suggestion for next month, Giff?" I led him into making his pitch.

"Yeah, the next 4 weeks are gonna be really busy for me. I have 3 different video shoots to produce and direct. I know I'm not gonna have any time to read. But I happen to know that TLA is having a classic movie festival starting soon, and I already saw their schedule."

TLA is the Theatre of the Living Arts, located on South Street.

Eric, one of our newest members, and a film student at The Art Institute, was immediately intrigued.

"What's on the bill?" he asked.

"They're showing a favorite of mine, *Rebel Without a Cause* on Sunday, September 9. We could go watch the movie together, then head somewhere for brunch and talk about the film."

"But I thought this was a Book Brunch," complained Chance, another new member, who was studying to be a school librarian.

Giff looked closely at Chance before speaking, trying to decide the level of snarkiness he should use with his reply.

179

"Chance, my young boy, I'm sure you know that this film is based on a book. I mean, with your librarian studies, you know all about that, right?"

Just a bit taken aback, Chance replied, "Of course I know. It's based on that new novel called...called...I think it's called 'The Cause of the Rebel,' or something close to that.

"That's your story? You're prepared to die on that hill, Chance?" Giff chided.

"Okay old head, you got me. I was frontin'. Honestly, I don't know the book or the movie."

Chance started laughing, mostly to cover his embarrassment. We all joined in. This wasn't a group where confrontations were expected or accepted.

"No worries, young buck," Giff replied. "First, you're gonna love the movie. And it is actually based on a book, though that isn't really common knowledge. It's called "Rebel Without a Cause" and it's based on a true story about a teenage criminal right here in Pennsylvania. The story was written by Dr. Robert Lindner in 1944, and the film came out in 1955."

As I listened to this exchange between Chance and Giff, I was distracted, watching Chance closely. I was a little unsure how to think about him. He was young, and very beautiful. Dressed elegantly, with fluid movements that seemed effortless, I thought of him as the embodiment of the best qualities of men and women. He was quite masculine, but he was also quite feminine.

I never told him this, but I thought of him as "femuline," my word for that mix of masculinity and femininity. In my experience, it's quite rare to find anyone who managed that so easily, so beautifully, with an air of sophistication and poise.

That's what I want to be, I thought. *I wish I could project that perfect image of refinement and elegance, without having to force it. It came to Chance quite easily and naturally. "I'd kill for that!"*

September 9, 2001, the second Sunday of the month, was such a glorious day that I somewhat regretted spending part of the day inside the dark confines of the TLA. All those thoughts disappeared, as I got caught up in the movie.

Every seat in the theatre was filled, as this film festival was a Philly favorite. Giff, Eric, Chance and I sat together, our eyes glued to the screen. Joining us were two other semi-regulars at the Book Brunch: Noah and Trayvon.

As I watched the drama unfold, I forgot about all my own troubles. Recently, I just wasn't feeling like myself. I had problems remembering certain things, and sometimes I felt like my imagination was taking over my life. I was growing more withdrawn socially, and sometimes I found myself in the middle of a conversation with...well, with no one else being there.

Having a few tests done by my doctor yielded no results, no diagnosis, no comfort for my growing fears. Or at least, that's how I remember it today. My memory is becoming increasingly unreliable.

Do people realize when they're going insane? I wondered. *Is that what's happening to me?*

Banishing those thoughts from my mind, I found myself back in the theatre, seeming to have missed part of the movie. I'm not sure where I went, or how I got back, but I was sort of getting used to recovering from these episodes. And I know the story well enough to have an intelligent discussion about it, without seeing the entire movie today.

We didn't even wait to get to our brunch spot before starting our instant reviews. Six gay men, all excited about the movie they'd just seen, all talking at once.

181

Noah: "The three stars just oozed beauty and sexuality!" (Referring to James Dean, Natalie Wood and Sal Mineo.)

Giff: "Teen anger and rebellion. I remember feeling that way. Sometimes I still do. Even now, I feel like I'm being controlled by the forces of society."

Me: "Did you see the devotion that Plato (Sal Mineo) had for Jim (James Dean)? So clearly in love, ready to do anything for Jim. I'd die for a relationship with someone who adores me like that."

Chance: "I can't believe I never even heard of this movie before. How'd I ever miss it? That was fuckin' awesome!"

Eric: "Seriously, I couldn't take my eyes off James Dean or Sal Mineo! Which one do you think was cuter?"

Me: "James Dean has that brooding teen look down perfectly. But for me, I'll take those dark piercing eyes of Sal over anyone else. He's a dreamboat!"

Trayvon: "You say this story is based on a book? Really? Like, that was a true story? Or did they change it up and make it all fictional?"

Giff: "Y'all do know that all three of the stars are dead, right? And they were all tragic deaths, when they were all still young."

We continued to discuss the film over a very late brunch. Our discussion was animated, informative and oh-so entertaining. I was glad that Giff had suggested this outing. Not that our group would ever stop discussing books, but mixing it up with an occasional classic movie, especially one with this level of drama (and implied homosexuality) was a good way to break up our normal routine.

James Dean died in a car accident on September 30, 1955. *Rebel Without a Cause* was released on October 27, 1955, almost a month after Dean had died. Some people still debate whether Dean was bisexual. Most probably, those people are straight and don't want to admit the truth. I'm convinced that he was quite gay.

Natalie Wood had a successful career as an actress. She died on November 29, 1981, at the age of 43. Her death occurred during a boating trip and has been described as under "mysterious circumstances."

Sal Mineo was nominated for an Academy Award as Best Supporting Actor at the age of 17 for his role as Plato in *Rebel Without a Cause*. Mineo, who publicly identified himself as bisexual, was living in West Hollywood when he was stabbed just after parking his car behind his apartment. He died on February 12, 1976, at the age of 37, as a result of that attack.

After an engaging and entertaining time with my Book Brunch friends, I was exhausted. Just before I fell asleep that night, I reminded myself once more that I had a dinner date tomorrow with Henry from Club Sanctuary. I can't forget to show up. He'll kill me if I miss his big announcement. Whatever that's going to be.

I'll find out tomorrow, were my final thoughts as I drifted into sleep.

CHAPTER SEVENTEEN

YANDI

Yeah, I had fun at Flaco's party, with them thirsty hot Mamis all up in my face. Well, not really in my face, they was actually aimin' lower than that, but you get the drift, right? Ya know, I aim to please and my aim that night was on point! Damn!

Later that night, El Jefe (The Boss) pulled me and Blanco over for a little talk.

"We got a delivery comin' in tomorrow night. Yous guys gonna be the pickups. Meet Chief at K&A (the corner of Kensington and Allegheny) at the usual time. Have a truck with yous. This package gonna be bigger than most. That's why I'm sendin' my two best boys. Ya feel me?"

We weren't supposed to know who The Chief was, but it was more of an open secret. He was a cop from our precinct. His delivery was fresh from the Evidence Room.

El Jefe had a deal with The Chief. Anything he could get out of Evidence, that was delivered right to us. Sometimes, it was even our own stuff that one or two of our boys mighta been caught with.

No evidence? That always led to a "Not Guilty." So our boys got off scot-free and then we'd be right back out on the street, makin' our profits.

K&A was a short ride on the El. But we couldn't ride the train tonight. Instead, we parked Blanco's brother's old '95 Ford pickup under the tracks, practically bouncin' in our seats every time a train passed overhead, waitin' for Chief to arrive.

Everything moved fast. It always did. None of us wanted to get caught.

As we were movin' the merch from Chief's car to the truck, Chief gave us a message for Jefe.

"We got some troubles down in the homo-hood. Tell Jefe the Big Boss wants some heat laid on them guys. Fags be gettin' outta pocket."

Blanco and I both nodded that we understood, tryin' to hurry and get the fuck outta there.

"Tell him we ain't lookin' for no one to get hurt, but if by chance a fag goes home with a broken arm or nose...well, we won't be investigatin' any assaults too closely. Ya got me?"

"Gotcha!" I replied.

That's why, a few nights later, me, Blanco and a couple other guys took the El down to Homo-Ville, lookin' to do some disruptin'."

Jefe told us to be packin', just in case we needed to show some extra force.

CHAPTER EIGHTEEN

HENRY

I reserved a table at Trust, one of my favorite restaurants, right at the corner of 13th and Sansom Streets, in the heart of the Gayborhood. Dinner could be served either indoors or at one of the tables outside. I opted for the latter, since it was a gloriously beautiful day, with moderate temperatures and no wind to disturb our enjoyment of the meal.

My thoughts were a hurricane, swirling at a million miles an hour, recalling the past, considering the present and wondering about the future.

I kept thinking about the times when Joey and I had first met and started our relationship. Not long after our first meeting, I handed him a sheet of paper.

"Do you know what an acrostic poem is?"

"A caustic poem?" he had answered teasingly, feigning innocence.

I threw him a look and laughed.

"Here, I want you to make one for me. Tell me who you are in four words."

He stared at the sheet of paper for a few moments. On it, I had written:

J

O

E

Y

Although I liked Joey at that time, liked him a lot, I wasn't sure if he had long-term potential. I was trying to find out if I should invest in making a future with him.

He hid the paper with his hand as he scrawled a few letters. Then, smiling, he handed me the paper which now read:

Joyously
Obedient
Eternally
Yours

Holy hell, I thought. *If this one ain't a keeper, I don't know who is.*

I thought my mouth might break from the huge smile I had as I read those words.

Then, Joey turned the paper over, where he wrote:

H
E
N
R
Y

"And who are you, good Sir? Tell me who Henry is in 5 words."

I thought carefully, then started writing.

"Read it and let me know if this is how you want me," I told him.

Horny
Every
Night
Riding
Your ass

"Fuck yeah," he whispered. "But hey, that's 6 words. I told you to only write 5."

"Did you really think I was gonna take directions from you? Now you tell me who the Boss is gonna be. You or me?"

"Ohhhh, it's gonna be you. I already know that," Joey told me.

I think that was the moment when we were both sure about what we wanted, and whom we wanted to be with.

I was about to test our relationship once more. I knew we had a strong bond, a true love, but I was going to be moving into a new world. I needed Joey's support.

Ever since moving out of Queen Village, with its suburban-like atmosphere, I felt liberated. I craved being surrounded by gay people, gay men. That was my comfort zone, my sustenance, my reason for being.

This meeting will be the first step in what I hope will be a new path for me. Yes, I love the club. I love Joey. I love our life. But I want to do more. I have bigger dreams.

I sent Joey and Billy out early, with instructions to busy themselves with an afternoon of shopping, telling them to be at Trust by 5:55 PM at the latest.

Alejandro and his boyfriend Kirk, who was now able to walk better with the aid of his new prosthetic leg, would also be joining us.

Fantasy, our newest Board member, wasn't able to attend, as she was spending a "Girls Only" week at the shore, as the peak summer season had just ended, with prices much lower after the glut of summer visitors had dissipated.

I had invited one member of the press. I wanted the gay press to break the story, that a young, intelligent, highly motivated Gay Black male was announcing his candidacy for a seat on City Council, representing the Gayborhood.

I figured that Harvé wouldn't be late, as he should be hungry for a story for his column. This might be, and actually should be, front-page news.

I strode up 13th Street at the stroke of 6. I couldn't even hide my delight when I saw the looks on my friends' faces.

"What the holy hell do we have here?" Jando joked, rising to greet me with an outstretched hand.

"I've seen you in all kinds of get-ups, but like Wow!"

I had decided to dress to impress. And totally against type. I spun around, enjoying the impression I was making in my brand-new, custom-tailored suit by Armani, shirt by Calvin Klein, square-toed dress shoes by Kenneth Cole and my extra-special Rolex gleaming in the late afternoon sun.

I felt glorious. Empowered. On top of the world. I truly believed I was taking my first step towards a new and powerful reality. Yes, I was going to start with City Council. But that was just the first step in my Master Plan.

I was seated facing north, towards Market Street and I'd arranged it so Joey would be at my side. Billy was next to Joey, which was his proper place as the lowest member of our tribe.

189

Across from us sat Jando, Kirk and Harvé. Drinks were already being served and my excitement was growing as I prepared to make my big announcement.

"First, I want to thank everyone for being here with me tonight," I began, nodding in the direction of each individual, acknowledging that their help in my plan was not only needed, but deeply appreciated.

"All of you know how I feel about this area. It's my home. My true home. I love being here and I love the feeling of community that The Gayborhood provides for us."

"Amen to that!" Kirk agreed.

"I feel safer here than anywhere else in Philly, but we also know there are problems. And some of the problems are clearly getting worse."

"So what can we do about that?" Joey asked, interrupting my speech, though, in reality, I didn't mind. He had my back for so many years; I could never be angry with him for any length of time.

"We can work to make changes from within," I answered. "We don't always have to be outside agitators. If we want real power, there's ways we can actually do that."

"What are you talkin' about?" Billy asked, his face screwed in a look of utter confusion.

"I'm talking about an election. There's gonna be a special election in a few months, to replace that rat who's been on City Council for years, and not doing a damn thing to represent our community."

"What I'm talking about is I'm declaring my candidacy for City Council, to provide real representation to our folks. Our people. Us."

I was in such a state that I was practically shouting.

"I'm going to be the very first, openly gay Black man to sit on Philly's City Council. And I vow to do everything in my power to keep us safe. We won't be pushed out, like some of them are trying to do. This neighborhood is ours.

190

It isn't Straightville. It's the fuckin' Gayborhood and it's gonna stay that way. Can I count on your support?"

Kirk slammed his fist on the table. "Hell yeah, we got you, bro!"

Jando slapped my hand with a high-five and I felt Joey hugging me tightly.

Harvé was so excited, he could barely spit the words out fast enough.

"This is huge news. Front page news, man. You're gonna make history. No, you **made** history already today! No one will ever forget what happened here on Monday, September 10, 2001."

I stood, ready to continue with my speech. trying to generate more excitement and talk about my proposed policies with this core group of friends and supporters.

Just then, I noticed a commotion, something happening at the corner of 13th and Market, about a block and a half away.

"That's the kind of thing I'm talking about!" I shouted, as I saw a group of 4 or 5 young guys running down the street towards us. They were smashing windows and knocking over kiosks, screaming. As they got closer, I could hear them shouting about faggots, queers and homos.

I didn't even have time to react. I turned and saw a look of fear on Joey's face. And then, something hit me.

CHAPTER NINETEEN

JOEY

I don't know how I got home. It's all a blur. Sirens, screams, pain all around me. Fear, confusion, more screams, questions, so many questions. In shock, I understood nothing that was going on around me.

By the time I woke up, it was already late afternoon. As I struggled to force the sleep out of my brain, the first thing I noticed was the quiet. Eerily quiet. The city was never this quiet. *What the fuck?* I thought.

Heading for the kitchen, totally naked, I started preparing the coffee, not even noticing the pile of bloody clothing on the floor of the bedroom.

Knocking at the door. A quiet knock at first. Easy enough to ignore.

The knocking turned to pounding. Voices frantically calling my name. Still confused, I peeked out and saw Jando and Kirk. They looked distressed. Worried.

I opened the door for them, turning to head back to the kitchen as they came inside.

"Fuck, Joey, we've been calling and calling you. Then we got scared you might've done something, so we figured we better come over and check up on you," Kirk hurriedly explained their presence.

Pouring my first cup of coffee, I turned to face them.

"What are you talking about? I might've done something? Like what? Why?"

"Oh my god, Joey, don't you remember what happened last night? And don't you know about today?"

Jando took my hand and led me to the sofa.

"Henry died last night. At the hospital. You were there. He got shot. In the head."

It was like his words were floating towards me through thick water. I started to gasp, suddenly remembering the night of terror, confusion, and pain that was only beginning for me.

I slumped into the cushions of the sofa. As the impact of last night began to torture my soul, I looked at my friends and sobbed. Quietly, no screaming. No throwing objects. The weight of the world came crashing into me. My shoulders heaved as my lungs struggled to find air.

Softly, Kirk whispered, "It gets even worse."

Worse? What could possibly be worse than this? I wondered.

That's when they turned on the TV. Expecting to hear something about a local murder, all I saw were scenes of unforgettable death and destruction.

"The country got attacked this morning," Jando told me. "I think it might be the start of a war."

I stared at the flickering images on the TV. It was September 11, 2001.

For many people, the world ended that day.

I still didn't really feel it, but my world had already ended the night before.

And then the darkness settled in over me.

CHAPTER TWENTY

HENRY

This page intentionally left blank.
Henry's voice has been silenced.
Stolen from him by an act of violence.
Anti-gay violence.

CHAPTER TWENTY-ONE

YANDI

After what happened at that restaurant, my instincts kicked in. I ran. As far and as fast as I could. I separated from my buddies. I could always catch up with them later. But this was survival. I saw what happened.

I got all caught up in what we were doin', causing a commotion to scare the homos. It got me all worked up so I just pulled out my gun and started shootin'. I wasn't really tryin' to hurt nobody.

That's when I saw that Black guy in the suit get hit right in the head. I watched it explode. Jesus H. Christ.

Then I did something dumb. I was really scared so I just tossed the gun into a trash can. Man, that was stupid. That might be the dumbest thing I ever did.

As I headed for the El stop, I tried to breathe. I couldn't draw nobody's attention. Not that this crackhead crowd would notice anything anyway.

I was pretty calm by the time I reached my cousin's place. Acting like nothing had happened, I sat down and started playing video games with him. By the time I was halfway through the second level, I was telling my cuz about my perfect aim, knockin' out the enemies on the screen.

Thinking about what I had just done, I felt no shame. Not really. Violence happens every day. Deal with it. Like I do.

By the next day, when I heard about the attacks in New York, I was a little shook by what happened up there. But for me, it seemed like a welcome distraction. No cop was gonna be lookin' into what happened in Homo Town when the whole world was on fire. For me, life was just gonna go back to normal.

Like the Chief told us, if anybody got hurt while we put the fear of god in some homos, well, the system would protect us.

***

Two weeks later, while I was hustlin' on my regular corner, I suddenly found myself surrounded by 3 cop cars. I almost started to run, but knowing how crazy some of these cops can be, I slowly placed my hands behind my head and knelt on the ground. I wasn't about to give them any reason to shoot me.

Damn! You can't even trust the cops these days, I was thinking as I was dragged into the cruiser.

CHAPTER TWENTY-TWO

JOEY

Days passed so slowly; every minute seemed to be suffocating me. With plenty of time to think, the details of what happened at the restaurant came back, eventually flooding my brain, ripping at my heart, and leading to an endless series of What-Ifs.

What if we never went to the restaurant?

What if Henry hadn't chosen that exact moment to stand up?

What if those hoodlums had come down the street earlier in the day? Or later?

What if? What if? What if?

Followed by Why? Why? Why?

More days passed and more questions consumed me.

Who am I anyway?

How do I fit in now?

What in the holy hell am I going to do now that Henry is gone?

"Henry" and "gone." Those two words just didn't seem to go together. Would someone please make this make sense?

There was no lack of company, a constant stream of visitors, consoling me, mourning with me.

Besides my personal tragedy, there was another cloud hanging over us.

September 11.

My mind would go from one tragedy to the other. I felt a despair that I'd never experienced before.

I couldn't watch the TV. All that horror and despair was too much for me to handle. I had to leave that mourning to others, as well as the fear that could still be felt in every corner of the city, probably in every state in the country. No one knew if another attack was coming.

My most vivid memory of that time was the absolute silence in the city. It was like no one could or would move. No traffic, no roar of passing buses, no crowds of people commuting in and out of the city, filling the restaurants at lunchtime. And not a plane in the sky. It was unnerving, to be honest.

Of course, the club was closed too. I couldn't even think about reopening, though I also knew that we had staff members who counted on earning their income there.

What am I supposed to do? I thought.

I am so grateful for all the friends who supported me by visiting and just spending time with me, so I wouldn't be eaten alive by loneliness and terror. Talking about little nothings helped me to forget the horror of what I'd witnessed. When I was alone with my thoughts, I couldn't stop seeing Henry, being hit, over and over, always in super slow motion.

I was hugging Henry, who had just announced his candidacy for the vacant City Council seat. He was getting excited about his plans for the future, and he stood up, wearing his beautiful new suit, the setting sun gleaming on his dark skin, his smile so bright, then interrupted by the commotion up the street. He turned to look at me and I was looking at him, more in love than ever, when I saw...

I can't even say the words. Bullets do horrible things to people. A bullet ripped my love away from me. If only I could have caught it, deflected it, kept it from ripping into him. But I've already done all the What Ifs.

I thought that music might comfort me, so I was listening to a lot of music, avoiding the news on TV. However, even songs that brought me joy before, now made me despondent. I'd sit and cry, listening to songs like:

"Bridge Over Troubled Water" by Simon and Garfunkel
"With or Without You" by U2
"I Will Always Love You" by Whitney Houston
"My Heart Will Go On" by Celine Dion
"Candle in the Wind" by Elton John
"Unbreak My Heart" by Toni Braxton

These are just a few of an endless list of songs that expressed the pain that was searing my soul.

Of course, Jando and Kirk were by my side almost constantly. I'm grateful for their comfort, but there was one person who was a delight and a surprise in my time of need.

We didn't see him often, but every once in a while, Henry and I would stop into Shawn's Shack, a homestyle soul food restaurant that had a huge, loyal following just north of Center City, not far from Sanctuary and just outside the Gayborhood.

Shawn had been friends with Henry for years; I think they met in grade school or maybe middle school. I remember one time when Shawn described to me how Henry had been stalking me in Rittenhouse Square, before we had met.

Now that Henry was gone, Shawn started bringing me a plate from the restaurant every evening, so I never had to worry about cooking. Many nights, Shawn would stay for an hour or two, sometimes talking, other times just sitting with me and listening to music.

We were both depressed, but I like to think that maybe I helped Shawn as much as he helped me to cope with our loss.

Billy came home a few days after *it* happened. He had been taken to the hospital for X-rays, after he'd fallen to the sidewalk during all the confusion. He was sent home later that night with a cast on his broken wrist, but he didn't come to our house. Instead, he went back to Willie.

In a way, I understand. Billy was hurt, too. Physically and emotionally. He needed to find a place of comfort, and for him, that was with Willie.

When he came to pack his belongings, I just had one question to ask.

"Billy, did he know?"

He stood there, first looking at me, then moving his gaze to the floor.

"Billy? Did you ever tell him?"

Shuffling his feet like a child caught in a web of lies with no escape, he shook his head, then slowly turned his head to look directly at me.

"Joey, he knew. Henry knew everything. I told him that same day. Sorry, but I'm not good at keeping secrets."

I was confused by this. I wasn't sure what it really meant.

"But Joey, remember this. Henry knew, and he was okay with it. He didn't fire me. He didn't leave you. He loved you, man. He really, really loved you."

In a way, I was devastated. That meant that Henry knew I was lying to him all those times he asked me for the truth. And though it was true that he never confronted me about it, I'll never be able to forget that he died thinking of me as a liar.

Why didn't I tell him sooner? I was planning to tell him that night...that night when he never came back home.

I have a few regrets in my life. But that is the biggest regret I have by far. I could have been honest. I should have been mature enough to admit the truth. And now I knew that Henry would have forgiven me. Really, he had already forgiven me. Every day, his actions showed me that he loved me, he had forgiven me, and I repaid him by not trusting him to accept me for who I am and for what I had done.

That hurts the most. In so many ways, I loved Henry. I needed him and counted on him for his love and support. If I had been asked two weeks ago if Henry and I trusted each other, I would have confidently said "Yes," even convincing myself that we did. But now, I saw things differently.

He knew the truth about me, and he still devoted his life to me. That shows the type of man Henry is...I mean, was.

On the other hand, I had now been exposed as a fraud. Even if I was the only one who thought of me that way, my feelings of self-worth were destroyed by my failure to trust the man I loved more than my own life. And now, I could never repair what I had broken. Our trust.

***

I didn't want to go to the memorial service. I didn't want to face the reality of my situation. But I had to do certain things, if only to honor the memory of the most important man in my life.

We waited ten days. A very long time, but there were obstacles, mostly due to all the confusion after the 9/11 attacks. But eventually, the dreaded day arrived.

Several people spoke before I did. I'm sure they talked about what an amazing man Henry was. About his intelligence, his leadership, his many contributions to the Philly gay community.

I couldn't hear any of them. All I could hear was my pounding heart.

Before I was ready, it was my turn. Standing in front of more people than I could have imagined, I began to speak.

"Hello, Community!" I began.

"I could probably name everybody here by name, but today, I think of us as a community. There's one person I have to thank for being the first one in Philly to welcome me into this community. And that is the one and only Mr. Henry Jeremiah Jackson. Today, this community, our community, gathers to mourn him and to celebrate his life."

I fought back the tears. I wanted to be heard.

"The first time I became aware of the power of community was way back when I was in the first grade, at the tender age of 6. Our school was having a holiday assembly, with each class planning something to entertain our parents. We spent weeks in Grade 1 practicing our song. On the day of the assembly, I was at home, sick with a fever. My Mom still went to the assembly, to see my sister who was in the third grade.

When she got home, my Mom told me how my classmates did such a good job with our song.

I looked up at her and asked, 'How did they do the song? I wasn't there.' Because of course, at that young age, I didn't realize that a community has to go on, even if one member can't be there for some reason."

"My mother didn't explain it very well, telling me that the class didn't need me there, which hurt my feelings at the time. And unfortunately, I lost both my mother and my sister not long after that."

"A community can be defined in many ways. It can also be based on different characteristics. As we know, the Gayborhood is a community. But that doesn't mean that gay people living in other parts of the city don't belong to the gay community."

"Henry taught me that our first community, which he actually called a tribe, was the two of us. Me and him. We shared a bond that I can't put into words. But our tribe, our community, had other branches. The club, of course. And Henry had his membership in CMMC, the Camac Malez Motorcycle Club."

"Of course, when our community loses a member, we mourn them. For me, the pain of losing Henry will never go away. But that isn't the end of the community. No, not even close. We have to go on. We have things we need to accomplish. Henry would say that 'We still have work to do.'"

"I'm here today to say my final public farewell to Henry. And somehow, life will go on. Our community will continue to thrive, to fight for our rights and to celebrate our lives and our achievements."

My misty eyes blinded me, making me unable to see if my words caused any reaction. But I said what I had come to say, to the best of my limited ability. No one expected words of infinite wisdom to come from my lips, least of all me.

I walked down the aisle, out the door, and didn't stop walking until I was home alone, in my empty, hollow apartment. Because even when a community is there to offer support, sometimes I just have to suffer silently and alone.

***

I know I'll be judged for this. I know I can be possessive and selfish.

A week after his memorial service, I took the urn containing all that was left of Henry and traveled by train to Atlantic City. I waited until nighttime, returning to the same beach where Henry had proposed to me. I couldn't stop crying, standing there motionless, frozen. Then I did what I had to do, scattering his ashes into the ocean waves, quietly whispering goodbye.

With a faltering voice, I once more said the words out loud.

"I love you, Henry!"

CHAPTER TWENTY-THREE

MISTER GQ

Writing my column about Henry's death was a most difficult task. Many of my columns were snarky, gossipy, and less than kind. That's the nature of the gossip business.

This column had to be different. I mean, I had witnessed the whole thing. Prior to that, I had been having doubts about my own level of sanity. Now, I was suffering from a severe case of PTSD (Post-Traumatic Stress Disorder).

One minute, we were having a moment of celebration, excited at the prospect of having an openly-gay Black man running for City Council, only to have that moment shattered by a bullet tearing into Henry's head, literally blowing him away.

I wasn't sure if I should go right out and buy a gun for my own protection, or to resolve never to touch a gun in my life. Right now, I'm just scared. I always thought of the Gayborhood as a haven, a safe place, but what about now?

Do I hide in my apartment, or what?

Luckily, the answer was provided for me. Alejandro and Kirk, two of the Board members from Club Sanctuary, came to visit me. They had witnessed the same horror as I did.

"We can't let this kind of shit happen here!" Kirk was hollering at me during the meeting in my office. "We have to fight back! They're lucky we don't declare war right now on those homophobic thugs!"

"Calm down, babe," Jando told him. "Harvé isn't the enemy. You don't have to scream at him."

Sitting down and composing himself, Kirk apologized to me for his outburst.

Being a disabled veteran of the war in VietNam, Kirk suffered from his own PTSD, as well as dealing with the constant reminder of the violence of war with his prosthetic leg, replacing the one that had been blown up during the war.

"First, an attack directly on our neighborhood," Alejandro was saying. "Followed the very next day by an attack on our country. We say it's time for us to make a statement. To take a stand. We want to promote peace and non-violence, but do it in a voice so loud that we can't be ignored."

"We want to protest against violence in general, but our specific focus is to bring about change in the Gayborhood. We have to let people know that what happened to Henry will not be tolerated. Because that one incident was bad enough, but we all know that Henry isn't the only one who was brought down by hatred and violence against us," Kirk added.

"What's the plan?" I asked, knowing that I could help them put out the word about whatever it was that they wanted to do.

"A protest, that's the main event," Kirk explained.

"And then a party, 'cause that's what we do best," Jando added.

I thought for a moment. "How about if we celebrate the power of our voices? Instead of weapons, or force, let's call attention to what I've been advocating for years. Using our voices as a force for change."

"The Power of Voice," Alejandro said thoughtfully. "I like it. The POV Party."

Kirk jumped in. "How about we call it the POV Protest and Party?"

"Yes," Jando agreed. "The Power of Voice Protest and Party. AKA the POV Protest and Party. We hafta turn this into our biggest event ever!"

There was a massive advertising campaign for this event. Every gay and lesbian organization in the tri-state area was notified, as well as every progressive, liberal, and gay-friendly organization. A march, set to begin at Club Sanctuary, going over to Broad Street and then down to City Hall, was planned for Saturday, October 13, just after the one-month anniversary of the brutal attack and murder of Henry Jeremiah Jackson.

After the rally at City Hall, the march would continue east on Market Street to Penns Landing, where a picnic/party would be held until nightfall. Later in the evening, the parties would continue at every club in the city that joined in this effort. It was expected that the biggest, most raucous party would be at Sanctuary, of course.

Asked to lead the initial march to City Hall was none other than the Camac Malez Motorcycle Club, whose members gladly accepted the offer.

That night, the line to get into Sanctuary seemed endless, and in fact, many were left outside. The club simply couldn't accommodate everyone who wanted to join their party.

I covered these events for the paper, trying to capture the details as tens of thousands of mostly gay men flooded the streets of Philly in a unified cause to bring attention to the violence happening in our midst. What began as a solemn affair, starting with the peaceful march, later turned into a celebration of our culture and lifestyle as the party continued into the night.

Even with a reporter's eye as sharp as mine, it can be difficult to see everything that happens during a crowded event. One question kept going through my mind.

Where's Joey?

CHAPTER TWENTY-FOUR

JOEY

My heart is in the darkest of places, from which there seems to be no escape. I can't leave the apartment, trapped in my swirling memories, my grief, my heartbreak.

Everything reminds me of Henry. Everything. Sights, sounds, smells. Henry was my life, so this is hard to grasp. I start to imagine that the whole thing is just a dream. Any day now, I'll wake up to find Henry's leg protectively draped over mine as we sleep. He always protected me. He'll return to keep me safe from all the surrounding horrors.

The flurry of visits eventually turned to a trickle, as people returned to their daily lives. But what can I return to? Where's my normalcy, my routine, my sense of security for our future?

Something else slowly crept into my life. **HATE**. I never hated anyone before, not that I can remember anyway. But when I was told about the young thug who was responsible for ruining my life, my hatred started growing each day into an uncontrollable rage.

I don't know what to do with this emotion. There's no way for me to release it. Screaming at the walls provides no relief. Sleep does nothing to erase my memories. Instead, I re-live the horror in my nightmares.

Screaming slurs.

Gangsters running.

Windows breaking.

Fear.

Panic.

A head explodes.

And then I awaken, shaking with fear and rage, soaked with the nervous perspiration of a man in turmoil.

What if?

What if?

What if?

The questions echo in my mind, and I begin to blame myself. Somehow, it has to be my fault. I don't know why. But I know I feel guilty. About something. About my dishonesty and my unfaithfulness. About my inability to protect Henry. I must be guilty, because I'm still here.

I'm still here.

I survived.

But what is survival? This isn't living, but I'm powerless to make things right.

Things will never be right again.

***

The wheels of justice grind so very slowly. The murder occurred on September 10, 2001. Clenching my fists, trying to hide my still-unreleased rage, I walk into the Criminal Justice Center with Kirk and Jando on either side of me.

"Criminal Justice, my ass!" I murmur as we pass the huge sign at the entrance. "I'd like to be the one to give him the justice he deserves; to rot in prison forever isn't even close to what that murdering bastard deserves."

Kirk and Jando remain silent. They know that no words will console me. They've already tried a million times.

I owe both of them so much. They stepped up and took over the complete management of the club. With Henry gone and my mental state in disarray, I needed someone to handle that. I knew I could trust both of them, and they did a great job under difficult circumstances.

When I saw that young, skinny kid enter the courtroom, I almost jumped out of my seat. I wanted to strangle that punk. That punk-ass bitch.

Already, Henry had been gone for almost a year, and here we are, with a trial just starting.

"He should have been fried in the electric chair the day they caught that sonofabitch."

"Silence in the courtroom!" someone shouted.

I didn't see the person who called for silence. I couldn't see the lawyers, the judge, the jurors.

They went about their work with no notice from me. I couldn't see them. I couldn't hear them.

I saw only one thing. Not a person. A thing. The object of my hatred. That orange-clad punk ass bitch.

I heard him say two words: "Not Guilty," in a strong, masculine voice that didn't seem to fit his scrawny frame. He seemed smaller than my memory of him running towards us, waving his gun erratically, shooting randomly. I wondered, just for a moment, if his time in the city jail, waiting for his trial, had any effect on him at all.

That thought left me as quickly as it came. I would not feel anything for this person, this murdering, homophobic bastard who bore sole responsibility for what happened to Henry.

Only one person pulled the trigger on the gun that hurtled the bullet in Henry's direction. It was that blur in orange. Without realizing it, I was sobbing. Kirk gently placed his hand on my knee, trying to comfort me.

Nothing would or could provide the comfort I needed.

Bits and pieces of the trial testimony seeped into my consciousness. Billy, who had the same view of the crime as I did, testified before me.

Lawyer: "Can you identify the person who shot the gun that resulted in the death of Henry Jeremiah Jackson?"
Billy: "I can."
Lawyer: "Is that person in the courtroom today?"
Billy: "He is."
Lawyer: "Can you identify which person, now present in the courtroom, shot and killed Mr. Jackson?"
Billy: "It was him."
With that, Billy pointed directly at the defendant, at Yandi, who refused to look at the witness, staring down at the table in front of him, nervously clutching his hands together.

When it was my turn to testify, I answered the questions robotically. The prosecutors had prepared me, so there were no surprises. The public defender had no questions for me. My part in the trial ended with no outwardly visible drama.

In my mind, I was in turmoil. All I could see was that person, that being, that...monster. I was seething inside. If I could, I would have spat on him, taken him by the head, bashing it against any solid object to cause the most injury and damage. I wanted revenge, but I had no avenue for achieving that.

My hatred continued to grow unabated.

Kirk asked me to meet him, outside my condo building. Reluctantly, I agreed, taking the elevator down to the lobby, spying Kirk waiting in his wheelchair.

"My leg hurts too much today," he explained.

"You don't even have to tell me," I responded. "You do whatever you need to do."

"Let's go down to the park," Kirk suggested. "Would you give me a push?"

Helping Kirk navigate the cruel sidewalks of Philly kept my mind from wandering anywhere else. At the park entrance, Kirk motioned towards a particular area. My area. Our area. Where it all started. Where I had met Henry.

Relaxing into our spots, Kirk asked me, "Who are you now?"

After a moment considering the question, I shrugged my shoulders. "I don't know. What do you mean?"

"I think you know what I mean, though I do believe you don't know the answer to the question.

I stared straight ahead into the distance, without focusing on anything.

"Do you remember when we met?"

I had to smile at that, if only a little.

"Of course. At the Veterans Service Center. You were telling your therapy group about trying to buy some porn from a bookstore, when you were still way underage, I might add."

"Yep, that's it," Kirk replied, also smiling at the memory.

"But do you know why I was telling that story?"

"To give every guy in the room a stiffie?" I joked.

"Well, that might have been a small part of the plan, but no, that isn't the real reason. You were only there for one session, so you never heard the full story. I was leading up to the most painful moment in my life. That moment when my leg got blown off in the war."

"Ohhhh," I said, suddenly feeling foolish.

"I hated the people who had done that to me. I couldn't focus on any one individual, because I don't know who actually caused my injury. But I knew I was mad, and I had

213

to be mad at someone. So I decided to hate an entire country. And that's a heavy weight to carry around."

"What are you saying?" I asked quietly.

"I had to learn to let go of that hate. And the group at the Service Center helped me do that."

A pause while I considered what Kirk was telling me.

"How? How'd they do that? How'd they help you?"

"First, I had to recognize and acknowledge what I was doing. The hatred was tearing me up inside. I started talking about it. Sharing with others what had happened to me. Finding common ground."

"You think I have common ground? Who the hell has gone through what I have?"

"Think about what you just said," Kirk advised me. "Do you think you're the first guy, even the first gay guy, to lose a partner to violence?"

I knew he was right. I wasn't sure that I was ready to listen yet.

Kirk placed his strong hand on my shoulder, gently massaging the tension away.

"We both lost something. Remember that. Sharing the story of your loss doesn't mean you have to find people with the exact same story as you. I lost a physical part of me, my leg. You lost someone who was also a part of you. It might not be that hard, to find people who can relate to you, and you can relate to them."

"Did you ever find forgiveness in your heart? Have you forgiven the person, or even the country, that caused your suffering?"

"It took a long time, but yes. I have forgiven them. Not just for their sake, but even more, for my own sake. I didn't want to be living my life with hatred burning inside my soul each and every day."

"Hmmmm. I hear what you're saying. I think you might be right about talking about what I'm feeling. But forgiving

214

that monster who shot Henry? I don't think that's ever gonna happen."

"Do you want me to help you find a group? For therapy?"

"Thanks, Kirk, but not yet. Maybe you and I can just talk every once in a while? Whaddya think?"

"Sure, Joey. No problem. I'd be happy to."

CHAPTER TWENTY-FIVE

YANDI

The wheels of justice do turn slowly, even from my perspective. The year I'd spent in the Philly jail system had been pure hell, just waiting for the trial.

The actual trial was even worse. All those witnesses, describing what they thought they saw. How could any of them be sure it was me? But still, they talked like they was 1000% certain, ready to lock me up for the rest of my life. If I couldn't be 100% sure who they was, how in the fuckin' hell was they so fuckin' sure about me?

Didn't I look exactly like every other thug on my block? Especially to these crackers. But I think they just wanna put someone away. They always jump all over us and then they say they doin' sumthin' about all the violence in the city.

They only care 'cause it happened in Center City. I know that for a fact. But we had to do it there, to put a scare in the fags and get them movin' outta that hood.

I ain't care 'bout nobody in that courtroom. Just like they ain't care 'bout me. I felt like I was invisible the whole time, a ghost just sittin' there, waitin' to get put away like an old pair of socks or sumthin'.

Though I couldn't see him most of the time, I could feel one pair of eyes burnin' into my back. I wanted him, that one guy, to leave me the fuck alone.

He's just a homo, I'd tell myself. *Why should I care if he lost someone? It ain't like they feel things like us real people do.*

216

But when I did catch a chance to see his eyes, they burned me. I ain't know why. I'm just sayin'. Sumthin' 'bout that one they called Joey got on my last nerve.

I had two different charges I was facing. Murder in the second degree in Pennsylvania means somebody kills a person while that first person (me) is also committing a felony.

Murder in the third degree means there was no premeditation and no other felony being committed.

No one accused me of premeditation, meaning I didn't set out deliberately to kill anybody.

The question for the jury, according to my public defender, was whether any other felony was being committed when that guy got killed.

And of course, as my boys in the jail kept reminding me, there couldn't be any hate crimes added because killing a fag ain't no big deal in this state. Even if I killed him 'cause I hated homos, that had nothing to do with the process in the courtroom.

I guess even the prosecutors didn't think that me runnin' through the Gayborhood, wavin' my gun like a maniac, screamin' at the top of my lungs about homos, knocking over kiosks and breaking windows, was any big thing. Because I wasn't actually charged with any other felonies. Just the charge of murder in either the second or third degree.

I admit I was shaking in the courtroom when the jury walked in, knowing they had reached a verdict. Murder in the second meant automatic life, with no chance of parole.

Murder in the third meant something very different.

Judge: "Have you reached a verdict?"
Jury Foreperson: "We have, your Honor."

No one in the jury looks in my direction. I was told if I saw that, to expect the worst, so I balled my hands into fists, trying to prepare for the impact of the next words in the courtroom.

An eternity passed while the bailiff walked in slow-motion in the direction of the judge, clutching some papers in his hand.

Inside, I was screaming. I wanted to turn and lash out at that guy who just wouldn't stop staring at me. Why am I facing a possible life sentence for killing a homo? The cops told us they wouldn't be hard on us if somebody got hurt.

Who did the jury care about more? Me, a young, tatted Puerto Rican gangbanger from the ghetto, or the young, Black, gay guy who was rumored to be getting ready to run for office, which might have caused big problems for the people who really run this city?

Let's find out, I thought.

"On the charge of murder in the second degree, we the jury find the defendant: NOT GUILTY."

With all my might, I tried to keep my cool and not let nobody know the relief that swept through me.

Behind me, I heard that guy, the one with the eyes, gasp and sob. I knew he had his friends there supporting him. *Why did he care so much? Did I really hurt him that much?* All during the trial, I hated the sight of him. *Was I wrong?*

I had the slightest hope that the jury might slap the homos in their faces and bring back a "Not Guilty" on all the charges. Maybe I could walk right out of here today. A free man. That would send a message, wouldn't it?

"On the charge of murder in the third degree, we the jury find the defendant: GUILTY."

Damn! They didn't go all the way.

My shoulders slumped, as my body tried to deal with the mix of anger, relief, and fear that I was feeling.

Anger that I had left behind evidence leading to my capture and trial.

Relief at not facing life in prison.

Fear because I knew that the state prison system would be my next home and I already knew that just about anything can happen in there.

My sentence was an automatic 10 to 20 years upstate. I already knew that, so no surprise there. Maybe you think I got off easy. Maybe you think society should throw me in a cage for the rest of my life, so y'all can just forget about me.

Not that anybody cared about me, anyway. Nobody was there for me that day, the day I heard my fate. Nobody from my family was in the courtroom. Nobody from the gang neither. Not one person alive cared what was gonna happen to me.

Even my defender, as soon as I was sentenced, simply turned his attention to his next case. He didn't say a word to me. He just let me go, a piece of trash being caught up in the wind, twisting and turning until getting swept up by the system. I was trapped and I knew it.

Next stop: Camp Hill, where I'd be evaluated and processed for placement in my "home prison," where I'd be for the next 10 to 20 years. That's so easy to say, isn't it? Ten to twenty. A snap, right?

Well, no. Not for me, not for all the other slaves in here. For me, that meant the entirety of my 20s would be spent livin' in a cage. And if they didn't let me out at my minimum, I'd be there for my 30s too. Imagine being 20 years old, then going away somewhere and comin' home when you're 40. What'll I even be like as a 40-year-old man? I ain't got no idea.

Oh, and you somehow object to me referring to myself and other prisoners as slaves? Slaves were freed after the Civil War, is that what you think?

Did you ever actually read the 13th Amendment? Right, I ain't think you ever did. But somehow you think you know what it say, amiright? I bet if you learned anything about it in school, they told you that slavery was "abolished." Read it and you tell me, where do you see the word "abolished?"

Section 1: *Neither slavery nor involuntary servitude, except as punishment for crime whereof the party shall have been duly convicted, shall exist within the United States, or any place subject to their jurisdiction.*

You're probably wonderin' how a dumb, uneducated thug from the hood knows about this stuff. I have to give credit to my first cellie, who was an old-head with 20 years already on the inside. He had time to study up, plus he was as smart as a whip.

I know you probably seen on tv sometimes, during a disaster, when convicts are shown "volunteering" to help the community, like rescuing people in flooded areas or fighting forest fires. You're being told that those prisoners are "volunteers" to make you feel better. In fact, they're being used as slave labor.

Or maybe you've been told that inmates are given jobs inside the prisons, to help them develop skills needed to survive once they're released.

That one really cracks me the fuck up! Inmates do get jobs inside; that part is true. Here in the Commonwealth of Pennsylvania, state prisoners are paid 19 cents per hour.

Nineteen cents per hour!

That can be done because the 13th Amendment defines prisoners as slaves, who are not covered by minimum wage laws, or occupational safety laws, or anything else. Besides taking advantage of inmates, the institutions save a ton of money.

If the prisons had to hire private citizens to do the work performed by inmates, they'd have to pay at least the minimum wage, raising costs substantially. Or if that 13th Amendment was changed or repealed, the inmates could earn a fair wage while performing work that needs to be done.

Anyway...

After a month of testing at Camp Hill, I was assigned to SCI Greene, a State Correctional Institution designated as Maximum Security, with a population of more than 1700 inmates.

At the time, I wasn't aware that Pennsylvania keeps more than 36,000 people trapped within its "correctional" system. There are 24 facilities throughout the state, many in rural areas, far removed from the everyday lives of the

221

citizens of the state. Of course, that's done by design. "Out of sight, out of mind" could very well be the motto of the PA DOC.

For the first few days, I was stuck in solitary. Why? That's just how they do it. To get you used to the idea of being completely oppressed by the system, which now is in complete control of me.

Once I was out of solitary, I found myself in Gen Pop (General Population.) Scanning the dining room during my first appearance at breakfast, I saw a few familiar faces. No surprise there, really. Lots and lots of guys from my hood ended up in the system.

At lunch, I almost jumped when I recognized someone.

Damn, is that even possible? I was thinking as my eyes followed every move. Plus, I was gettin' chubbed out, my cock already stretching up and out, though no one would ever notice inside these baggy clothes.

I ate quickly because I was hungry, which I soon discovered would be a constant state for me. With no money on my commissary, there'd be no snacks or other food to fill my belly. That can make a bad situation worse really fast.

I tried not to stare at him during every meal, which was the only time I saw him. He didn't seem to pay me no mind, so I wondered if I was wrong 'bout what I was thinkin'.

On my fifth day inside, he walked right up beside me and sat down on my left. I stared straight ahead, not wanting to look. Maybe he was mad that I kept on eyeing him. You never know what people might be up to.

"Hey...I don't really know how to say this, so I'm just gonna be blunt. Are you from Philly? Do we know each other? Is your name...?"

I pushed my leg against his, feeling his muscular leg tense up.

"I think you might be the guy I been lookin' for. My name's Yandi. Mi nombre Yandi."

I was shaking with desire.

"Y tu?"

"Eloy. Mi nombre Eloy! I'm your 'Coqui Boy', remember?"

He whispered a few words from the poem he'd written back when we were in the shelter together.

Solo me, solo me
Just like the little, lonely coqui
He wants to be found, by making his sound
Just like me.
Coqui! Coqui! Coqui!

"Man, I never forgot you, never," I told him. "You were the only one who..."

I stopped, not sure it was safe to talk about what happened between us back at the shelter in Philly. Maybe for him, it was just *boyz bein' boyz.*

Then I felt him place his hand on my knee and give it a hard squeeze. Just for a second, but that's all it took to send me the right message. The one I was hopin' he'd send me. An invitation.

"We got a lot to talk about," I said quietly.

"We gonna do a helluva lot more than just talk. If you into it, of course," he replied.

I know I can be a selfish bastard. Even though I had just re-connected with Eloy, I had a thought that some might consider evil. I was hoping that he'll be in here for at least 10 years. I know, I'm a creep. I don't know if it's possible for two guys in here to have a "thing" or not. But right now, my hopes are hella high. Plus, my dick is drippin'.

223

CHAPTER TWENTY-SIX

JOEY

What is the shape of grief?

I try to grapple with it, but I can't really get a handle on it.

It seems to be in constant movement, shifting shapes, moving into places where I thought I might be safe.

I want to package my grief into some sort of physical shape. It could be a cube, a cone, a cylinder, a sphere. Anything that I can grasp and handle, take it and put it away, only letting it out when I want it.

No? Those shapes won't hold my grief? How about a pyramid? That might work. Did the ancient Egyptians build their pyramids to contain the grief they felt at the passing of their gods, the Pharaohs?

Despite my best efforts, my grief slips out, eluding my efforts to capture it. I envision a diamond, thinking that an object formed from pressure might be the perfect container. If I squeeze the grief with just a little more force, will that transform it into something tangible, something that can be controlled and eliminated?

It's even worse than trying to capture smoke in the air, or trying to imprison the fog that seems to appear out of nowhere early in the morning, when I wake up from another night of horrors, dreams from which there is no escape. The terrors when I'm awake seem even worse.

Somehow, I have to escape this.

Kirk, though not a trained therapist, was a huge help to me as I tried to navigate the uncharted waters of life without Henry. I guess he learned a few techniques during his own therapy sessions, and he seemed to be there whenever I needed him.

"Do you ever think about the kid?" he asked me.

"All the time. I can't get him outta my head. He haunts me. If only he knew what he did, how he destroyed me, destroyed us," I answered.

"Why don't you tell him?"

Well, that was an unexpected suggestion. It never occurred to me to actually communicate with the kid. How could I do that?

I soon discovered it wasn't that hard to communicate with him. All I needed was his name, inmate number and the SCI (State Correctional Institution) address.

The really difficult question: *What am I gonna say to this kid?*

"Whaddya think, Kirk? Should I lay him out, tell him he's a monster that destroyed me and my family? Tell him he's a no-good motherfucker and I hope he rots in jail forever?"

"Would that make you feel better? He might already hate himself. We don't know. And what's your purpose? If the goal is to hurt the dude, then go ahead and tell him all that."

I decided not to write in haste. I wanted to think about what Kirk said. If I do write to the kid, why am I doing it and what do I really wanna say?

I wish I could capture my grief and send it to the kid. Let him live with it. I don't want it anymore. I never wanted it. My plan was for Henry and me to live fabulous gay lives, doing as we pleased, traveling, experiencing new places and things. It was all gonna be so awesome. It was awesome. For quite a long time, until...

Trying to push the grief away wasn't working. I knew I couldn't give it away. No one else would want it. What's left, then? Maybe it was time to try something different. What if I embraced my grief? Celebrated it? And if that's what I decide to do, how do I accomplish that?

An important date was approaching. Soon it would be May 27, 2003. That was our shared birthday. The year before, I spent that date hiding in my condo, crying, trying to drown my sorrows in a bottle that proved to be totally unfulfilling. This year...something different.

I thought about telling Kirk and Jando what I was planning to do. But sometimes, I just have to do certain things on my own. I truly appreciate the support of my friends. I'd be lost without them. Still, I know I can't depend on others for everything.

Tuesday night, May 27, 2003. I chose my outfit carefully. Nothing leather. Nothing like the recent outfits that I wore to excite and arouse Henry, who craved seeing me in submissive-mode.
Casual, but beautiful clothing. Expensive, but not ostentatious. Not somber, either. Though I loved to dress in fashionably all-black outfits, not tonight.
Standing at the door to the club, I walked into Sanctuary for the first time since Henry died. Catching a view of myself in the mirrored wall, I thought I looked quite grand in my classic, creased black trousers, cream-colored oversized shirt, accessorized with a thick gold chain from which my precious phallic pendant hung. The same locket

that Henry gave me the day we got our tattoos. The one with the inscription of our wedding date: 12/25/80.

As I began to feel the music move me, I could see my reflection changing. It was no longer the "present me" that I saw. Instead, I saw a younger, more innocent, more naive version of myself, watching me, wondering what my next step would be.

Since it was Tuesday, the club wasn't crowded, though it wasn't empty either. My reflexes took over and I did what I almost always did at the club - I got up on the dance floor and made my moves. It didn't matter if anyone watched me or joined me. This was the real me, the "dancing queen," the one who always enjoyed the nightlife and the promise of whatever the night might bring. I let myself go, drifting with the flow of the music.

I felt myself letting go. I was letting go of the guilt, the hate, the horror. And finally, finally, I felt my grief just beginning to disappear.

I suddenly realized that I wasn't alone. Jando and Kirk, who had been managing the club since "the incident" had joined me on the floor, dancing their hearts out.

Instinctively, I now knew what I had to do. About the kid. About the letter.

But even more importantly, I had to do just one more thing. Without telling anyone what I was doing, and hoping that no one would even notice, I took the last remaining bit of the physical Henry, the small bit of his ashes that I had kept locked away in the pendant he had given me when we were marked with our tribal symbol, our Pride tattoos. With one wild swing of my arms, I released the rest of him onto the dance floor, into the atmosphere of this place where we had shared so much.

He belonged here. He should rest here. Henry should always be a part of Club Sanctuary and the club will always be a part of him.

Henry will never leave my heart. I understand that now. I can keep him there, treasure him, and enjoy the memories. I can find joy in the fact that we had met, fallen in love and built a life together.

But I also didn't have to let the past hold me back. Henry wouldn't have ever wanted me to live the life of a grieving widow. Henry loved life. He would want me to do the same. I was never as sure of anything in my life.

Emerging from the darkness into the light which had been eluding me, I spent the night on the dance floor, letting the music, the lights, the friendships bring me back from the depths of my despair.

When I got back home and fell into bed, I had the first good night's sleep in a very long time. No nightmares. No terrors. No monsters. No demons. No guilt.

And while I can never say that the grief is gone, it no longer controls me. I recognize it; I acknowledge it; I accept it. It is now a permanent part of me. Just like Henry.

**

The letter I sent was very simple.

Yandi,

I'd like to be given the chance to talk with you. I'm asking for permission to visit. It might be a difficult time for both of us, but I'm willing to take that chance if you are. Please consider this as an opportunity. Write back if you add my name to your visitor list.

Joey

Below that, I added all the information he'd need to give to the DOC (Department of Corrections) for me to be allowed to visit.

Now, all I gotta do is wait for a reply.

CHAPTER TWENTY-SEVEN

MISTER GQ

I know I'm not completely well, and that incident at Trust, where our dinner group was attacked by those hoodlums made me re-think my ideas about my personal safety. It's bad enough that I was just slightly paranoid before that horrid incident.

At this point, I haven't actually made a final decision about staying or going.

The Gayborhood is changing, though, no doubt about that. And some of the changes are happening really fast. I wonder if the city really is making a deliberate attempt to move us out.

Many parts of Center City Philly, including The Gayborhood, used to be a rundown, ghetto-like area.

In 2000, Philly enacted a new program, called a tax abatement, to incentivize new construction. It provided major property tax breaks for people buying new or newly-rehabbed properties.

After years of seeing no new construction in Center City, it suddenly became a hotbed. The Richie Riches, newly interested in urban living, began flooding the area. And no, these weren't gay folks. Straight people started arriving in droves, including singles, couples and yes, families with children.

This movement has its advantages and disadvantages. A major problem being faced by long-time residents of the area was the rapidly-increasing cost of living here. Rich people want to live in areas with lots of amenities and as you are well aware, everything...and I do mean everything, comes at a price.

I consider myself to be an expert in gay culture. That statement isn't made in jest. Seriously, I've been studying our culture closely for decades, documenting it in my gossip columns, gaining a large following of fans, and expanding my career as I now have a syndicated column and I want to expand my outreach. Maybe a radio show. It would be so cool to have guests on my show, talking about what's happening in gay society.

I also admit to having strong opinions, and I pride myself on basing those opinions on facts and experiences. Allow me to provide one brief example.

When I'm at the Book Brunch, I've already read the book. I've probably also read many books that might be similar to the one being discussed, allowing me to compare and contrast. I believe that makes my opinion more valid than someone who simply reads the back cover of the book, has no idea of the nuances and themes contained therein, but whose voice at the table is spoken with authority. As if! I object, your honor!

That opinion, based on the Reader's Digest version of a book, carries little weight with me. And yet, I see these wannabes, speaking dramatically, but without authority, trying to cast me aside and replace me as the "new" arbiter of taste in this town.

My advice? Do the work, honey. Till then, I just say, "Bye Bye Bye," like the pretty boys in my new favorite video from NSYNC.

Anyway, I do digress, as I so often do. I think I was talking about the next Sunday Book Brunch, and if I wasn't? Well, my mind is already there.

The second Sunday of the month, April 13, 2003. Our group decided to try a new place to eat and chat, and it was just one block from my building on the Benjamin Franklin Parkway.

I'll share a little secret. I had suggested the change of venue, not just for my convenience, but also because I was still feeling a little hesitant about spending too much time in the Gayborhood. Every time I traveled there, I just had a sense of dread, along with the vivid memories of that awful day. I could barely walk along 13th Street anymore. The memory of Henry's body crumpled on the ground...

Oh dear, let me get back to what I was saying. I'm looking forward to hearing what Giff thought of our book for this month: *Before Night Falls* by the Cuban poet and novelist, Reinaldo Arenas.

On a beautiful day like today, I enjoy eating outside. Check that. I *used* to enjoy eating outside. Not anymore. You know why. I don't feel safe. I have to be hyper-vigilant, which takes the joy out of the meal. Would you enjoy constantly checking your surroundings while trying to enjoy a sumptuous sirloin, or a grilled-to-perfection salmon, or even a simple martini?

Thanks, thug! I think as I enter the restaurant.

For the past two years, we'd kept the same group of guys gathering for the brunch. Consistency is sometimes a good thing, and I was thankful to have no need for new recruits at this point in my life.

Today, though I lived closest to the spot, I was the last to arrive. Slightly miffed, I saw that Giff was sitting in my seat, the one facing the entrance. Because, well...you know...I have to watch to see who's heading in my direction.

I know I'm not the only one who lives this way, in constant fear of my life whenever I'm away from home. Some people live that way because of the choices they've made in their lives. But that isn't the case for me. Before witnessing the brutal, cold-hearted murder of my friend, right in the heart of an area that I had considered to be a safe zone...well, that takes a toll on you. On me.

Knowing how I thought, Giff quickly changed seats, explaining that he had been "keeping it warm for me."

Really? I thought. *Or did something (or someone) catch your eye and you were striving for a better view?*

The waiter hovered close-by until I was seated. Once I became aware of him, I was enthralled with his beauty. Dark features. Tall, slim, smooth. The way his trousers clung to his ass. His beautiful, soft-looking hands. That smile as he pranced around the table, filling our glasses with unasked-for water, as my friends chit-chatted incessantly.

Meeting his eyes as he handed a menu to me, I didn't immediately notice the card that was attached. However, since I had never eaten here before, I couldn't just order "the usual" so eventually I tore my eyes away from this vision of male beauty to consult the list of offerings.

On the card was a simple and direct message:

"Hello! My name is Felipe and I'm happy to be your waiter today. Though I'm deaf, I'm perfectly capable of serving you. If you speak distinctly, I can read lips. If you prefer, you can point to items on the menu, or even use the notepads on the table to write a message. Thank you!

Giff ignores the directions and deftly uses ASL to speak to the waiter. I speak in a normal voice, though slightly more slowly than usual, asking if Felipe would recommend the goat-cheese and cherry tomato frittatas or not. His enthusiastic thumbs-up made me once again notice his strong, masculine hands, and I momentarily wished his thumb could somehow find its way inside me.

Where exactly? Oh, babe, anywhere will do just fine. Your choice! I was thinking as I watched Chance mouth the words as he placed his order.

"Don't be so ignorant!" I chastised him, actually slapping his wrist lightly. "Mind your manners and act like a normal person."

Noah, Eric and Trayvon all placed their orders, as Felipe moved quickly to the kitchen.

Pulling two books from his bag, Giff asked, "What did everybody think? I hope y'all finished the book this time."

Why does he have two books? I wondered, before noticing the different titles.

Giff continued, saying, "I read it twice. First, in English, as we all did, with the title *Before Night Falls*. I thought it was just so beautiful, but things do get lost in translation, you know."

I shouldn't have been surprised. Giff was always the one with the best insights about every book we discussed.

"Here it is in the original Spanish, under the title *Antes Que Anocheza*."

Without asking, I picked up the Spanish copy. Flipping through, I wondered if I'd be able to appreciate the beauty of the prose as it was originally written.

Throughout our meal, we discussed many aspects of the book, as we always did. Many of us appreciated the frank, sometimes brutal language.

Eric was the first to bring up the letter from the author that was included at the end.

"I can't imagine the courage it took to write that final letter. Such honesty is rarely seen, I think."

Reinaldo Arenas died in New York City on December 7, 1990, at the age of 47. The author decided to end his own life via overdose, as he was dying from complications due to HIV/AIDS.

For me, the unbearable weight of knowing that this particular virus bore responsibility for the premature deaths of so many artists, authors, musicians, actors, and others across the full spectrum of life, forced me to appreciate the very act of living.

Already living in fear of a disease for decades, now I was being forced to fear a different disease - violence.

How am I going to cope with this? Can I survive an onslaught of hatred on top of all the other problems facing our community? It felt like there was never any relief. Just layer after layer of problems being piled on, much as I would use layers of bedding to warm me at night.

But these layers, instead of warming me, left me cold, bitter, angry, and worried.

Despite everything, we do find ways to celebrate. That's why I'm grateful for places like Club Sanctuary. I can go there to escape the outside world. I can immerse myself in a world of glamor, glitz, fun and frivolity.

When I get sad or lonely, I look back through the copies of my old column, reading about the fantastic nights at the club, where we could just celebrate being our true selves. Even if tomorrow would bring a new day of pretending, trying to fit into a world that was really never made for us, and only sometimes tolerated us, the club scene for me always represented something powerful.

The power of me. The power of us. The power of a community willing to embrace our individuality and our

235

commonalities, no matter how Queer we might seem to outsiders.

I will continue to treasure that until my dying day.

After returning home, slowly, I walk over to my silent friend, Chlorophytum comosum, and stroke his branches. On days less formal, I just call him Spidey, but today, his full name is preferred.

"See, that irritating bulge around my waist is finally going away," I tell him. "I guess it's because I've been getting in some pretty good workouts."

Chloro turned away from me, as I lifted my shirt over my head to remove it, exposing those ever-growing black and purple lesions now covering so much of my body.

Ignoring them, I inhaled deeply, sucking in my gut, wanting to show my physique to Chloro.

Don't worry about the lesions. I already know. I got my diagnosis almost two years ago. I wasn't really surprised to learn that those nights spent in the orgy room at the baths had finally caught up with me.

I know I'm running out of time. But I'm keeping it quiet. My fear right now is that the last Book Brunch may very well have been my last Book Brunch, the finale in a rather long series. I had been hoping for a renewal of the series, hahaha! But now I think it is not to be.

CHAPTER TWENTY-EIGHT

JOEY

My state of anxiety only grew as I got closer to the prison. When I pulled into the parking lot, I just sat in the car for a while. First, the setting itself was enormous, a group of buildings surrounded by gates, towers, barbed wire.

How many prisoners does Pennsylvania have? I wondered. *This one institution looks like it can hold thousands. Are there really that many people in this state who have to be kept away from society? And why are they here anyway? Rehabilitation? Punishment? I admit, I never spent any time thinking about prisons or prisoners.*

Except for that one time when Javier had been sent to the jail in Philly, this was totally outside of my experience.

I arrived early on a Tuesday morning, in a rural part of the state that seemed desolate and deserted. Thinking back to the visit I made to see Javi in Philly, where hundreds of other visitors waited their turn, I was the only person who seemed to be visiting here today.

Is that what it's like for the inmates here? Many of them were convicted in courts in Philly, then they find themselves incarcerated in some far-off corner of the state, making family visits very difficult. That's part of the prison culture. Isolate the inmates from the support of family and friends. Make everything difficult. Enforce thousands of rules and regulations designed to place obstacles in the path of anyone who really does want to rehabilitate themselves. Dehumanize the inmates, making it easier for the COs, (Correctional Officers) to treat them with cruelty and hatred. No matter what had brought them to this unfortunate, forbidding place.

Eventually, I found myself in a large room designed for visits. Vending machines lined one wall, in an area where prisoners weren't permitted to enter, but visitors could buy snacks and sandwiches to share with the inmate they were visiting. A few tables were scattered around the room, but most of the seats were attached to the floor, two seats together, where an inmate and visitor would sit side-by-side.

My breathing was becoming difficult and I felt light-headed. *Did I really want to talk to this guy? This was Henry's murderer. What was I thinking?*

Watching him walk towards me, his impassive face betraying no emotions, I was struck by his frailty. Maybe it was the over-sized uniform he wore, but he seemed so much smaller than the man I watched in court during the trial. Before, I saw a monster...now, I wasn't really sure.

He sat down next to me, staring straight ahead. An awkward silence ensued.

"I want..." I began to say, interrupted by his hand raised in my direction, as if I had encountered a stop sign on the road here.

"Please, just give me one sec," he said, his voice trembling with emotion. "You're the first visitor I ever got here. I just need a minute to think first."

Then, I heard him sobbing, so quietly, desperately trying to hide his emotions, but unable to, and I thought I could actually hear his tears streaming down his cheeks.

The part of me that wanted to violently attack him, the part that needed to get revenge, the part of me that felt nothing but hatred, started to melt away.

I waited a moment, then broke the silence of his tears, with the simplest of greetings.

"My name's Joey," I said.

Recovering control of himself, squaring his shoulders and holding his head high, but still staring ahead without seeing me, he replied, "I'm Yandi."

"How in the hell did we end up in a place like this?" I asked rhetorically.

Yandi slowly shook his head. "The fuck if I know."

Unsure how to start the real conversation, I asked, "You hungry? I have some money for the machines."

"Yeah, I could go for some chips right now. The food in here tastes like shit. Might be nice to taste sumthin' real."

After spending a few minutes at the vending machines, I returned to my seat with a couple bags of chips, some sandwiches and sodas. I already know that sharing food can be a good way to break down barriers.

He spent a few minutes concentrating on satisfying his hunger. Not really used to snacks from vending machines, it seemed to me that a steady diet of all this salt and sugar could literally rot a person on the inside. But, considering my surroundings, I ate a few bags of chips and cookies myself.

Suddenly, he stopped eating in mid-bite. "I have sumthin' I wanna tell ya."

Turning, I looked at him, seeing his profile as he never looked at me directly.

"What is it?" I asked.

"I never realized until later what I really did to you. Not when it happened. Not even during the trial. It was being in here when I saw what I actually done."

"You mean it's because you got caught and now you're being punished?" I asked, thinking maybe the prison system had served its stated purpose.

"Nah, nothing like that," he told me.

"Then what?"

"Before, I never knew what it was like to have anybody care about me. And I didn't know what it really meant to care about another person."

I took a moment to think, trying to comprehend what he was saying.

"I don't understand," I told him.

He took a deep sigh, then emptied the crumbs from a bag of chips into his mouth, chewing quietly.

I heard him swallow. Then he took a deep breath, trying to explain to me.

"I mean, out there, back in Philly, I was on my own. All the time. For years. I had my bros, of course, but not like what I wanted."

He hesitated before continuing, lowering his voice to a whisper, though no one was anywhere near us.

"I found out what it means to have feelins for someone. For a...you know...for a guy."

With those words, a shock went through my system. *What did he just say?*

Thinking back, trying to remember the fear that struck me that day, when a homo-hating thug, running and screaming through the streets of the Gayborhood, fatally attacking my beloved Henry...is that same guy now telling me that he's...GAY?

For the first time, he turned to face me directly. The sorrow etched into his features tore at my heart. I came here with the intention to try to explain the damage he had done. To make him feel shame. Though I wasn't sure he was capable of an emotion like that.

It seemed that something...or someone...had already beaten me to the punch.

Still facing me, he gazed downward, suddenly afraid to return eye contact.

"I never really knew what it meant to have someone who's important to me. Just one time, years ago, I felt like maybe I had a connection. But we was just kids, stayin' in a shelter, and once we separated, that was it. I never saw him again, but I never stopped thinkin' about him."

"Yes, I know what you're talking about," I assured him, as his eyes once more brimmed with tears.

"So ya see, I ain't never cared about nobody. And nobody ain't never cared about me. So when I took someone important away from you, I really didn't know what that meant. I didn't think I hurt you real bad 'cause I didn't understand. But now, I'm tryna tell you that I get it. The harm I did finally got through my thick noggin.

Shaking my head, I started to see the bigger picture. How loneliness and fear can shape our behavior in ways that we sometimes don't understand ourselves.

Yandi continued, "When I got here, I found the guy. Right here. The one I'd been thinkin' about for years. The one that I...that I...well, I think I loved him all that time."

Now my eyes were starting to tear up.

"And you know what I found out? That he missed me, too. But then he got into some trouble and he ended up here, and then somehow I ended up in the same place and we found each other again."

The words were pouring out of his mouth now.

"We actually started spending time together, and well, and doing stuff together. You know what I mean, right?" He lowered his voice again. "Sex stuff."

"So now you..." I began.

He cut me off. "Now I understand what I took away from you. I just didn't get it before. But now, as I spend time with him, and realize the feelins I got for him, for the first time I get what you had with your dude. And if anyone ever took my guy away from me, well, I'd wanna..."

He stopped dead right there.

I clamped my lips together. "Yes, I know. You'd wanna hurt the guy or worse. I'm pretty sure I know how you feel."

"I came down here for this visit for one thing. I had to tell ya just how fuckin' sorry I am about what I did. If I could take it back..."

Now it was my turn to raise my hand, to signal for him to stop.

I wanted to scream at him in fury, but what would be the purpose? Was I trying to hurt him? Because looking at him right now, it's apparent that the dude is already in pain.

The pain we inflict upon ourselves is often greater than any pain inflicted on us by others.

"I don't even know what to think right now. I have a whole lot to think about. I came here not sure what to say, but I never thought I'd end up hearing you say anything like this."

"I can't stay too long, 'cause I have a long drive back to Philly. But I have one more thing I wanna tell you," I said towards the end of our conversation.

"I loved Henry with all my heart. I still do. And if there's one thing I know about Henry is that he lived with love in his heart. His whole life, he tried to make things better for others, especially me. So I know what he'd want me to do now."

I thought I saw Yandi flinch a little; maybe he thought that Henry would want me to beat him to a pulp. Nothing could be further from the truth.

"I guess things are pretty rough in here for you, right?" I asked.

"I try not to let most of it bother me," Yandi replied. "I know I put myself here and the fact is, at least I have the company of a guy I love, though we don't let nobody know about that in here. The worst part I think is the hunger. They don't feed us nearly enough."

"I didn't know that," I replied. "But I do know this. Henry wouldn't want you to be hungry. He'd want to try to help you. Even after what you did, Henry would be the first one to recognize that there's goodness in you too."

Clearly, Yandi was confused by these words.

"Your man, your Henry, would want to help me?"

"Yeah man, he knew what it was like to feel pain and to act out in the wrong way. He had a forgiving heart. He even forgave me."

Yandi chose to ignore that final statement.

"So I guess this is good-bye," he told me.

"I do gotta get back on the road, but first, I wanna make a promise to you. We...that's both me and Henry...want to help you. Even if it's just a little. So I'm gonna set up a monthly payment to your inmate account. I hope $100 a week will come in handy, and help keep you from starving. But I'll set up a monthly payment, $400 a month. And every time you receive it, promise me that you'll think about Henry."

"You don't even know how much that's gonna help. And not just me, but my boy too. Maybe someday, I'll be able to help somebody instead of causing hurt, like I did to you."

I didn't say anything, but I knew that Yandi was already helping somebody in there. That boy he was with. I didn't ask for his name. That was none of my business.

Yandi shook my hand as I stood to leave.

I sat in my car in the parking lot, sobbing uncontrollably.

***

Some habits have to be broken. I still remember the struggle when Henry and I tried to quit smoking cigarettes. It took more than a few tries, but we ended up being successful. Mostly thanks to Henry, who was much stronger than I was, in every way, including his self-control.

Society forced me to quit the habit of dropping 'ludes every time I went to the club, when that drug was prohibited from being manufactured in the US.

Other habits remain. That first cup of coffee upon awakening. Sometimes a second.

Saying "I love you" to Henry every night before I fall asleep. You may think that habit ended when he died. You would be wrong. I still say those words. Out loud. I have to. Even as I was able to let go of the worst of the grief, that didn't mean that I let go of the love. That's still a part of me. I hold it close to my heart and I cannot allow that to disappear into nothingness.

Love is real to me. It's tangible. I can feel it and hold it, caress it and feel its warmth. Holding it close to me, I can mold it into shapes, sizes, whatever works for the time that I'm feeling it.

That's because I believe that love is not only an emotion, but it also has a physical presence. It envelops me. I hope it surrounds all of us. I know that love lives within my heart, but it also surrounds my heart, protecting it. If it wasn't physical, how could love do that?

Maybe you don't believe me. That's okay. I know what I can do. I will hold onto the love that existed...I mean, that exists...between me and Henry for as long as I breathe. Nothing will ever change that.

I have another habit. Henry actually got me started. Every time I walk along Arch Street, I turn at a certain corner. Henry told me never to walk past that one restaurant, the

244

one where the owner was talking to me when I took Zumi to the park.

Today, I'm changing that habit. I find myself standing outside the restaurant, on the other side of the street, trying to peek discreetly inside, while walking by as if I had no interest in that place.

I'm not sure who I was trying to fool. Myself? Henry? The owner? The passers-by?

No one cares if I walk by the restaurant. I'm trying to convince myself to believe that. I think I care. Maybe the owner cares. And I'm sure Henry cares. But his voice is silent. He doesn't warn me to stay away. Maybe I have nothing to fear.

The next day, I find myself staring at the restaurant. Feeling a bit foolish, self-conscious, thinking that others might be observing me, when in reality, I was just a person standing on the street, in the constant chaos of mid-day Chinatown.

I thought I could see him, the owner, Tuyen, looking in my direction, but my eyes have been known to deceive me. I find myself wondering whether he would even remember me. After all, our conversations had occurred quite some time ago, and they were always brief affairs.

I wasn't even sure if he was gay. Did we ever talk about that? Was he a customer at Sanctuary? I can't be sure. If I think about it too much, I find myself even more confused. Why am I standing here?

I felt Henry tugging at me, like I was on a leash, but he wasn't leading me away from the restaurant. Rather, he was guiding me in that direction.

I pulled away. I wasn't ready. Henry would have to give me a stronger sign than that.

Now I was developing a new habit. On Day Three, I started circling the block, so I'd pass by the restaurant several times. I pictured Henry walking me, guiding my steps, coaxing me along with encouraging words such as "Good boy!" and "Atta boy!" and "Who's a good boy?" Just like he would back when I was his pup.

Crazy, right? But I know what I feel. When I resist, I feel like I'm being strangled, pulled along forcibly, by an invisible leash attached to an invisible collar. Led by an invisible, but very strong presence. It could only be Henry. No one else had ever had that kind of influence on me.

I'm not really good at keeping track of dates, but I think it was on Day 4 or 5 when I turned the corner and saw that he was waiting outside the store. For me. I'm quite sure of that.

I started to walk across the street so I'd avoid walking directly up to him. Then I stopped and thought about that. I've been trying to get his attention. Why am I now thinking of avoiding him? Maybe it's the dance we all perform at times, that mating ritual where one acts shy while the other pursues the prey.

By the time I finish that thought, it's already too late.

"Hello," he calls out. "Welcome back to my neighborhood."

"Hello," is my simple reply.

"I'm sorry if I embarrassed you before with my little game," he told me.

I didn't know exactly what he meant. Maybe that's why Henry was so upset that day.

Then I noticed a small jar in his hands.

"This is a gift for you. I heard about what happened, of course."

Holding the jar in my direction, I saw the label that said "Joey's Sweetness."

What the holy hell is that?

"I made it myself. Though perhaps 'made' isn't exactly the word I want to use."

Twisting open the jar, I was met with that unmistakably sweet odor of honey. Fresh honey. Home-made honey. It smelled delicious, tickling my nose with the promise of a delightful sensation when tasted.

"May I?" he offered, showing me a small plastic spoon in his breast pocket. "You would like a taste now?"

I hesitated for a moment, suddenly realizing that the jar of honey wasn't the only sticky sensation I was having. Just standing here had brought my honey comb to full attention, a fact not unnoticed by my companion.

"Someone told me that using plastic utensils can ruin the taste of sweet things," I lied, in an attempt to get a taste of more than the honey.

"Would you find it rude if I used my finger as a spoon?"

I felt like my manhood was doing an impression of a flowery pistil, loading up my stamen to the breaking point, ready to pollinate my own pole, right there, inside my pants, without a touch from any buzzing bees...or anything else.

"Come with me," he ordered, guiding me with gentle pressure applied to the back of my waist, towards the back of the restaurant.

I found myself in the cramped back office, with a desk and chair, a filing cabinet seemingly overrun with papers, a wall map of Southeast Asia and a time clock. I stood, unsure of what was expected of me.

"Shirt off!" came the command, as he sat with his legs spread wide open. "Pants off!"

I obeyed without question. I knew what was coming next. Or at least I thought I did.

His dark eyes were smoldering with desire and his nostrils flared in heat. "Already wet, I see," he told me, seeing the wet stain on the front of my red bikinis, a sure sign of my readiness to serve.

"Down on your knees!"

247

I didn't notice that he had brought the jar of Joey's Sweetness into the back office with him. Dipping his middle finger into the jar, he then held the finger less than an inch from my face, slowly rubbing the honey on my lips, covering them with sweetness. Taking a fresh drop of honey from the jar, he then pushed that same finger into my eager mouth, as I moaned with lust and desire.

"I think you're a derrty boy," he told me, mispronouncing the word "dirty." But there was no doubt what he meant.

Rubbing more honey onto my erect, quivering nipples, he toyed with me, flickering his tongue against the pleasure peaks on my chest.

He took a moment to open his pants, lowering them enough to reveal his tool of dominance, erect and throbbing, veiny and uncut, hairless except for the small patch of black hairs at the base. His balls were already tight, as if he was ready to explode so soon after we had started.

"You like my mighty sword?" he asked me. "Much bigger than your little dagger, trying to be released from its sheath. Maybe I should name you 'Tiny,' just to remind you about your little bird dick."

He was stroking himself slowly as he talked, clearly enjoying himself and wanting to put me into a submissive frame of mind.

He took more honey, letting it drip slowly from his hand onto the sheath of his manhood, then pushing my head down. I opened my mouth and swallowed.

Licking and slurping, I felt a desire that I hadn't experienced in months, reaching into my undies as my mouth worked its expert magic on him. A few quick strokes had me grunting, my eyes half-closed, experiencing the utter joy of having a cock inside my mouth, feeling the dribble hitting my tongue as I swallowed the sweet offering.

"Up!" he said, in a sharp bark. "Turn around."

I felt him pulling down my underwear, first feeling his breath against my white, meaty cheeks, then feeling myself being opened as he spat hard against my waiting port of pleasure. I knew the ship would be docking in there soon enough.

He took two condoms and expertly wrapped himself, then he pulled me down so hard that I had no time to adjust to the invasion. His strong arms bounced me up and down, up and down, and I heard him grunting as he released his own honey into my warm and welcoming beehive.

He rose up as if to disengage, telling me to get back on my knees.

"Let me see it," he said in a gruff whisper, still recovering from his quick orgasm.

Pulling my underwear down in the front, my rigid member aching, it flopped against my belly. Leaning back, he spat expertly, finding his target as the head of my cut dick almost exploded.

"No, derrty boy, not yet. And don't touch."

Kicking off his shoes, he positioned his legs so he could use both feet, encasing my quivering member, caressing it and teasing it with his feet. Rubbing up and down, then moving a foot to grab my nipple with his toes, I was flooded with desire.

Returning both feet to my rod, rubbing, faster and faster, he gave the order.

"Shoot your little gun, your tiny pistol. I want to see what a wet, derrty, sticky little boy you are."

My fountain of love squirted everywhere as my body writhed in pleasure, touched only by the feet of the Master, who had me under his complete control.

The whole scene took about 5 minutes. It wasn't love. It was quick, dirty, nasty and oh so pleasurable! It seemed to me that much more than a temporary sexual tension had been released.

"I want you to be here the same time tomorrow. Don't keep me waiting."

I agreed as he quickly ushered me towards the door, needing to get ready for his first customers.

There was no doubt that I'd be back for more.

CHAPTER TWENTY-NINE

TUYEN
JOEY

Tuyen:

"Is this all there is to you? Just a hole for me to fuck every day in my office? Is there anything else you have to offer?"

No doubt I had fun playing with Joey in my office. He's a good boy: obedient, respectful and sexy as fuck. I'm interested in moving on to the next level, but only if he has something to offer. Besides sex. Is he ready for a new emotional attachment? Is he even interested in me in that way? I don't know.

"If I may speak freely, I'm not sure what you want," he told me. "You want me to be one of your boys? Or do you want something exclusive?"

"Get dressed," I told him, tucking my manhood back into my pants after just having creamed inside the boy once more. "I want to take you somewhere."

I left orders for my manager to run the restaurant for the rest of the day. "I won't be back until tomorrow," I told him, speaking in our native tongue.

A few minutes later, I was barreling up I-95, with Joey in the passenger seat, headed towards the Walt Whitman Bridge. Crossing into New Jersey, I pulled over at a spot that most drivers would pass without notice.

Opening the trunk, I pulled out a large bag, placing it on the ground.

"You carry that," I commanded.

I saw the look of hesitation in his eyes. We've all heard horror stories of young men being kidnapped, tortured, even killed.

"Do you trust me?" I asked him.

He stood there, thinking.

"If not, get back in the car. I'll drive you back home and we'll never see each other again. I promise."

"No, I got it," he told me, picking up the bag. I led him away from the highway, into a patch of woods.

Before long, the woods opened into a meadow. My meadow. Smiling, I saw my white wooden boxes, my hives, located at various spots throughout the field.

Joey stopped in his tracks. "What the hell is this? What're we doing here?"

"I'm here to teach you a lesson. Several lessons, in fact," I told him.

"Where did you think my honey comes from? How do I get Joey's Sweetness? You think it just drops outta the sky?"

"Well, I didn't actually think about it," he told me.

"You see, that's part of the problem with you. You should be inquisitive. Interested in learning new things. Interested in learning about me," I scolded him.

"I am interested. I wasn't sure if it was okay for me to ask," he protested.

"I know you were busy because I always had my cock up your ass. You like that a lot, I can tell. And I enjoy talking to you about that, how I'm the man inside you and you are...what's the right word I want to use to describe you...You are my bitch, right?"

I enjoyed watching Joey's face turn red. Even with all his experience being submissive, I could still embarrass him. That was a good sign.

I started to put on my bee suit. "I have an extra one for you. Put it on."

"You wanted to know more about me, right?" he asked.

"Yes, I do. Let's talk while we collect honey."

"But that's the thing, Sir. I'm scared of bees."

"I told you I brought you out here to teach you some lessons. Before I teach, let me ask you, what do you know about bees?"

"Well, I know they make a loud buzzing sound with their mouths as a warning when they're gonna bite you. I think they're screaming a warning, but the sound we hear is a buzz. Then after they bite you, they sting you too, sometimes like a thousand times. People drop dead right after a sting. I think I read that somewhere, like in a Science book or something like that," he told me.

"Is that what they teach you in your American schools?' I said, trying to contain my laughter at his complete ignorance of bees.

"In my country, we learn different things. That bees are necessary for agriculture. That we can use their honey to include in delicious foods, or even to just eat as a sweet treat. Nothing you told me is based on fact. None of it, you understand me?"

"Show me that you trust me and put on your bee suit."

I like when they obey without question, so it set my heart pounding faster as I watched him dress into his protective suit.

"First, the buzzing sound is made mostly when they beat their wings to fly, though they also buzz when they shake their bodies to remove pollen from flowers onto their bodies."

Getting close to the first hive, I continued the lesson. "Bees can communicate with their buzzing sounds too, and they also use their wings for warming and cooling."

253

"I never knew any of that. I'm not too much of a nature boy, I don't think," my handsome and sexy companion told me.

As I began to collect the honey, I told him, "For me, the most interesting part of the bee community is how their roles are so clearly defined."

After I showed him how to collect the honey, I told him, "Now it's your turn. Just do the same as I did."

Watching him perform the task, under my direction, increased my feeling of power over him. I felt my stinger growing in length and girth. I wanted to pollinate him right here, right now, but I knew he had to concentrate.

"The three different members of the hive are the Queen, the workers and the drones. The Queen's only job is to lay eggs. The drones are the male bees. Their only job is to mate with the Queen. You understand so far?"

"Yes, I'm listening," Joey replied as he worked carefully extracting honey.

"And then we have the worker bees. They have different roles, but each worker might perform several different roles during their lifetime. They work as housekeepers, nurses, attendants to the Queen, architects, ventilators, guards and foragers."

"Wow, they have a lot of responsibilities," Joey was saying as we finished collecting our prize, the golden-sweet honey that would soon be put to good use at the restaurant.

Walking towards the car, I explained to my worker, "Clearly, I am the Queen bee. But since we are not bees, I will be called the King. Like the Queen in the hive, I will be the one who will be served. Do you agree?"

By this point in the conversation, I wanted to inject this boy with my massive stinger and ejaculate my sweet juices deep in his body. Still, I waited.

"Yes, that sounds right."

"No, you do not understand. I am the King. I am your King. You do not simply say 'Yes' to me."

"Yes, my King. You are the King here. You are my King."

"Now you are beginning to understand. Let's think about your role now. It's clear that you cannot be a drone. You will not mate me. Your tiny stinger will never penetrate me. Is that clear to you? Do you understand and more importantly, do you agree?"

"Yes, King. I agree."

"You once told me that you and your Henry used to switch roles sometimes. That was between the two of you. It is not the same between us. I need you to understand this and accept it without question. You will never, and I mean, never, penetrate me with your male member. Tell me again, agree or disagree?"

"Yes, King, I understand and I agree. I am never to be permitted to penetrate you."

"Before I forget to tell you, there's one other very important difference between me and your former Master. I do not want promiscuity. I do not want threesomes, foursomes, or any other number-somes. If we do this, it's only you and me. I will leave all my other toyboys alone. You will submit only to me."

"I think you mean boytoys, King."

I snapped. "Toyboy, boytoy, shmoyboy, boyboy, toytoy. The words don't matter. If I have you, I have you totally. Completely. No sharing. No cheating. No sneaking. Is that what you want or not, toyboy?"

I used the wrong word, toyboy instead of boytoy, just to make my point.

He didn't ask for time to think about it. I think he was ready to make this decision. He could have a life adrift in a sea of Dominant men, with no clear path forward, or he could choose to be my one and only submissive.

"Yes, my King. I agree with everything you said. That is what I want, to be your toyboy."

I liked the way he also used the wrong word, just to show he understood his new role in life.

I continued my lesson with him.

"I love the way the lives of the bees are organized. Now, since you are not the Queen, and you are not a drone, that means you must be a worker. Yes?"

"Does every worker have to play every role you told me about? he asked.

"No, they do not. But let's review them and decide what suits you the best."

I listed each role.

"Housekeeper? Hmmm, I doubt it. We can use others for that. But in an emergency, you can fill in, I guess."

We both laughed a little at that. I was thinking he might look cute in a sexy maid's outfit. But we could have that conversation some other time.

"A nurse? Hell no! We go to the doctor's office or hospital for medical emergencies."

"An attendant to the Queen. Yes, I think that role suits you perfectly, but you will be an attendant to...who?" I prompted him.

"To you, to the King, of course," he replied correctly.

"And by being my attendant, you will be required to service all of my sexual needs. When I want. Where I want. And anything else I may require of you. Can you handle those responsibilities, worker bee?"

"I know I can do it, my King. But even more than that, I want to do it. I need a King in my life and it's clear that you're the perfect King for me."

I continued listing the roles, smiling with satisfaction at this obedient, beautiful boy in front of me.

"Architect? No! Ventilator? No! Guard? No!" I did not want the toyboy performing those duties.

"Finally, a forager. Sometimes, I want you to go shopping for me. For us. But mostly for me," I told him. Any problem with that?"

"No, Sir. No, my King. I love to shop!"

I smiled, knowing that my new toyboy was going to be perfect for me.

As soon as we got into the car, my pants were open and I was forcing his open mouth down towards my rigidity.

"Give me service, worker bee. Service me and I reward you with all my golden honey."

It only took a minute before Joey was swallowing my nectar, then licking me clean before we headed back to the city.

Quite purposely, I did not give my worker bee permission to satisfy himself. I wanted to watch him pleasure himself later on, when I could concentrate on the show he would give for me. It was more enjoyable for me if the pleasure was mixed with just enough pain to be sure my boy could feel my presence strongly.

***

Joey:

Henry had been my soul for a very long time. There's no way I could ever forget him, or even stop loving him. But I know I need structure in my life. Henry could no longer provide that. I knew that Tuyen could and would guide me in the ways I needed guidance.

It also helped that Tuyen was strong, athletic, handsome, sexy and dominant. Those were the qualities I looked for. Tuyen had them all. If he had a fault, and I would never say anything to him about it, it was his premature ejaculations. He explained it by saying that the warmth and tightness of a man's back entrance were just too

257

pleasurable for him. That's why he made extended foreplay a requirement for every sexual encounter he had.

I had no problem with that. Sometimes. he'd allow me to spill my seed. Other times, no. He decided. I complied. Some things in life are made simple when we have roles that fit us and that we want to play.

"It's Saturday night. Come to the club with me tonight. I haven't been there in a while."

"No," Tuyen told me. I'm not a club kid. Never was."

"Please. Just for me."

Tuyen let out a loud sigh. Sometimes, on rare occasions, he would agree to something I suggested. Maybe it gets tiring to always be the one to make all the decisions.

"Okay, this one time. Go put your party dress on."

He was teasing me, of course.

He dressed simply, with a white dress shirt, black trousers, sensible shoes. His shirt was open to display his thick gold chain with the emerald dragon pendant. I wanted to give him just a touch of make-up, to enhance his dark eyes and emphasize those very high cheekbones, but he would have none of that.

I think he was surprised that I knew so many people. I also don't think he was prepared for the size of the crowd and the wide variety of the individuals who showed up to party.

I shouldn't have been surprised when I saw that he knew people, who weren't shy about coming up and greeting him.

I was hoping he'd dance with me, like Henry sometimes did. But at first, he declined, stating his preference to sit at the bar and enjoy his vodka tonics. I sat next to him, watching the dancers, with waves of memories washing over me, crashing into me, a force of nature that felt heavy and difficult to manage. The energies from those gone for so long sometimes seemed to become a physical presence for me.

So many guys gone, so many nights of fun, dancing, gossiping, making out, getting high, and yes, having sex. The first time Henry dominated me right out there in the middle of the dance floor, proclaiming himself (and rightfully so) as the "real boss."

"This gives me an idea," Tuyen told me. "But let's not discuss anything serious now. We're here to have fun, right?"

And with that, he took my hand and led me out to the dance floor, where we bumped, hustled, vogued, twisted and even waltzed until we were both out of breath, laughing our way back to the bar, and having one helluva night.

***

Tuyen:

"I don't want to move into the place you shared with Henry," I told Joey.

I'd never feel comfortable there. It's like his spirit or some part of him is still present. And I don't want to replace Henry. I want to be a unique experience for Joey.

My place, basically a studio above the restaurant, was too small for us. We have to make some decisions about where we'll live because of course, I want us to live together. For now, I have to insist that we meet at my place. There are no ghosts here. Almost every night, Joey sleeps in my apartment, in my bed, which is exactly where he belongs.

But before we make a final decision, we still have our lives to live and a big part of my life is returning to my homeland once every year, to visit friends and family.

"I'm planning my trip to VietNam for next month," I told Joey, over drinks as we waited for our meals at the Hard

Rock Cafe. "I want you to go with me. I want you to see how beautiful my country is, and to meet my grandmother and the rest of my family."

He gave no sign of hesitation, agreeing immediately.

"Wow! My first trip to Asia. I've seen pictures of course, but I really wanna experience it in person!"

I was happy to see his enthusiastic response.

"Are you sure about me meeting your family? I don't wanna give your Grandma a heart attack or anything!" he joked.

"Leave that to me, baby. I can handle my family. I think my grandmother, my cousins, all my family, they're gonna love you. Not as much as I do, but they'll love you just enough," I assured him.

***

Joey:

I could write an entire book about the week Tuyen and I spent in VietNam. Instead, I'll give you the travel brochure version.

First, the trip to get there was very long. You don't realize just how far away some places are until you make the trip. Tuyen was a great comfort to me, a relatively nervous traveler, as we flew cross-country and over the Pacific.

Occasionally, we would switch seats, so we could take turns looking out the tiny window, but no matter where I sat, Tuyen would keep a protective hand over mine as we shared the armrest. I appreciated that, especially when we encountered any turbulence.

VietNam is a country of contrasts, at least in my opinion. Stunning views, both in the cities and in the countryside. Modern in some places, but that changes as you move beyond the urban areas.

What was consistent was the friendliness of the people. Considering the history of US/Vietnamese relations, I was relieved when we encountered no hostility.

We visited Hanoi, the capital city in the northern part of the country, as well as Ho Chi Minh City (Saigon) in the south. For me, there were so many highlights, I barely know where to begin.

The night markets, with dizzying sights, sounds, and the smells of exotic dishes being served to throngs of people.

A trip along the Mekong River, on a multi-passenger dragon boat, with the carved dragon head at the front, a wooden tail at the back and brightly-painted dragon scales along the hull. As we sailed, we saw fishermen in basket boats, in search of the catch of the day.

The mix of cultures, with influences from France and the United States, along with the native Vietnamese culture provided an exotic mix of sights and sounds. Buddhist pagodas and Catholic churches along the streets, high-rise apartments, single-family homes and huts were all visible as we traveled around the area.

Meeting Tuyen's family was quite the experience. It seemed to me that every relative was present to greet him as we gathered for a family feast. No one spoke English, but it was clear to me that they loved Tuyen and they accepted me. No one seemed to question our relationship. At least, not in any obvious way. Tuyen assured me that there were no problems, and the smiles and friendly faces of his relatives gave me no reason to doubt him.

***

Tuyen:

I'm so happy to have Joey here with me to meet my family. I believe that my "wife" must have the approval of

261

my family members, and once my grandmother gave her approval, everyone else was sure to follow her lead.

Should I use the word "wife" to describe Joey? I know that most of the politically-correct crowd back in Philly will be clutching their fake pearls when they hear that.

Do I care about their opinions? To be honest, no. If you must think of us as equal partners, be my guest, but that is to deny our reality. Joey is not my equal. He is submissive to me. If he wasn't, then we would not be together. That's a fact, Jack, as I once heard someone say.

I'm going to ask Joey to marry me. I want him to agree to be my wife. I don't want him to be my husband, my partner, my significant other, or anything else the liberals in America would insist on, trying to force me to fit our relationship into their pre-conceived notion of who and what we are.

However, I have to discuss something with him first.

I'm seated on the bed in our hotel room, away from friends and family for now.

"Sit here, baby," I tell him, indicating that he should join me on the bed.

Instead, Joey sits cross-legged on the floor in front of me, looking at me with pure love in his soulful eyes.

I nod my approval.

"You know I like things to be orderly, like the structure of the bee society that I showed you back in Philly."

Joey sits quietly, listening intently, not wanting to miss a word I say.

"I know that you and Henry had a long relationship, one that changed over time. Am I right about that?"

"Yes," Joey replied. "We tried to be equals, even though he was always stronger than me. Later on, Henry took over. It worked better for us that way."

"I see the wisdom that Henry had. Trying something with you and when it didn't really make either of you happy, he adapted and made things better."

The look on Joey's face told me that he was in awe of me. My wisdom. My power. My authority.

"In a world where many are powerless, I want to feel power."

Pausing, I let those words sink in.

"I don't need or want power over everything and everybody. I couldn't get that even if I did want it."

Another brief pause, then an emphatic:

"I do want to feel power over you."

Again, a purposeful pause.

"I want to feel power. The question is, do you want to feel my power? Will you accept it, embrace it, take it as it is intended? To control you. To rule over you? To dominate you? Not just in the bedroom. That part is already decided. I'm asking about your whole life. Our lives. I have the power. You do not. Think about what that means."

I didn't ask Joey for an answer to those questions. His answer to the follow-up question would provide all the answers I needed.

"I have something to give you, if you want it. It's a ring. A ring for my wife. Not a female. My male wife. That's what I want you to be."

Joey started to speak, but I motioned for him to stay quiet.

"Do not interrupt me," I told him. "As I was saying, I have a ring for you. This ring will go on your finger. The finger that tells the world that you are married. But right now, you already have a symbol on that finger. Your tattoo. And I understand what that means to you, but this ring will cover the tattoo. You have to understand that."

Joey's eyes broke from mine as he looked at the tattoo on his ring finger. The two initials. The capital "H" for Henry and the small "j" for Joey. It not only symbolized their names, but also their positions. I admired Henry for the power he had over this boy, who I hoped would now agree to be my male wife.

"I don't want you to lose that symbol. I know it means a lot to you and you're always going to have a place for Henry in your heart. So I want you to think of this ring, not as something that hides the older symbol, but as something that protects it."

"I believe that Henry is with his ancestors, now," I continued. "I don't want us to hide from him or pretend he never existed. This ring will embrace your finger, but it will also embrace the symbol of the memories that you have about your past life. But only if you accept the ring and the conditions that go along with it."

A brief pause.

"Will you, Joey, accept my offer and become my wife?"

"Yes, I do accept the offer. I will be your wife."

Then Joey extended his hand and I slid the ring onto his finger, feeling him trembling at my gentle touch.

Handing another ring to Joey, I extended my hand, saying, "I, Tuyen, accept you, Joey, into my life as my devoted, loyal and obedient wife. I will protect you and love you always."

He slid the ring onto my finger, making this the happiest moment of my entire life.

***

Joey:

The most casual conversations can sometimes lead to long-term and consequential changes.

Chatting with my long-time friends Alejandro and Kirk over lunch at The Garden, a restaurant that led the city's food renaissance when it opened in 1974, I shared my latest news.

"Tuyen wants to take me on vacation, for a week, and he wants me to pick the location. How cool is that? He said we can go anywhere I want. So...do either of you have any ideas?"

Jando didn't miss a beat. 'Honey, I've been telling you for years now that Puerto Rico is an awesome vacation spot. I can tell you all the places to go."

"We went last year," Kirk added, "and the island is so beautiful. To be honest, I didn't want to leave."

"It really has everything. Beautiful weather year-round, gorgeous beaches, and the food is awesome. And don't even get me started talkin' about the gorgeous men!" Jando could talk for hours about his beautiful native island.

"Not to mention, there is gay nightlife there. Quite a few clubs. Beaches too. Gay beaches. Nude beaches. All kinds of beaches."

It sounded like Jando and Kirk were ready to go back for another visit soon.

Later that night, back home, I asked Tuyen what he thought.

"Great idea! I've never been there before. Have you?"

"No, never," I replied. "I guess that makes both of us Puerto Rican virgins!"

With his approval, I could begin making our plans for a week-long adventure in Paradise.

It was clear that Jando and Kirk weren't exaggerating when they described this magical place. I fell in love with the location instantly, especially since we had left a frigid Philly at 17 degrees F for a tropical 83 degrees F upon our arrival.

265

We did every activity we could squeeze into a 7-day trip. Scuba-diving, parasailing, sightseeing tours, hikes in the tropical rain forest, and soaking up as much sun as we could during daily trips to the gay beach, located in an area called Condado, a section of San Juan popular with tourists.

We were walking along Ashford Avenue, the main drag in Condado, when Tuyen saw a sign, announcing that a large building, formerly a restaurant right on the beach, was up for sale.

Circling the place at least three times, we looked for flaws. He was silent, clearly contemplating something, and I wasn't about to interrupt him. I had been well-trained to read the silent signals he gave about my expected behavior.

Then we stood in front of the building, on the beach, in a popular tourist destination, as Tuyen took me by the hand.

"Do you like it?' was his simple question to me.

I had already decided what I thought. "I love it. It's perfect."

There was no need to tell Tuyen that the final decision was his. He already knew that. My opinion wasn't going to have any effect on the final decision. I was well aware of that, and indeed, that was exactly how I wanted my life to be.

"I'm going to call the agent. We're going to stay here for a few more days. I like the possibilities I see here."

A few days later, we signed the Agreement of Sale. We'd close in 30 days. A very quick transaction, but what would be the purpose of dragging out the process?

"This is a great location for a new restaurant specializing in Vietnamese cuisine," Tuyen was telling me.

"May I suggest something?" I asked hopefully.

"Yes, you may. I'm listening."

266

"What do you think if we made it into a combined restaurant with a club, or at least a bar or maybe a lounge? We know the clubs here are open till 5 AM. But maybe we don't have to try to attract that young crowd that wants to party all night. How about a safe place for gays and lesbians and our allies to kind of hang out, hear some good music, relax, maybe even dance a little? And, serve a full menu, of course."

Tuyen was laughing, but not in a negative way. He was considering what I said.

"Someone once told me that you can take the kid out of the club, but you can never take the club out of the kid. Or something like that."

"I like your idea," he continued. Especially the part about making it a place friendly to gays. I know that's always been important for you."

"Have you thought about a name for the place?"

Tuyen was laughing again. "You're gonna think this is a funny name, but I already know what I want to call it."

Promising myself that I wouldn't laugh, I asked, "Well, what's it gonna be?"

"I want to call it ToyBoys. And it's all because of you."

I did laugh, but not because I thought the name was silly. I sort of liked it, and I was sure the name would grow on me. But I didn't understand what I had to do with it.

"You don't remember, but one day, maybe it was the first time I took you out to see the beehives, I was talking about boytoys. But I made a mistake and called them toyboys."

"Yes, I do remember that," I told him.

"You corrected me at first, but then, the next time you used the term, you used it wrong, like I did. That was a sign that you respected me and honored me. Even in a mistake, you wanted to join me in it, and not make a big deal to prove that you were right. That told me a lot about you and it was exactly the right thing for you to do."

267

Again, simple conversations can sometimes have profound meanings and consequences.

I've seen the glazed look in the eyes of my friends when I describe every detail about our move to Puerto Rico. They don't want to hear about every step as we:

1. Sold Club Sanctuary for an insane amount of money to an entertainment conglomerate, but first ensuring that our current staff could stay on if they wished and that the Board of Directors would retain their positions, with profit-sharing as one of their major perks.

2. Ended the lease on the apartment we shared in Philly, since we had decided against buying a new home for the time being. That ended up being a fortunate decision, since it was much easier to end a lease rather than having to sell a house.

3. Said our goodbyes to some very dear friends, with promises to visit and stay in contact. And of course, invitations were extended to visit us in our new location.

4. Left Tuyen's restaurant to be run by his family members.

5. Said goodbye to Philadelphia, a city that had adopted both of us, welcoming us into various segments of the community, but especially all the beautiful LGBTQ people we had grown to know and love throughout the years.

6. Made many trips between Philly and San Juan, planning the new layout and design for our new adventure, a brand-new restaurant/bar/lounge right on the beach.

***

We've been living here in San Juan for a little over six months now. Toyboys has become a huge success and we both enjoy our lives and this new place for us to work and grow our relationship with each other. We're also finding plenty of new friends in a Queer community that's brand new for us.

The drag culture in Puerto Rico is so fierce, I think, as I wave to our hostess, Miss Gloria Las Tetas, who took her name in honor of Cerro Las Tetas, two mountain peaks that remind everyone of the biggest titties you ever saw, located between Salinas and Cayey, a short drive from here.

Maybe someday, Miss Joey X-Drag-a-Vaaaahnza will make a return to her proper place on the center stage of the club, but not today.

Though we planned to keep the club/restaurant somewhat lowkey, we did want to draw a crowd. Hiring drag divas and gogo boys as staff members and entertainers ensured that our place, ToyBoys, quickly became a hotspot for both locals and tourists.

I'm enjoying the sounds of the newest reggaeton hits being played by the DJ. "Dile" by Don Omar, the King of Kings of Reggaeton, draws a few couples to the dance floor.

Tuyen joins me as we sit in lounge chairs, facing the Atlantic Ocean, quietly lapping at the shoreline. On this moonlit night, I enjoy seeing the reflection of our bright blue neon sign visible in the stillness of the ocean, beyond the waves. ToyBoys.

Signaling to the bartender, I have two of our signature drinks, the ToyBoys Twist, brought out to us.

"Do you have any regrets, Joey?"

"Not about this, no, not at all."

But then I continued.

"I think that a life without regrets is a life unlived. I wouldn't want to live a life where I never made a mistake, never learned anything from my experiences, never had to adapt to changing conditions. So yes, I have regrets. But I wouldn't change my life for anything in the world. I've had the love, the real love of two of the most beautiful,

269

wonderful men who have ever existed. First Henry, and now you. How many guys get to say something like that?"

"Sure, I enjoyed the good times I had, the easy times. The minor inconveniences and annoyances in my life back then just seem so trivial now. And that's because I experienced the darkness, the raw grief of losing someone that I thought would be with me forever."

"I couldn't have escaped that bleak hole without the help of others. My friends, certainly. They helped so much. But my real savior, that was you. Gradually, step-by-step, inch-by-inch, you led me out of that darkness and back into the light, where I can live and breathe again. And now we have all this!"

Tuyen was silent for a moment, thinking about what I'd said. Sliding his chair closer to mine, he stretched out his leg, protectively covering my leg with his. Then he took my hand and just held it tightly.

"I love you, Joey."

Turning my gaze from the ToyBoys reflection in the darkness of the sea to the glowing face of the full moon above, a slight dizziness overcame me. Slowly, the moon began to spin, then disintegrate into a thousand kaleidoscopic pieces, each reflecting a distinct memory.

First, every shard of the now-splintered moon displayed an image of Henry, as memories of our many years together came into sharper focus. As those images faded, I could see the faces of so many dear friends, most of whom had left far too soon. Lonnie, Stephen, BJ, Georgie, Jian, Finn and Travis, the Four Williams, Peter and Paul, Alejandro and Kirk, BaeBae, even Yandi, appeared as my life story was reflected in all the broken pieces of the moon.

To me, it seemed that the spinning images lasted for minutes when in reality, it had only been a second since Tuyen spoke to me.

I replied with confidence, knowing that I was exactly where I was supposed to be, and with the exact person I was supposed to be with. As the moon returned to its natural state, I thought to myself, *I love you, Henry.*

Then, turning to face my man, my partner, my husband, my savior, I declared in a voice so strong that it seemed to echo along the shoreline, "I love you too, Tuyen."

The End

A Message to Readers
of CLUBBED THREE

Thank you for reading CLUBBED THREE: Darkness and Light.

If you enjoyed the book, please give it a rating, which helps me in my book promotions. Of course, reviews are always welcome.

If you have any comments or suggestions, you can contact me at:
robert.karl.author@gmail.com

Please visit my website for updated information at:
robertkarlauthor.com

The CLUBBED series was written to help keep the history and culture of the LGBTQ+ community alive.

In the darkest of days, may you always find your way back to the light.

"Everybody at the club has a story, and every story deserves to be told."

Other Books By This Author

CLUBBED: A Story of Gay Love: Trials, Tribulations and Triumphs (Book One in the CLUBBED: Stories of Gay Love series)

CLUBBED TWO: Anxiety, Anger, Activism (Book Two in the CLUBBED: Stories of Gay Love series)

Links

Website: http://robertkarlauthor.com

Instagram: https://www.instagram.com/robertkarl_inpr/

Twitter: https://www.twitter.com/rkarl

Facebook: https://www.facebook.com/robert.karl.3154/